# how sweet the sound

# how sweet the sound

## stories inspired by the hymns we love

*T. Wyatt Watkins*

## T. WYATT WATKINS

*To Bruce, with very best wishes! Keep making a joyful noise!*

**Judson Press**
VALLEY FORGE

*How Sweet the Sound: Stories Inspired by the Hymns We Love*

© 2001 by Judson Press, Valley Forge, PA 19482-0851

**Library of Congress Cataloging-in-Publication Data**

Watkins, T. Wyatt.
    How sweet the sound : stories inspired by the hymns we love / T. Wyatt Watkins.
        p.   cm.
    Includes bibliographical references.
        ISBN 0-8170-1382-2 (pbk. : alk. paper)
        1. Christian fiction, American. 2. Hymns—Fiction. I. Title.
    PS3573.A8447 H69 2001
813'.54—dc21                                                    00-060275

Printed in the U.S.A.

07  06  05  04  03  02  01

10 9 8 7 6 5 4 3 2 1

*To my wife, Donna,*
*whose life puts in my heart a song*

# Contents

# Preface

HOW SWEET THE SOUND REVISITS IN STORY THE HYMNS God's people love to sing. It is set in the same quiet grove of maple and ash as my earlier volume, *Gospel, Grits, and Grace.* In that book I brought my love of story to bear on a young pastor's experiences in a little country church. Now I continue my account of the courtship of pastor and people in the arena of a second love: music. True-to-life accounts from my treasury of experiences at Ashgrove Baptist Church are mingled with the texts and tunes of nearly a thousand years of Christian hymnody.

Anyone who attends congregational worship knows it to be true: people care deeply and viscerally about the hymns they sing. For as long as Christians have been raising voices to God, they have fanned the flames of passion about hymnody. The hot-button issues of the modern church, for all their buzz, can't generate a fraction of the "noise" in the pews reserved for congregational song.

How Sweet the Sound plays up this truth in the peculiar affairs of the family at Ashgrove Church. Each chapter marries a beloved hymn text to a contemporary story line of need and blessing. The hymns themselves have their own tales to tell—both of poems and poets. These become intertwined with the lives of ordinary people seeking grace and guidance for faithful living. In the process, a church comes to sing the message of grace in a truer key. Following the stories are brief reflections on the hymns themselves, their tunes and texts as well as their composers.

Whether you are coming home to Ashgrove for a second visit or stepping into the world of our quiet grove for the first time, I welcome you here to a special place where grace always sings loud and true in the end!

# Introduction

I N THE MID-1980S, A YOUNG PASTOR LEFT SEMINARY AND entered the crucible of ministry. The setting for this maiden pastorate was the far west side of Indianapolis. There, in a quiet grove surrounded by cornfield, I grew up in ministry and in life. A child of the city, I confronted the country head on, and the country confronted me. But over some time and turmoil, a pastor and a people found a middle ground. They resolved to take their pastor as he came, oddity and all. I, meanwhile, fell gradually into the tranquil rhythm of rural life. We managed a meeting of minds and hearts. Nowhere was this truer than in the arena of music!

We have each been shaped by our experiences with song. In the Christian church, this has meant above all the formative influence of hymnody. Some people grow apart from the sacred songs of their heritage. Others continue to embrace them gladly. But none can outrun their hold on the heart. In decisive moments throughout our lives, old texts and tunes manage to reassert their sway. Through the daily acts of living and dying and blessing, we learn to hear them again for the first time.

Coming to a pastorate in rural Indiana, it did not take me long to recognize my own musical heritage as rather uncommon. My favorite hymn growing up was John Bunyan's "He Who Would Valiant Be." A best friend and I would be on alert at all times for hymn requests. At the instant they were asked for, our hands were in the air. With our stupid grins and eager gazes, it was only a matter of moments before one of us was called upon. Without fail we would blurt out, "Number 252!" That hymn number sat at the ready in my cerebral filing cabinet, right next to my school locker combination and Chicago Cubs' batting averages. The hymn had three verses, each of which concluded with words of our heart's longing, which I still cannot explain. We sang, "There's no discouragement shall make him once relent his first avowed intent"—and then, in conclusion, leaning toward one other and raising our heads high, we cried, "TO BE A PILGRIM!"

At Ashgrove Baptist Church, no one had ever heard of John Bunyan. Neither did my personal catalogue of the great hymns of the church impress anyone. These ranged, I believed, from the ancient Latin and Greek poems of the pre-Reformation church, to the inspired English texts of Isaac Watts and the Wesleys, to the solid German lied of Lutheranism and Pietism, to early American hymn tunes and the later verse of intellectual and social conscience. My list expanded to include traditional spirituals, Southern harmony tunes, and even the 1960s summer camp songs of my youth. But there was a great gaping hole in my knowledge of congregational singing. I seemed to be the only Baptist in Indiana who knew nothing of the songs of the great revivals. Somehow I had made it to adulthood without learning the gospel texts of nineteenth- and early twentieth-century America and England or the cheery tunes that delivered them.

I came to the little church on the county line of westside Indianapolis a classically trained musician. I knew the key signatures by heart. Solfege was to me as natural an act as blinking or swallowing. I could recognize the sonata form and pick out the subjects of a fugue while whistling "Dixie." My favorite composers were Johannes Brahms and Sergei Prokofiev. But I had never heard of Charles Gabriel or Philip Bliss, my feet had never left the blood-red church carpet singing "I'll Fly Away," and I had never walked "In the Garden," alone or with anyone else. I did not even know that Fanny Crosby had been blind!

Within two weeks of my arrival at Ashgrove Church, it became apparent to the members that, musically speaking, they were dealing with an infant and, quite possibly, a heathen! After their initial shock, they took upon themselves the task of my remedial music education. While I was their pastor, I learned easily 150 new hymns, though they preferred to call them the oldies but goodies. Almost all were from the English and American revival traditions. Sometimes the theology nearly turned me red, and the tunes made me queasy. But, over time, I found among those songs many sincere expressions of faith, void of pretense and strong in conviction.

Meanwhile I sought among the congregation a hearing for the texts and tunes that I loved and that brought me into the presence of the holy. I introduced them to the history and theology of hymns. I argued that hymns don't have to sound happy (to be in a major key) to move the heart to joy or have snappy rhythms to coax tired bodies up out of the pews. I shared my passion for tunes like *Ebenezer* and the plainsong tune *Divinum Mysterium*. I extolled the solid marriage of words and music in hymns like "God of Our Fathers" and "Be Thou My Vision." And I sang my heart out on "Balm in Gilead" and "Go Tell It on the Mountain." Sometimes I got gawks or stares of incredulity. But now and again there shone in some a glimmer of recognition, as if a deep sleeping spirit had been stirred to consciousness. And whatever else was true, together we always had "Holy, Holy, Holy," "Great Is Thy Faithfulness," and "Amazing Grace"!

What follows are stories of hymns that have inspired the lives of a frail yet faithful people I love, and their pastor right along with them. With any luck, they'll stir a song or two inside you as well. And together, we may hope, the many songs our lives sing will reach their final goal in God and join the grand psalm of all life, the final text and tune of heaven.

*Soli Deo Gloria.*

# CHAPTER 1

# Consecration

## "Take My Life and Let It Be"

THE DISTRIBUTION OF HUMAN TALENT IN LIFE IS A MATTER OF grave inequality. A chosen few possess an embarrassment of gifts. Everything they attempt receives the Midas touch. Excellence seems to flow from them like water from a faucet. They have an uncanny knack for getting things right. These are the people the rest of us love to hate.

Others appear to labor in vain. In these cases, diligence resembles water down the drain, and practice makes pitiful. These are the ones who help us sleep at night. It is as if God wishes the human race to wrestle with the twin sins of pride and envy. We could get a little miffed at the Creator for this if we weren't so busy gloating and sneering at each other instead. It is a cardinal truth, however, that everyone is especially good at something—even if it happens to be gossip, backseat driving, or just lazing around all day still as a scallop on the ocean floor.

The members of the choir at Ashgrove Baptist Church had special talents and abilities of all sorts. Phil Simpson

# Take My Life and Let It Be

## Written by Frances Ridley Havergal

Take my life and let it be Consecrated, Lord, to Thee;
Take my moments and my days—
   Let them flow in ceaseless praise,
Let them flow in ceaseless praise.

Take my hands and let them move
   At the impulse of Thy love;
Take my feet and let them be Swift and beautiful for Thee,
Swift and beautiful for Thee.

Take my voice and let me sing Always, only, for my King;
Take my lips and let them be
   Filled with messages from Thee,
Filled with messages from Thee.

Take my silver and my gold—Not a mite would I withhold;
Take my intellect and use
   Eve'ry pow'r as Thou shalt choose,
Ev'ry pow'r as Thou shalt choose.

Take my will and make it Thine—It shall be no longer mine;
Take my heart—it is Thine own,
   It shall be Thy royal throne,
It shall be Thy royal throne.

Take my love—my Lord, I pour
   At Thy feet its treasure store;
Take myself—and I will be Ever, only, all for Thee,
Ever, only, all for Thee.

could whistle three octaves and summon one of his blood-hounds from a distance of better than a mile. Jett Burges had won spoon-playing contests in his twenties and sometimes carried a pair of silver-plated ones in his pocket just to prove it. And Heidi Hapness had a knack for smiling wide on every vowel sound and every pitch, from low F to high C—or as close to it as she could come. Like any group in any place or time, the members of the Ashgrove choir could be made to seem very gifted indeed if you cast the talent net widely enough.

The trouble was that nearly all fifteen of them shared one critical deficit: none could sing to please a chipmunk. Serve up the Mormon Tabernacle Choir—hold the melody, harmony, and rhythm. This was the sound that emanated from the Ashgrove chancel on Sundays.

Things were no better out among the congregation at large. They seemed to make it a point to follow the choir's lead, which one supposes is how it is meant to be. But standing on the platform with the worshipers before me and choir members behind had a way of making surround sound seem more like a new form of torture than an advance in technology.

The Ashgrove choir never sang anthems. Instead, they alternated arrangements of the twenty or so hymns they knew best and loved most. "My Savior's Love," "Wonderful Grace of Jesus," and "What a Wonderful Savior" were three of the peppy ones. In a more reverent vein, they favored "Ivory Palaces," "His Eye Is on the Sparrow," and "The Old Rugged Cross." For variety, the men would sing a verse, and then the women, and occasionally a soloist got a turn. The last stanza was always full chorus again. Due to my sadly sheltered upbringing, almost nothing on their list had ever before greeted my ears. For the first three months there, I struggled to keep up with all these new hymns. I also found, though I am now embarrassed to admit it, that I didn't care much for most of them. Ivory palace language made me think more of the Taj Mahal than of heaven. The refrain of "The Old Rugged Cross" sent me back to the Bible in a panic to see where I'd missed out on the promise of crowns in heaven. I searched in vain. And hymns like "Wonderful Grace of Jesus" were plain hard to sing. Many of these hymns were more difficult than folks seemed to realize. When we think we know about something, we aren't always as afraid of it as perhaps we should be. This principle is true of driving at high speeds. It applies to white-water rafting. And it certainly has stood the hair up on the heads of many fine electricians. But it is doubly true of hymnody. Every Sunday I left worship with the feeling that, whatever merit there might be to these hymns, we weren't doing them any favors.

A pastor longs for a people who can sing. What if our world was suddenly turned upside down and ministers were invited annually to evaluate their congregation's performance over the previous year? (This is a practice I heartily endorse, by the way.) What evaluative tool would they use? Near the top of the form I would devise would be the following statement: Cooperates in the pastor's preparation to preach his/her best. But how would the typical pastor weigh the evidence on this question? Statements such as Refrains from calling the pastor at home on Saturday evenings or Avoids voicing grievances five minutes before the worship hour come to mind. But these would not factor on my list. My criterion would be simple: the congregation that cooperates in the pastor's preparation to preach is a congregation that can *sing!*

Over time, the most maddening of circumstances can come to seem humdrum. By the fall of my first year there, music at Ashgrove Church was fast becoming a mere annoyance. Then, in early November, congregational song came once again to top the charts of pastoral concern. The Plainville-Nebo Association of Churches was in the habit of holding a combined worship service on the Sunday evening before Thanksgiving. Ashgrove Baptist had recently joined them. Learning of this venture into ecumenism had caused my heart to swell with new enthusiasm. The latest news, however, tempered my zeal. Church choirs provided special music for these services on a rotating schedule. This was accomplished in an alphabetical manner. It had taken most of the 1980s to cycle through the roster: from Bridgeport Christian in 1981, to Grace Lutheran in 1982, then Hills Road Friends Meeting, Nebo United Methodist, and Plainville Presbyterian in 1983, 1984, and 1985 respectively, and, finally, the high-church Episcopal parish of St. Cecelia, patron saint of music. All of this wound things fatefully back around to the beginning—to the new beginning: Ashgrove Baptist Church. We were slated for our choral debut. Our moderator and volunteer music director, Harold Hatch, had been contacted, and he enthusiastically recruited the Ashgrove choir. I, however, was busy making plans to be out of town that weekend.

But this was not to be. So often, bad situations only worsen before they resolve. It seemed that Harold was having difficulty recruiting male voices for the service in question. He had begun to scrape bottom. Finally, as a last-ditch alternative, he came to his pastor.

"You want *me* to sing?" I said. "In the choir?" I added.

"You think you're a bass or a tenor?" Harold continued.

"Baritone," I answered. "What are you going to sing?"

"Well"—Harold, always the quick thinker, the diplomat—"what do you think we should sing?"

The bouncing ball back in my court, I pondered a moment. Here was an opportunity not to be wasted. As it happened, I had just been reading up on revival hymnody and had come upon the name Frances Ridley Havergal. Her best-loved hymn was one of the few I had recognized at Ashgrove. It was a good hymn, I thought. I had always liked it. I'd grown up with it.

"'Take My Life and Let It Be,'" I said. Perhaps "take my life and let me be" is what I had been thinking. But now it was out.

"Good!" Harold answered quickly. "It's all settled then!" And immediately he began to walk away. He had me, and we both knew it. "It's all settled" meant I would sing. "Oh!" he added, turning back, "I'd say you're a tenor. We could *use* a tenor!" And he was gone.

My next sensation was that of a live goose in a boiling pot. In a gathering of Lutherans, Presbyterians, and Episcopalians, I would be singing in the Ashgrove choir. Here, before even my third clergy meeting, my reputation was cooked. Then something came to mind that restored my hope. In reading about Frances Havergal, I had discovered that her father, Anglican clergyman William Henry Havergal, had found himself in a situation not unlike my own. In the 1840s, the quality of English congregational singing was stuck at low tide. William Havergal had poured his energies into a reformation of hymn singing at his parish. His strategy had been simple: raise the level of singing by improving the quality of song. Havergal had reintroduced the strong texts and tunes of early English composers. Apparently the effort had borne fruit. The great American hymnist Lowell Mason had noted that the quality of music in William Havergal's parish exceeded any in the rest of England. Maybe things would get better, I consoled myself. The greatest solace for pastors in their moments of misery is the realization that they are not alone.

But it was Frances Havergal herself whose example led me down an even richer path of understanding. She had been a musician of no mean talent. As both singer and pianist, she might well have been sought after, gone places, done things, made a splash around the Continent. Instead, she had had only one true passion: singing for Jesus. She had spoken five languages, composed inspired words with ease, and had charm to burn. Yet she had given away her mere forty-two years in single-minded devotion to the cause of consecrating souls to Christ. She had even lived out rapturously the verse in "Take My Life" about offering silver and gold, boxing up and shipping off to the needy those few prized trinkets she had had to her name. Frances Havergal had been possessed by the thought that her life was not her own.

The deeper meaning of all this came in an unexpected fashion. The Ashgrove choir had been hard at work rehearsing for the Sunday evening Thanksgiving service. At the final rehearsal, I was increasingly annoyed at the choir's chronic inability to carry through a simple phrase without breathing, especially on the opening line: "Take my life and let it be *consecrated!*"

"Do we have to stop?" I blurted out at last. "Is there some reason why we can't sing the phrase through and finish the thought—that we are asking God to let our lives be *consecrated?*"

"But," Heidi Hapness spoke up in her trademark tone of utter innocence, "what is 'consecrate' anyway? I don't even know what the heck it means!"

Others shook their heads—but up and down this time in agreement, not side to side in their usual disdain of Heidi. She has sounded a chord in them.

"Well?" Harold said, looking my way. "You want to comment?" He said it in a puckered up sort of way, as if holding back a very big grin.

But I sat stunned, smitten. The fact was that I had never bothered to consider it. Synonyms raced through my head: *offer, dedicate, give, present* . . . But these would no longer do. Heidi had touched off a chord in me as well. Suddenly, for the first time, it came to me just what consecrated was all about.

"It means *surrender*," I said at last. "It means you give up, entrust to God everything you are and have and care about—because you love him."

In Jesus' parable of the talents, a master entrusts to each of three servants a different portion of his assets. When later he checks on their progress, something comes clear: the master is looking not only for a positive yield on his investment but also for a definitive sign of love and devotion. According to Jesus, the point is not only to make best use of the gifts you've got but also to give yourself to the God who offered them.

Consecration! This is what it all boiled down to. However we calibrated the taste meter, wherever we fell along the talent continuum, in worship we were consecrating ourselves to God. Nothing else really mattered. It is what Frances Havergal seems to have done. Little wonder she was remembered as the "consecration poet." "Take My Life" was a song of solid ground for every singing soul.

Now it was clear to me. It was not for the Plainville-Nebo Association Thanksgiving service alone that this hymn was being programmed. It was for my benefit as well that we sang it. It was to be my personal act of consecration. Here I would surrender all my presuppositions about taste and style. I would lay them down before the throne of grace. From here forward, I would strive to sing lustily any and every song in the hymnal. I would champion any text, however corny, and any tune, however quaint, so long as they were offered to God with thoughtful and sincere hearts. I doubted whether the flock would follow suit. Probably few would come overnight to hold a candle for Mozart or Bach. But at least I would be modeling something as close to the heart of the gospel as I could think: that to worship the God of surpassing grace meant to practice such grace in our worship.

And wasn't this principle of praise already at play all around us? Didn't all sensory experience shout aloud, cacophonous canticle to God's handiwork? The great chorus of nature, from the rustle of wind in the trees, to the rush of a river and the chatter of a stream, from lark to locust, from crow to cricket; and the rich canvas of color, from the greening of spring to the steamy yellow of high summer to the busy calico of late autumn to the still white of deep winter; and the exquisite tastes of sugar and salt and everything in between; and the feel of soft fur and polished wood, and the smell of cinnamon and daffodils and a smoked hickory barbecue. Each of these revealed a calculating grace and, together, a Creator worthy of praise.

Why should worship—especially worship—be excepted from this rule of the cosmos? Every song, every prayer, every recital of words, every *Amen!* in response, every physical gesture—all standing and sitting and kneeling and hunching and stretching and swaying and genuflecting; all pipes and strings, bells and chimes, shouts and whispers, coughing and throat clearing, and sweet silence itself; all art and architecture, banners and paraments, crosses and crucifixes, and every depiction of Jesus, whether spirited or sad, solemn or sweet; and the smells of old hymnals and Welch's grape juice and incense and heavy perfume in the pew; and the gestures of a handshake, or a hug, or a kiss on the cheek; and laughter, and tears, and contrition and release; and the sound and look and feel of unrestricted joy.

Weren't all these made for God's good pleasure? Did not each warrant a place in the grand panoply of praise?

Take our lives, O God! Let them be consecrated! Take our hands, our feet, take our voices and lips, our moments and days, our silver and gold, our wills and hearts, our lives and loves—take our very selves! Consecrate us, dear God! Until we will be ever, only, all for thee! Ever, only, all for thee!

At the Sunday evening Thanksgiving service, the Ashgrove Baptist choir and its pastor sang their lungs out. On the last verse, the whole congregation stood tall and joined the chorus. It was not an especially stirring sound we made, but any who could not feel the pleasure of the Lord there must have been not unlike a certain young pastor who once mistook the sound of praise for the God who bends low to bless it.

After Thanksgiving, I joined the Ashgrove choir tenor section and never missed a Sunday. I still prefer Bach, Beethoven, and Brahms, but those ivory palaces seem to reach a little higher toward heaven with each passing week.

## ♪ Hymn Notes ♪

In life, gifts are given, and God's people must choose how to honor them. Frances Ridley Havergal (1836–1879) was endowed with a lovely voice, a talent for piano, and a charming personality—gifts that will travel. But Havergal appears never to have strayed from her single ambition to press them into the service of the gospel. In a word, Frances Havergal consecrated all that she had to the evangelical cause, or, as she put it, to "singing for Jesus."

The circumstances surrounding the writing of "Take My Life" shed light on the evangelical spirit of her setting. In 1874, as Havergal visited friends, she began to pray,

"Lord, give me all in this house!" Before her visit ended, Havergal reports, her prayer had come to pass. All ten persons in the home "had got a blessing." Unable to sleep for her excitement, she spent most of the night in prayer and penned the poem that finished "Ever, only, all for thee."

The hymn unfolds in couplets, each emphasizing aspects of our consecrated lives: moments, days, hands, feet, voice, lips, silver, gold, mind, will, heart, love. The phrase "take myself" compliments the hymn's opening phrase while again summarizing the whole of what one has to offer.

Havergal composed hymns over a period of thirty-five years, publishing them first on leaflets that periodically were consolidated into volumes with titles such as *Under the Surface* (1874) and *Loyal Responses* (1878), in which "Take My Life" appeared. From her considerable output, only a handful of hymns are still widely sung. Among these are "Take My Life," "Another Year Is Dawning," and "Lord, Speak to Me, That I May Speak."

The tune most frequently used with "Take My Life" is *Hendon,* composed by H. A. Cesar Malan (1787–1864). Worthy of note is that Havergal desired this text to be sung to her father William Henry Havergal's tune, *Patmos.* Her wish was fulfilled among American Baptists and Disciples in the 1970 *Hymnbook for Christian Worship.*

## CHAPTER 2

# Voice of the Trinity

## "Holy, Holy, Holy"

TOM TATMAN WAS A MYSTERY, STARTING WITH HIS AGE. Was he in his twenties or sixties, I had long wondered. It was difficult to tell on account of his face—the soft, smooth skin of a babe in arms but the droopy eyes of a man who had known much pain. He had been with the church for a mere number of months that might as well have been days, for Tom was shy. Words from his mouth were rare as June bugs in January. When they came at all, they were timid, broken, halting. Tom Tatman was a stutterer.

Tom had first come to the church as a guest of Billy Burton, after Tom's failure as a factory line worker. Billy was a foreman at a local canning plant. He had taken Tom on, confident he could make a fine line worker out of well nigh anyone. Instead, Tom's performance had been well nigh awful. After just two weeks, Billy had pronounced the whole thing a failure.

"Tom just couldn't hack it," Billy explained. "You could see the strain in his eyes. It was hard to watch." Billy had made a point to befriend Tom, he said, to try and help him make the grade. "But in the end," Billy lowered his head a notch to tell it, "I had let him go."

"You fired him," I qualified.

"Had to," he said. "He was a danger to himself. The whole thing's a matter of speed, of timing. Tom just couldn't keep up. Nothin' more I could do," Billy concluded.

Except ask Tom to church, that is. The day after had giving Tom the pink slip, Billy had resolved to invite him to

## Holy, Holy, Holy

**Written by Reginald Heber**

Holy, holy, holy, Lord God Almighty!
Early in the morning our song shall rise to Thee;
Holy, holy, holy! Merciful and mighty!
God in three persons, blessed Trinity!

Holy, holy, holy! All the saints adore Thee,
Casting down their golden crowns around the glassy sea;
Cherubim and seraphim falling down before Thee,
Which wert and art and evermore shalt be.

Holy, holy, holy! Though the darkness hide Thee,
Though the eye of sinful man Thy glory may not see;
Only Thou art holy—there is none beside Thee
Perfect in pow'r, in love and purity.

Holy, holy, holy, Lord God Almighty!
All Thy works shall praise Thy name
   in earth and sky and sea;
Holy, holy, holy! merciful and mighty!
God in three persons, blessed Trinity!

morning worship at Ashgrove Church. "Just seemed like the decent thing to do, somehow," Billy explained.

Surprisingly, Tom had accepted with thanks. He had walked into the vestibule that Sunday and been greeted straightaway by Harold Hatch. Harold had peered into those droopy eyes as if into a mirror—eyes that wince at a world gone mad, a world whizzing by out of control. Harold had beheld the countenance of a soul mate.

For several years, Harold Hatch, painting contractor by trade, had avoided taking on help, convinced the institution of apprenticeship had faltered. All young labor was inane and impatient. Impatience was the worse half. Tradesmen of all types were too much in a hurry to excel at anything. No one any longer had a heart for the art of it all.

"I'd rather work alone and starve to death than hire noodleheads," he often said.

Then Tom had turned up, and Harold had begun to believe again.

"Slow, is he, you say?" he asked Billy.

"I'm afraid," Billy said.

"Good," said Harold.

This had been the sound of music to Harold, who lived in hope that the word slow might still mean "careful." Besides, Tom didn't talk much, and this was especially favorable since Harold himself talked enough for a painting crew of ten. "Ah! Someone to mold!" Harold thought. "Someone who'll take the time to ponder a bare board before he paints it."

At the close of worship, Harold slipped up on Tom in that way of his, so that as Tom turned around, he came immediately eye to eye with his destiny.

"Can you paint?" Destiny asked.

"No," Tom Tatman replied.

"Good!" said Destiny. And Harold and Tom each flashed the other the same squint-eyed smile.

Even Billy was pleased with Tom's new painting career. "Some things just seem meant to be," he philosophized, "and this gets proved out over time . . . "

For as long as anyone could remember, the only soul who read Scripture from the pulpit of Ashgrove Baptist Church was the pastor. When I first began to float the idea of lay readers, the reaction was swift and decisive. "The pastor does that! It's his job!" But I early suspected this to be a cover. Reading was not a congregational strong suit. People avoided the lectern for fear of embarrassment.

"I'd like to start a lay reading class," I announced at the monthly deacons' meeting. "I'd like to train a team of first-rate Scripture readers for worship." Herb Chestnut, chairman of the board, choked on those words. He was of the view that if anyone other than the pastor or moderator were to speak from the front of the church, it should by all rights be the head deacon. Herb approached that possibility with all the fervor one feels toward a root canal.

"You won't get many," he cautioned. "People around here are awful shy about gettin' up in front. Besides, we've always thought readin' the Holy Bible was the pastor's job!"

"Yes, I know," I said.

Undeterred, I had prepared a flyer:

WANTED: EAGER READERS OF SCRIPTURE!
COME AND EXPERIENCE THE JOY
OF READING GOD'S WORD IN WORSHIP!

I placed a sign-up sheet on a clipboard in the vestibule. Then I waited. For the first two weeks, shyness prevailed and the sheet remained empty. Herb scouted the table, peering down at the blank paper from time to time approvingly. Then, as a matter of sheer inevitability, Heidi Hapness signed her name. Others, convinced they could do no worse than she, followed suit. After four Sundays, I took the clipboard into my study and made an appraisal.

Nine lines were filled in, but one of the names was illegible. Its letters were irregular, as if the pen had jerked with every stroke. "Some child!" I thought to myself. And I had put it out of my mind. There were eight others who had signed up—all of them women—yet I was exceedingly pleased with the response. The Ashgrove Baptist Church lay readers' class would commence at last.

This was not the only new worship team at Ashgrove Church. Nearly from the beginning of my tenure there, it became evident that my approach to hymn selection wasn't working. People complained about the hymns more than they sang them. Even if the complaints persisted, I felt that at the very least we could spread around some of the blame. Harold Hatch, our song leader, Shelly Higgins, the church pianist, and I gathered at our maiden hymn selection meeting.

"Let's start with hymns we all know," Harold suggested, convinced of the value of common ground. "There must be at least a few of these." I rather doubted this at first, but soon we compiled a list of more than twenty hymns, excluding Christmas carols. At the top of the list, outranked only by "Amazing Grace," was the nineteenth-century English hymn "Holy, Holy, Holy."

"This one should work well," I said, "since we're coming right up on Trinity Sunday!"

Harold and Shelly shrugged.

"A very old church festival," I explained, "dedicated to the Holy Trinity."

"Holy, Holy, Holy" had been written for that very day of the church year. The author was Reginald Heber, an

Anglican bishop and missionary to India. Heber had been born into wealth and privilege. Biblically literate at age five, fluent in Latin by age seven, he had been the sort of child who makes the rest of us feel stupid. All rankings of intelligence flatten in the face of genius. But Heber's heart had been tender. Before he had left for boarding school, his parents had sewn his tuition into the lining of his coat for fear he would give it away to the needy along the way. As a missionary in India, he had preached mightily against the caste system the very day he died of heat stroke at forty-three.

In the intervening years, Heber had pursued among other things his passion for excellence in congregational hymn singing. At the beginning of the nineteenth century, most Anglican churches had still been singing the psalms exclusively. Heber had wanted musical texts to inspire congregational singing, fresh words to enrich worship according to the ecclesiastical church year. Finding none, he had begun to write his own. "Holy, Holy, Holy" was a catalogue of epithets versified in threes—a "trinity of words"—to evoke the mystery of that doctrine. The God who is "holy, merciful and mighty" is also perfect in "power, in love, and purity," and eternal (he who "wert and art and evermore shalt be").

"Some churches change the words," Harold pointed out. "Not everyone likes the Trinity, so they sing the 'wert' and 'art' part more, I think."

Then Shelly, an old Baptist, said she recalled growing up singing a different ending. Instead of "God in three persons, blessed Trinity," her church had sung "God over all and blessed eternally."

"What's the point of that, do you suppose?" she asked.

"About five hundred years of church history," I said.

The remarkable thing was that for all these differences, "Holy, Holy, Holy" remained a hymn that almost everyone sang. All Christians seemed to claim it equally. Something in it spoke to everyone.

"Now, we'll be reading for meaning," I said. It was a Thursday evening in April, and we were convened in the sanctuary for our first lay reading session. "Naturally, clarity and projection are important as well," I added. "We want our hearers to be transported into the text, to experience its colors, its contours—to see, smell, and taste the setting, to believe that they are present on the scene of the story as we speak . . . "

I had phoned all eight people on the list and invited them. All had come. Our first task was to tackle the drama of a story from the Gospels. Mark 9, we chose, an account of exorcism, of the healing of a man with an evil spirit. It had bound his tongue and caused him to convulse.

"Epilepsy!" Addie Cox exclaimed. "Just had it in Sunday school!"

"Maybe," I responded. "But they didn't know that. We want to read it as they would have experienced it—as some formidable demonic power."

"Oh," she said.

They began a bit timidly, but soon they were reading with true spirit.

"If you are able!" they recited Jesus. "All things can be done for the one who believes!"

"I believe;"—now the words of the father—"help my unbelief!" each one read in turn, until they nearly wept with sympathy for the poor man.

"You spirit that keeps this boy from speaking and hearing," declared Jesus, now with mounting fervor and assurance, "I command you, come out of him, and never enter him again!"

"Bravo!" cried the pastor. A fine beginning indeed!

Meanwhile one who still stuttered in speech sat idly at home—one whose handwriting shook so badly that the pastor had coolly dismissed it.

"Might've looked into it, you know—inquired." It was all Harold Hatch said. It was enough. He had heard from the women about the splendid time they had spent at the first ever lay readers' class. He had heard from Tom Tatman about the tiresome time he had had at home, unaware the session was even going on. I had explained that the signature was simply illegible, impossible to decipher.

"You might have thought to ask," he said. "To follow up."

"Well, to be honest," I told Harold, "I'm not so sure about Tom—whether this is the best place for him. He talks awfully—"

"Slow." Harold finished my sentence.

"Reading Scripture well is not an easy thing," I argued. "It takes—"

"Practice." He had done it again. "Have you ever sat down with Tom," Harold asked, "taken the time to have a proper conversation with him?"

I hadn't.

"You know," Harold continued, "Tom's just about the best painter I've ever had work for me. He's slow, careful, precise."

"But doesn't he shake a lot? How can he do all the detail work?" I asked, ashamed of myself.

"Some of it he can't. But most of it he manages. There's a lot going on behind that shy face a' his. He's a young man with a way, if you'll let him find it! . . . Maybe you should give him a chance."

When Harold held you in the grip of wisdom, there was no purpose served in trying to wriggle free. Best just to nod and be silent, to heed his advice and be the better for it. I phoned Tom that very night.

"Hell . . . hell . . . *hello?*" Tom answered.

"Tom," I said, " . . . you free next Thursday night?"

"Prais, prais, *praise* the Lord! O, O, O give thank, thank, *thanks* to the Lord, fo, fo, *for* he is good; for his stead, stead, *steadfast* love endures forever." The women sat motionless, without expression, as Tom read, his voice shaking audibly, his head buried in the page.

"Who, who, *who* can utt, utt, *utter* the mighty doings of the Lord?" As he asked this question, not one of them could think of a polite answer. It was hard to watch, Billy had said of Tom on the factory line. Here in the sanctuary of God it was hard to listen.

This was the second gathering of the Ashgrove Baptist lay readers' class. The assignment had been Psalm 106. "This is a psalm of praise," I had explained, "but also of confession and a prayer for help."

"Sav, sav, *save* us, O Lord," Tom, the psalmist, continued, and "he, he, *he* regarded their dist, dist, *distress,* when he heard their cry . . . "

"Good, Tom!" I lied. "Now, speak up, and look up more, too. We want to be able to hear every word." And I did my best to say it all matter-of-factly.

At the end of the hour, I walked Tom out to his car. "It's really coming," I told him.

"No, no no! It's aw, aw, awful," he said, "and you know it!"

Then I remembered my own description of the psalm: words of praise but also of open, honest confession, of truth telling and petition.

"We'll work on it, Tom!" I said. "It'll be good, it'll be fine . . . " And I drove home with droopy eyes.

"Mild C.P.!" my wife blurted out. It gave me such a start I dropped the screwdriver and nearly fell off the ladder I had climbed to hang venetian blinds. I flashed her a look somewhere between confusion and consternation. I didn't like ladders to begin with, certainly not when they shimmied to my shuffle five feet off the ground.

"Not you!" she joked. "Tom Tatman! I think he has a mild case of cerebral palsy. I've watched him," she said. "I think it's why he stammers."

Suddenly it all made sense: the shyness, the slowness of movement, the indecipherable handwriting. Hypoxia of the brain, fixed from birth, ill-fated as blindness. I had seen it close up in its more severe forms, including jerkiness, facial contortions, and difficulty walking. Once I had heard described the spasms of muscles unwilling to relax, the relentless bodily tension never releasing its grip. I had marveled at the determination of those who suffered with such conditions, who willingly expended twice the effort to do each little thing while the rest of us took all our ease for granted.

Once again I thought of Tom. Whatever his true condition, he had often been bruised by disappointment. Yet he had not given up. Yet he painted! If he could learn to paint, then why not read? Why not in public, why not in worship? "Oh, who can *utter* the mighty doings of the Lord?" I asked. "Why, Tom Tatman, of course!"

Lay reading in worship at Ashgrove Church commenced at last on Pentecost Sunday, the day the disciples first caught the Spirit and shared the gospel with the world. They were just ordinary Janes, but on that day their tongues were loosed by fire. It seemed too poetic a parallelism to resist.

Gladys Hatch led off with a reading from the Gospel of John, chapter 20. "Peace be with you," she announced tenderly. And a second time—*"Peace be with you!"*—this time with such evident emotion that some present reported feeling the blessing of Jesus himself. Then Hassie Longstreet, our Louisiana transplant, read the story from Acts 2. Her elegant Southern drawl dignified the occasion further. As flawlessly she called the role of nations from Parthia to Pamphylia, Herb Chestnut's jaw dropped in awe. Had it not been frozen in place, he might have cried out, "Mercy sakes, can these ladies really dress up the Word!"

After worship, all the women lay readers congregated to celebrate an auspicious beginning. "Who'll read next?" they wondered aloud. Who would dare, after the perform-ances of Hassie and Gladys? Meanwhile, Tom Tatman stood at a distance, looking away and feigning indifference. Naturally he had taken in every word. His expression revealed nothing, but his eyes had their trademark droop, long the facial bellwether of impending disappointment. His eyes said, "It's, it's, it's over! We'll, we'll, we'll never read from up there!" But this time his droopy eyes were wrong—I knew it deep in my gut.

I knew it because of the remarkable occurrence earlier that morning during the Sunday school hour. Pauline Jones had been engaged in an innocent Bible lesson with her juniors. Walking from the vestibule to Fellowship Hall, I became party to it and couldn't coax myself away. She had been reminding students as frequently she did that God loved us enough to die on the cross. Mitchell Cox, Winslow and Addie's youngest boy, had perfect attendance. He was hear-ing this now for at least the tenth time. It was almost out of compunction that he finally asked the thing about which he'd wondered for weeks:

"But how could he *die,* if he was God?"

There was a brief silence in the room, while the full extent of Pauline's impotence in the face of such a question came home to her.

"Well—he wasn't really *God* at the time, Mitchell," Pauline answered at last, having some faint recollection this might be right.

"Huh?" Mitchell had grunted.

"Well, hold on now," threw in Pauline's husband, Maynard. "Yes he was, too!" Maynard was Sunday school treasurer. He had slipped in to collect the basket offering but then foolishly forgot to mind his own business within his wife's province.

"Well, not God the *Father,* I didn't mean," she scrambled. "God, the *Son* I meant! —it was just Jesus, the *man,* that died!" Then, "Maynard, don't you have somethin' to do?" And she shot him her worst "How dare you!" look.

As Maynard hurried from the room, I turned myself quickly about face so that I was staring at the portrait gallery of former pastors, hanging along the opposite wall. "Oh, morning, Maynard," I said, jerking back around as though he'd caught me unaware.

"Women!" he fumed.

Glancing down the pastors' gallery of six self-assured faces, I wondered briefly whether one of these held the answer to Mitchell's question. "No," I resolved, "not likely . . . "

How, after all, could God be both alive and dead at the same time? Or both human and divine? How was God both three persons and one substance? How could two persons, Son and Spirit, proceed from the third without being subordinate to it? The early church fathers had not resolved these matters. The councils of Nicea and Chalcedon couldn't settle them. Christians had been doomed to stumble over such questions all the way down to the present day. Wars had been fought over them. Martyrs had paid the ultimate price. Meanwhile the masses continued to offer their highest allegiance to creeds they couldn't begin to understand. Wasn't this just the way of words? Finally all speech was stutter, a mumble of meaning. To speak at all was to aim at truth and miss, I thought. Then a strange idea lodged in my brain.

On Trinity Sunday, everything happened in fours. Four hymns were sung, four prayers were prayed, and four fresh lay readers stepped to the pulpit for the first time. One of them was Tom Tatman. I had asked him to read a portion of Revelation 4, which I had divided into four sections for each of my four readers. The briefest yet most important of these sections went to Tom.

There was a rationale for this. It had to do with the special relationship between Revelation 4 and Reginald Heber's hymn, "Holy, Holy, Holy," which it had inspired. Both wished to tell us what God was like. Each accomplished this not by explaining things but through poetic imagery, little glimpses of holiness.

The nature of God is a mystery, the Trinity, unfathomable doctrine. Better to leave it that way. But one thing seemed clear beyond a doubt: a God as grand as ours merits more than one "holy." Both the Book of Revelation and Reginald Heber had offered God three. Not bad, I thought, but we could do better. After all, we had Tom Tatman.

It had all hit me the week before, as Pauline squirmed over a question too wise for our own good. Tom was the ideal lay reader for Trinity Sunday. As a circumstance of nature, he spoke everything in threes anyway. Tom Tatman was a trinitarian by birth. If anyone could bring to life this doctrinal mystery in our worship, it was he!

Tom stepped into the pulpit, trembling, as Harold said later, "like a paint shaker." Then, casting those droopy eyes down on the page, he began.

"Holy, holy, *holy,*" he intoned in a tentative voice. Then again, stronger, "Holy, holy, *holy,*" gaining in strength and confidence. And finally a third time, his voice by now booming: *"Holy, holy, holy! The, the, the Lord God Almighty, who, who, who was and is and is to come!"*

Tom Tatman, stutterer, spoke a triple trinity of holies. Not since Nicea itself had the grandeur of God been more meaningfully expressed. Then Heber's hymn was sung. Worshipers stood to intone a whole new string of holies of their own. All in all, it was about the holiest service of worship anyone could recall.

And after worship, the lay readers' class of Ashgrove Baptist Church huddled in the vestibule, all eight women surrounding the single shy man. What a fabulous morning it had been, they exclaimed. Who would read next, they wondered? Who would dare, after Tom "Trinity" Tatman!

It was as Billy Burton had said: "Some things just seem meant to be, and this gets proved out over time!"

## ♪ Hymn Notes ♪

Bishop Reginald Heber (1783–1826) was one of the first and best hymn writers in the nineteenth-century Romantic Movement in England. Kind-hearted and prodigious, he distinguished himself early as a leader in Anglicanism at that moment when upper-class gentry were first aligning themselves with the evangelical wing of the church.

One of Heber's chief interests as a pastor was improving the quality of congregational singing. Most Anglican churches, including his first charge in the small town of

Hodnet in Shropshire, still sang the Psalter. "My psalm-singing continues bad," he wrote to a friend. Heber began to compose hymns of his own, based upon texts from the Gospels and Epistles and the Nicene Creed.

One of these, published the year after his death, was "Holy, Holy, Holy, Lord God Almighty" (1827). It appeared in a posthumous collection of fifty-seven works entitled *Hymns Written and Adapted to the Weekly Church Service of the Year.* Intended for use on Trinity Sunday, "Holy, Holy, Holy" is probably the best known of all Heber's hymns. The text paraphrases Revelation 4:8–11 while drawing on the formula for God's persons, Father, Son, and Holy Spirit, as put forth by the Council of Nicea.

However one interprets the trinitarian language of the creed, the scene of worship Heber's hymn portrays is one of utter unity. Gathered are all the saints, the cherubim, the seraphim, and the testimony of all God's works in earth, sky, and sea—that is, everywhere. God's deeds as well as God's being conspire to elicit praise on earth and in heaven.

John Bacchus Dykes (1823–1876) wrote the tune *Nicea* expressly for this text. It first appeared in *Hymns Ancient and Modern* (1861). Its title is a clear reference to the council where the trinitarian doctrine was formulated.

# CHAPTER 3

# Home to Erin, Home to God

## "Be Thou My Vision"

RAYMOND WAS EVERYWHERE. NOT A BUSY WESTSIDE intersection escaped his sway. When you least expected it, he would appear—at the next traffic light, around the next bend, at the top of the next hill. From his corner perch, he lay psychological siege to everything on four wheels. He would stare at oncoming traffic, his eyes rolling up into his head, and draw curious customers like a vacuum cleaner. But they would leave with a broom instead. Raymond Slane peddled sweep brooms for a living. He made them at night in his cramped apartment on Thompson Road. Then, from dawn to dusk, Monday through Friday, Raymond sold them on the curb.

He would choose a spot and stand, broom in hand, still as a guard at Buckingham Palace. Those on errands returning in the opposite direction were especially susceptible. They would cast unwitting eyes on him a second time, standing in the precise pose in which they observed him perhaps hours before. Then they would exhale a stupefied sigh, signaling surrender. Even the cold-hearted hyperventilated on his proud, preposterous air. Before they could regain their composure, they would fabricate some pretext for needing a new broom and pull off the road to buy it. They would trudge weak-kneed to his side, cash in hand. Raymond would wait patiently as they made a selection.

# Be Thou My Vision

From *The Poem Book of the Gael* translated by M. E. Byrne
and edited by Eleanor Hull.
Originally published by Chatto & Windus.
Reprinted by permission of The Random House Group Limited.
Copyright © the Estate of Eleanor Hull

Be Thou my Vision, O Lord of my heart—
Naught be all else to me save that Thou art;
Thou my best thought by day or by night—
Waking or sleeping, Thy presence my light.

Be Thou my wisdom, be Thou my true word—
I ever with Thee and Thou with me, Lord;
Thou my great Father and I Thy true son—
Thou in me dwelling, and I with Thee one.

Riches I heed not nor man's empty praise—
Thou mine inheritance now and always;
Thou and Thou only be first in my heart—
High King of heaven, my treasure Thou art.

High King of heaven, when vict'ry is won,
May I reach heaven's joys, O bright heav'n's Sun!
Heart of my own heart, whatever befall,
Still be my Vision, O Ruler of all.

Then he would inspect the broom carefully before accepting the eight-dollar payment with one hearty "thank you!" All this he did without ever once looking up. This was just as well. Raymond Slane was blind.

Because I was his pastor and cruised the west side as much as any licensed driver, I was predestined to be Raymond's best customer. Having pulled off early in my pastorate to buy a broom, I had thought in the future simply to drive on by. After all, I reasoned, he would never see me. He would be none the wiser.

"Heard you drive by the other day, Pastor," Raymond announced offhandedly one Sunday.

"Oh? Really?" I responded, stunned.

Ray had said it with just a bit of the Irish, I thought, with that Gaelic flair of irony that can cause the hearer to stand accused. It was a quality in his voice long noted by members of Ashgrove church. Especially given their prevailing Kentucky dialect, it stood out in stark relief.

Thinking fast I asked, "Now, when was that, Ray?"

"Last Tuesday, around noon," he answered without hesitation. "Engine squeals a bit, Pastor. Might ought to have the radiator belt checked for tension."

Later, reviewing my mileage record, it had all come back. It had been a Tuesday, and I had been in between hospital calls. Over the noon hour, I had detoured two blocks south to a Burger King drive-through window. I had been biting into a chicken filet sandwich when the light turned red, and I had idled in a line of vehicles for nearly a minute. It was then that I had spotted him, standing tall, still, and stoic on my side of the road. And I had passed him by . . .

Closing the mileage book, I vowed never again to leave Ray and his brooms in the dust. Consequently, by the sixth month of my pastorate, a Raymond Slane sweep broom hung on a nail behind every door of our home. When Ray dropped bills in the Sunday offering plate, I sometimes contemplated the percentage of his generosity for which I was personally responsible. At least a little was coming back to God, I consoled myself.

The same did not appear to hold for Ray himself. He had attended Ashgrove church for several years but had never joined. He was a self-proclaimed agnostic. "Just can't quite see my way clear to God yet!" he would joke. "Not even a burning bush would do me any good!" But the whole truth was murkier than that, I had thought. Behind those eyes, Ray harbored secrets he was unwilling to disclose.

A case in point concerned the multiple theories of Ray's history of blindness. Some were certain Ray was a victim of arguably the worst form of visual impairment: stricken in the prime of life. They set forth as evidence Ray's frequent allusions to the experience of sight. Some had heard him speak of the great beauty of his mother's eyes and hair and gentle face, or describe the raging descent of the falls on the Niagara River, or paint a verbal picture of that spectacular spray of light and color in the night sky on the Fourth of July. Once, he had even recounted his experience at the precipice of the Grand Canyon, how leaning into its empty vastness had nearly hollowed out his soul. Surely only the sighted had such words for such things.

If Ray were indeed a relative newcomer to blindness, its cause too remained shrouded in mystery. Had it been an injury—head trauma, perhaps, from a fall or a car accident? Was it some condition or predisposition—diabetes or a brain tumor or macular degeneration? His own silence on the subject only fueled the rumor mill. Ray kept us all groping in the dark.

But there was another lens through which to interpret Ray's words. Maybe he had always *seen* as a blind man. After all, couldn't the blind behold beauty with their hands? Or survey size and distance with their ears? Or perceive contrasts of light and darkness in the eye of the mind? Didn't the blind learn to see with their other senses in a way not given to the sighted? Though this was a minority view, it took root in me and grew my desire to explore the hidden contours of beauty, to see the world through the eyes of Raymond Slane.

My curiosity settled especially on the name itself: Slane. From the moment he first introduced himself, it had conjured in me a faint recollection. I had heard this name before, but I failed to pin down time or place. Slane, the man and the cognomen, remained a tease on my consciousness.

Raymond reported to work each day on foot, walking the west side with a stack of brooms, sheathed on his back like a quill of arrows. He had rarely lost his way, except in deep snow, and only once had nearly come to harm. A thief had jumped him near dusk on a lonely street. But Ray was strong and had managed to pin the man with a broom by his neck and bloody his face before help had arrived to save the poor thief's life.

Ray knew the feel and smell of only one car, and it belonged to Phil and Jeannie Simpson. The Simpsons had introduced Ray into the fellowship of Ashgrove church several years earlier, and Ray rode with them on a regular basis. When Phil, a church trustee, had assumed responsibility for the purchase of janitorial supplies, he had placed his dear wife in charge of procurement. The church needed brooms, and Jeannie had found them one day, driving by the corner of Twelfth and Granville. Ray's were such fine specimens that she had tracked him down again to purchase more for herself. Word had spread around the congregation until other wives commenced buying from Ray direct at his apartment. Soon Ray had caught on like a cheap plumber. From there, it was only a blind step or two to the precipice of church participation. Several ladies began to take pity on a poor, lost bachelor with no soul to attend to his basic needs— needs like home cookin'! The lure of baked goods from the kitchens of Madge Spires and Alberta Rump had weakened his resistance to the point that, with an invitation to the summer fish fry, Ray finally had stepped off into the abyss.

Now Raymond rarely missed a Sunday. He sat on the aisle halfway up from the back of the sanctuary, with Phil and Jeannie to his immediate left. Unlike some of the sighted worshipers, Ray never closed his eyes to sleep through my words. He sat rigidly in the pew, with hands on his knees and an expressionless face, like the statue of Lincoln at his Memorial in Washington. There was one difference. Something long and wooden jutted up from the floor between Raymond's legs and rested against his clavicle bone. It was a broom handle without the broom, Ray's version of a blind stick, which he would slap emphatically, driving anything with ears well out of his path.

The presence in the pews of a blind man and his broomstick held both fear and fascination for children. For once, they could stare at something strange in the freedom of anonymity—at least until their mothers glared at them disapprovingly or their fathers boxed their ears. Once out of earshot of either, they would trade nicknames for Raymond—Blindman and Mr. Broomstick, or, most favored of all, Blindstick. Raymond knew of these appellations. His ears soaked up sound like an acoustical tile. But Ray didn't seem to mind. Ashgrove was home now, insofar as he even believed in the concept.

Then, one day, the light of heaven shined down on Ray and caught us all up in a story of remembrance and illumination. At the tail end of a monthly church potluck dinner, the men were finally giving up on desserts after second and third helpings and the women were beginning to clear away food. A well-satisfied Raymond Slane reclined peacefully in his chair at the table, gauging the noise about him toward no particular end. It was then and there that young Andy Burges mustered the courage to approach Ray with a question.

"Do you know how to *use* one 'a them things?"

Ray had been twirling his broom handle between the palms of his massive hands, as if trying to light a campfire from friction. Andy had been watching him. He was Jett Burges' youngest son and as good-hearted as all the rest. But his knack for combining pure innocence and astonishing impertinence into a single question rivaled that of Dennis the Menace.

"You mean, can I use a *broom,* young fella?" Ray asked in good humor.

"Sure," Andy answered. "I mean, you make 'em all day—can you sweep with em?" Andy was less interested in Raymond's sweeping talent than in the blind man himself. He had fallen with the other boys into the nicknaming fun, but his curiosity went deeper than most. Andy seemed as eager to search behind those eyes as was his pastor.

Ray offered Andy no answer but a grin. Then he raised himself up from his chair to his full height of six feet, three inches, and glancing in Andy's direction, said, "Follow me!"

Feeling his way to the kitchen, Ray quickly traded his broom handle for one of his own brooms, hanging from a hook on the wall. "Down there," he said, pointing Andy to the far wall of Fellowship Hall. Andy on his heels, Raymond Slane felt his way to the end of the room with the aid of the broom handle, then turned it on end and began to sweep the floor of the hall in its entirety. The clean-up crew, taking down the last of the tables, was careful to step around him as he worked methodically from one end to the other, never once losing his place.

Meanwhile, from the opposite end of the hall, Harold Hatch, Shelly Higgins, and I were discussing worship for the coming month. Sermons would focus on select miracle stories from the Gospel of John. Each story suggested a worship theme, and we were working our way through the outline in search of appropriate hymns to compliment them.

Watching Ray from our corner brought to my mind a chess master who can play several matches at once, blindfolded. Gradually every speck of litter and debris on the tile floor was checkmated into a dustpan, then tossed by Andy into the trash. I marveled equally at Ray's performance and Andy's response to it: awe!

But Ray was rapidly sweeping our way, as we turned to a text from John 9, the story of Jesus' healing of the man born blind. In John, I commented, "blindness" meant failing to understand who Jesus is—that Jesus is God's grace revealed. Were there hymns, I entertained, that wrestled with the questions of physical and spiritual blindness and sight? And with every certain stroke of the broom, Ray grew nearer to our conversation, and I grew more concerned to stop it. But it was too late.

"Well," Shelly offered categorically, "the very best hymn about blindness is 'Open My Eyes, That I May See!'" She began with great flourish to sing out the refrain, as if already convinced I did not know it:

*Silently now I wait for thee,*
  *Ready, my God, thy will to see;*
*Open my eyes, illumine me, Spir—it divine!*

"Now there's an oldie but goodie," Shelly had finished.

It was a blessing she played the piano, I thought, but my lips were busy conceding this was a very nice choice—"for a final hymn," I added.

"But we've got to sing 'Turn Your Eyes Upon Jesus,'"
Harold weighed in. *"That* oughtta be the invitation
hymn—*everybody's* been askin' for it, and seems like this
would be an ideal time to work it in!" Then, either to
honor Shelly's precedent or to poke further fun at my ignorance of good old hymns, Harold too took up a chorus:

*Turn your eyes upon Jesus,*
  *look full in his wonderful face,*
*and the things of earth will grow strangely dim,*
  *in the light of his glory and grace.*

"Okay," I agreed. "Those two hymns. You work out the
order, but we still need one more, and I have one to sug-
gest. It's not in our hymnal, but I brought another along."
Without further explanation, I rose to to my feet, intoning
a whole verse of one of my favorite hymns. If they wanted
old, I would give them old—a Gaelic melody from eighth-
century Ireland:

*Be Thou my Vision, O Lord of my heart—*
*Nought be all else to me save that Thou art;*
*Thou my best thought, by day or by night—*
*waking or sleeping, Thy presence my Light.*

By now, Raymond's broom was near enough to sweep up
our feet. But instead he came to a halt, still as on a sales
day, stuck at attention at some busy westside intersection.
Raymond had been listening as I sang, eyes rolled back,
wearing his trademark blank expression, confiding nothing. Then, suddenly, something in Raymond had changed.
He faced me squarely and spoke with an urgency I had
never before encountered in him.

"I know it!" he began. "I know that song—not the
words, but the melody. I know it! My mother sang it when

I was little. She said it was from home . . . I still hum it sometimes—out there," he pointed beyond the walls, "during the day: 'With my love on the road . . .'" Ray started, and then he fell silent.

I glanced down at the hymnal and let my gaze settle on the bottom left corner of the open page. In an instant, scales fell from my eyes. Next to the designation Hymn Tune was the word I had long wrestled with as something faintly known. It read, *Slane.*

"Those words you sang," Ray asked. "The words to that hymn—what do they mean?"

Next day, I sat at home in my study, poring over books on Ireland and Celtic Christianity. As I scanned the literature, I replayed the remarkable conversation of the day before. As Harold and Shelly listened in, I had read to Ray all the verses of the hymn with a tune bearing his family name. Then I had sought to unveil their meaning to the extent I understood it.

"God is our life," I had begun. "The Celts—the people of your name—had a deep awareness of this truth. This hymn is like a prayer to God to *be* God in all of one's life: to be vision, and best thought, and wisdom, and true word, and inheritance, and treasure, and victory, and heart, and ruler . . ."

"And *light,*" Raymond had interjected.

"Yes, and bright heav'n's sun."

"And *vision,*" Ray had finished—just like the hymn itself.

"Right," I had agreed, "and especially vision."

"He's my eyes, you know!" Ray's voice had inflected a rare passion. "More, too— He's my great Father—with me since . . . " Ray had stopped to think.

"He was a Catholic," Raymond had suddenly begun to recollect, this time of his own father, "and a rogue! That's all I know. As far back as I can remember he was already gone and I was already blind."

"Then, at one time you *could* see?" I had asked. I had asked this as if he had been party to the long congregational debate on the subject. But Ray hadn't seemed to mind.

"Yes, but I can't remember much, really . . . " Another silence. Our incessant question stuck to each of us like a terrible itch. Ray had sensed it. So he had chosen at long last to put us out of our misery. "I fell, Mother told me, and it left me blind. I don't know how or why. I don't recall it. It's just what she said. That, and that it was meant to be. And, she told me never to worry—that we had other ways of seeing. I've always remembered that."

And she would sing to him, Ray had added—Irish songs, mostly—like "With My Love . . . , " and "The Bells of Shandon," and "We May Roam Thro' the World."

"What happened to your mother?" Harold had asked.

"Oh, she died along the way of things . . . Seems we traveled nearly everywhere in search of a home. Then we came here, and she passed not long after. She had a brother not far who was a priest. He died as well. So I stayed. I made brooms. I found you—and so here we are!"

And it was a remarkable place to be, I had thought.

Holed up in my study, I read through the morning. Slane, I discovered, was a city near Dublin. It was also a hill in County Meath where it was said Saint Patrick, in the fifth century, defied King Loigaire by lighting a fire of faith on Easter eve. With this and other acts of love and daring, Patrick had founded more than three hundred churches, baptized more than 120,000 persons, and single-handedly Christianized Ireland. The record of his deeds was steeped in legend, of course. Beyond his own autobiographical *Confession,* there was little to go on. But objective truth is by nature elusive. Some things come true after the fact, like a game-deciding call of an umpire or a mistaken stock market projection prompting a financial panic. The events of the Sunday to come, however, were neither self-fulfilling prophecy nor products of wishful thinking. For Raymond Slane, who lived by faith, not by sight, spiritual truth resided in a place deeper than cold, hard fact. Now Ray was becoming reacquainted with more than the power of his old name—Slane; he was beginning to come to terms with the name of God in his life.

Sunday arrived, and with it the worship theme of blindness and sight. Either as an act of defiance directed at me, or of sensitivity aimed at Ray—I thanked them either way—Harold and Shelly had placed both their hymn selections at the front end of the worship order. Long before the sermon, we had already asked the Spirit to "open our eyes" and then "turned those eyes upon Jesus." This was not bad, I had granted, as we joined Jesus in Jerusalem to witness his restoring of sight to a man born blind.

I began the sermon by retracing the outline of the story itself: Jesus heals a blind man on the sabbath. The powers are not pleased. A drama of interrogation unfolds, defining the terms of blindness and sight. There were many ways of seeing, I continued, just as there were many ways to be blind. All of us are sight-impaired in some way, whether physical or spiritual. But to be blinded to the reality of God's gracious love in Jesus is the genuine tragedy. The real journey of the man in the story was from physical blindness to spiritual sight. The real way to see, John's story made clear, is to come to the light of God's love. This is true sight.

I spoke these things in earnest, yet felt presumptuous at having uttered them at all. Who was I to speak of blindness? Meanwhile, I joined every child of the church in my preoccupation with the person of Raymond Slane. I watched vigilantly for his slightest reaction to my words, but Ray sat as always, hands on his knees, still as sleep. The sermon ended. It was time for the closing hymn, and so I stepped out of the pulpit and down into the center aisle. There I introduced the final hymn to the congregants and directed them to the words only, printed on an insert in the bulletin. All who knew the tune were welcome to join in from the start, I had offered. Others were encouraged to blend their voices as ears allowed. With Shelly at the keyboard, Harold and I began to sing the first verse. Soon it became apparent none would join us. On verse 2, things were only a little better.

This made all the more resounding the unexpected hum that came to fill the sanctuary like bagpipes. Its source was a seat halfway up the aisle, a remarkably resonant bass that shook Phil and Jeannie in their pew like Jell-O. It was Ray, intoning the tune of his youth. He had rarely sung a Sunday hymn. He knew none of the words. But on the final verses, Ray carried us home. We sang:

*High King of heaven, my victory won,*
*May I reach heaven's joys, O bright heaven's Sun!*
*Heart of my own heart, whatever befall,*
*Still be my Vision, O Ruler of all.*

And when it was done, Ray was on his feet, and those feet were on the move. Blind Ray—who held a broom handle tight as a lover, who swept a floor smooth as a baby's behind, and who once had beaten off a robber with his blind stick like a kung fu warrior—Raymond Slane dropped that stick and let it roll under the pew. Then he stepped into the aisle, solo, and made his way to the front of the sanctuary, forward to a giddy pastor and his singing sidekick, up and into the Light.

## ♪ Hymn Notes ♪

Blindness and sight are prominent themes in the life of faith. Christian sources for these date back to biblical times, but they come to rest especially upon the Gospel stories of Jesus, who restored sight to the blind. This is particularly true of John's Gospel. Here Jesus is the "light of the world" (John 8:12) and spiritual blindness and sight are key metaphors for the nature of sin and salvation. To see is to recognize that Jesus comes from God and embodies God's gift of redemption ("If you have seen me, you have seen the Father."). To be blind is to miss this revelation and remain in the darkness of sin.

There are many hymns about blindness and sight. English evangelical and American revival hymns especially develop the theme. "Open My Eyes," "Turn Your Eyes upon Jesus," "The Light of the World Is Jesus," and "Amazing Grace" ("I once was blind, but now I see") are examples of the predominantly sighted world sharing and overcoming the fate of blindness, here in a spiritual vein.

"Be Thou My Vision" is one of the oldest hymns still sung in the church. Surviving its eighth-century origins in ancient Gaelic verse, it was translated into English prose by Mary Elizabeth Byrne (1880–1931) in 1905. Seven years later, Eleanor Henrietta Hull (1860–1935) versified it in *Poem Book of the Gael*.

The lovely and infectious Irish melody to which the text is set has long been known as *Slane*. The melody was harmonized by David Evans (1874–1948), a prominent Welsh musician, and it appeared in its current form in 1927—twelve hundred years after the text was first penned!

# CHAPTER 4

# Friends in High and Low Places

## "A Mighty Fortress Is Our God"

I T WAS AN IMMACULATE MORNING. THE SUN WAS SQUINTING-bright. Its rays danced on the early dew before steaming it out of existence. The celestial thermostat was set at seventy-five, with a mere tap-on-the-shoulder of a breeze to accompany it. From nearby woods, a hoot owl bid the world good night, while a lone bobwhite commenced anew its never-answered question. Not far to the west, the city was buried in the hum of hurried life. But here, on the county's edge, all was still but early birds and bees—and one lone, proud figure, tramping across the lawn of Ashgrove Baptist Church.

Russ Ingersol's gait had a higher than normal arc to it, owing to the altitude both of the grass and Russ's excitement. This was only his second week with the toy of his dreams. Ever since the trustees had finally yielded to temptation and purchased their own Kubota tractor, and built a pole barn to house it, and placed him in charge of

# A Mighty Fortress

Written by Martin Luther
Translated by Frederick Henry Hedge

A mighty fortress in our God, A bulwark never failing;
Our helper amid the flood Of mortal ills prevailing.
For still our ancient foe Doth seek to work us woe—
His craft and pow'r are great, And, armed with cruel hate,
On earth is not his equal.

Did we in our own strength confide
   Our striving would be losing,
Were not the right Man on our side,
   The Man of God's own choosing.
Dost ask who that may be?  Christ Jesus, it is He—
Lord Sabaoth His name, From age to age the same,
And He must win the battle.

And tho this world, with devils filled,
   Should threaten to undo us,
We will not fear, for God hath willed
   His truth to triumph thru us.
The prince of darkness grim, We tremble not for him—
His rage we can endure, For lo! his doom is sure:
One little word shall fell him.

That word above all earthly pow'rs—
   No thanks to them—abideth;
The Spirit and the gifts are ours
   Thru Him who with us sideth.
Let goods and kindred go, This mortal life also—
The body they may kill, God's truth abideth still:
His kingdom is forever.

its operation and upkeep, Russ Ingersol had been living in a janitor's paradise. It was fortunate for him that most of the trustees had grown up around tractors, owned their own riding mowers, or were hemorrhoid sufferers. From the very date of purchase, Russ had been given the keys to the Kubota. It was his alone to ride, maintain, and protect.

They might just as well have been the keys to the Kingdom. As he neared the shed, Russ threw back his shoulders, lengthened his stride, and assumed the proud posture of a nobleman come to survey his stables and barns. The fantasy would have been complete had he not been laden down with a heavy gas can from the custodial supply closet. But Russ was also a royal procrastinator. He had yet to transfer any maintenance supplies from the church building to the shed. The tractor had come with a full tank of gas, and this was all but used up. Even with a heavy load, however, Russ Ingersol's spirit was as light as a feather.

Then, ten feet shy of the pole barn, Russ dropped the gas can and stared dead on. The lock to the pole barn had been jimmied. Its doors were slightly ajar. Russ swallowed hard, then drew near with the caution of a bomb detonator. He cracked the door and peered into the dark, letting his eyes adjust. Soon he was staring at the back of the empty barn. The Kubota, new joy of his life, was gone.

What would the trustees say? Russ had purchased the padlock on his own. Kip Quarfarth had declared it inferior.

"Better take it back and get a *better* one!" he had said, but Russ had neglected to save the receipt. Now the tractor was stolen, and Russ was left only with the dreadful assurance that he was to blame.

"I've gotta get it back!" Russ said aloud. On the ground, still soft from recent rain, was a set of fresh tire tracks leading out to the road. At points along the path they had made deep indentations in the mud. "There's dirt tracks out there for sure," Russ reasoned, shaking a thoughtful finger in the direction of the street. He ran to his truck, revved it once, then squealed away like a mad herd of pigs. From high in a blue sky, the bright beams of the sun shone down to light his way, as a caressing breeze swept the plain, carrying the canticle of songbirds to stir the heart and still the nerves. It was an immaculate morning—but Russ Ingersol no longer noticed.

The trustees of Ashgrove Baptist Church met only one evening a month during the year, except in the summer, when they rarely gathered at all. Assemblage in the summertime was reserved for matters of direst urgency only—fire, air conditioning trouble, or Russian invasion. Summer was for fishing, gardening, baseball, and lounging. There were exceptions, of course, and these invariably put board members in a foul mood.

Russ sat in Fellowship Hall, his head bent low, still burning-red with chagrin inside and out. Six sour-faced trustees were in special session. It was the Saturday morning after the day of Russ's great misfortune. As he had sped down the county line road south, Russ had met up almost immediately with Winslow Cox, driving back in the other lane. He had recognized Win straightaway by his trademark, blue-and-white-striped farmer's cap, sticking out on the horizon from the seat of Ashgrove Church's new Kubota tractor. Win had spotted the tractor an hour earlier, the church name stenciled in black on its body, ditched in a field along Old US 40 at Six Points. He had returned with gasoline and the other set of keys and was riding it home.

"We're just lucky it was a'runnin' on empty," said a sullen Sarge Grimshaw, chairman of the board, "and that them hot-wirin' thieves didn't get back to it before you did, Win!"

"Well, it's like I always say," followed Kip, looking Russ's way, "a door's only as strong as the lock that's on it!"

"Okay," continued Sarge, "so what're we gonna do?" A silence ensued—nearly time for six lonesome fishermen to cast out and reel in Saturday supper in their minds. But their daydreams were cut short by a voice from an unexpected quarter.

"Well, I'd like to handle it myself! . . . I've got some ideas . . . " All eyes turned to the speaker. Russ knew that after only a year as church custodian he had hardly earned the esteem of a board that, as Harold Hatch put it, "would find a way to be crotchety on a sunny day in Beulah Land." But Russ was running on the bold fuel of righteous indignation. The Bible said that love casts out fear, but anger had its own way of putting the freeze on fright. Russ rose up out of his chair and leaned forward, pressing his fingertips firmly on the tabletop like an army general laying out a battle plan. The transformation was palpable. For the first time in his life, Russ had a group's undivided attention.

"Motion lights," he began. "One over the door, two at the corners. I'll put 'em up myself. And titanium steel padlocks, two of them, maybe three. And I'll pay for all this out a' pocket. I'm not about to let that tractor drive away again!"

It was a well-known fact: The key to a successful church proposal was its benediction, the good word at the very end. The best word went, "And it won't cost any money!" Nearly as pleasing was its corollary: "I'll pay for it myself!" Led out by either of these, a proposal had legs, and God's good people were apt to join hands and bless it along its way.

"Well," Sarge had shrugged, "I can't see as we shouldn't let him go on ahead with it! What about it, folks?"

Heads bobbed in agreement like a half dozen fishing poles all getting bites at once. Then the meeting was over.

Russ drove straight to the hardware store. He put it all on his charge card, knowing full well that his wife, Polly, wouldn't like it. But it was all a matter of pride now. He was guarding more than a barn. Russ Ingersol's very reputation was on the line.

Days passed without incident. Russ had installed the new padlocks that same afternoon. With some help from Ed Garrett's son, Eddie, an "electrical whiz," as his father referred to him, Russ had run power to the pole barn and mounted the motion lights. Most evenings at dusk, just for peace of mind, he would drive to the church and trip them himself. They flooded light in a twenty-foot radius around the shed. Anything caught in their beams would be clearly visible from the road. Russ Ingersol, keeper of God's benevolences, had defended against the night and gained the day. Once again his shoulders were back and his head was high.

But it couldn't last. There came the fair, grass-cutting morning when Russ awakened to smashed motion lights and hasps hopelessly mangled from a crowbar's prying. One of the locks was missing. Another was partially sawed through. But the barn was not penetrated. The would-be burglars had stopped shy of the prize, and this was some consolation.

"They'll be back, though," Russ warned himself, "to finish the job." Meanwhile he was back to the hardware store for more security: a vertical deadbolt that sank into the concrete floor of the barn, a long, thick chain to secure the tractor with bolts to the same, heavier hasps, and more motion lights. But the thieves appeared determined. On one occasion, they ripped one door off by its hinges while failing to cut through the chains to free the Kubota. On another, they took pot shots at the door locks, splitting them into fragments but puncturing a tractor tire in the process.

Russ, meanwhile, was no longer sleeping at night. His nerves were fraying fast. The county sheriff's department had been notified of each attempted break-in, but with no leads they could do little but a random night patrol. Russ had thought of camping out at the church to catch the crooks red-handed, but Polly had begun working nights at the new Wal-Mart, leaving Russ at home with their daughter, Jenny. Polly Ingersol would never have stood for such foolhardy bravado at any rate.

It was a difficult situation. Sarge Grimshaw summed up people's thoughts on the subject: "We don't need no lousy pole barn," he said. "What we need is a cotton-pickin' fortress!" He had muttered this well under his breath, but Russ had heard it, clear as a bell.

So things stood when the pastor of Ashgrove Church climbed into the pulpit to pursue another, unrelated line of defense. It involved the congregational singing of hymns of the least savory variety, so far as most were concerned—those of German Lutheran origin. There was a handful of ex-Lutherans in the pews, and, curiously, they were the ones most opposed to Lutheran hymnody. Perhaps they were haunted by childhood memories of gloomy worship in a dry-as-dust style. Maybe the sluggish hymns with more verses than fingers to count them were emblematic of the fidgety torture of time standing still. At best they resembled a relative of mine who ate so much peanut butter as a child that now he grew ill at the very sight of it. Whatever caused the sentiment, I felt an obligation to justify my programming of all Lutheran hymns, including and especially their exemplar, "A Mighty Fortress Is Our God."

"This next hymn takes us back to the founder of the Protestant movement of the Christian faith," I led out. "In fact, this very hymn is one of the reasons we are here today at all!" Martin Luther, I explained, vilified both by a pope and a king, wrote the words we were about to sing at one of his greatest hours of danger. "If it weren't for Luther's steadfast faith, you and I might be chanting in Latin this morning!"

It was a dangerous world, I had continued, one in which our fondest hopes could slip into the clutches of evil at any moment. Luther understood our single assurance to be the power of the word—"one little word," to be exact, the Name above "all earthly powers." God's "Spirit and the gifts" could still stir souls to repentance and hearts to praise. As we sang of God, our mighty Fortress, we should do so just as we should live our lives—not "in fear," not "in our own strength . . . striving," but by allowing God's "truth to triumph through us." At the end of the road stood the promise: God "must win the battle." This was our sure and certain hope.

With that, Shelly Higgins had begun to pound the harmony in the watered-down duple rhythms found in many American hymnals, and the congregation had taken up the tune. While it was hardly a rousing rendition of the hymn, people had at least endeavored to sing along. Even the ex-Lutherans had troubled their mouths to move to the text, and their pastor had left the pulpit all smiles.

But Russ Ingersol had exited worship with his face chiseled in sternness, the kind of gravity often associated with German ancestry. Indeed, Russ possessed those roots. "Ingersol's an old German name," he was fond of saying. "Grandpa came around turn a' the century from . . . well, some place over there!" Russ could never remember the name. But in worship that morning, he had become charged with a fresh sense of provenance and destiny. He had taken my words to heart. This is every preacher's first hope. But

Russ was poised to put Luther's words into literal, fateful action. "God must win the battle!" Russ repeated again and again like a mantra. "God must win it!"

That evening Russ phoned me with a question. Did I know where he might obtain a cassette tape of Lutheran hymns?

"Why, Russ!" I fired back, delighted. "So you're taking an interest in the hymns of Luther!"

"Well, yeah," Russ answered, "sort of am, I 'spose—but, really, Pastor, what I need is to have that one we sang today—that 'Mighty Fortress' one! That's the one I'm lookin' for!"

"You liked it, huh?" I said, pleased with myself. "Well, I've got a tape you can borrow. It has several German hymns, some that I think you may know: 'Now Thank We All Our God,' 'We Gather Together,' 'When Morning Gilds the Skies'—even 'Silent Night'!"

"Well, that'll be fine, Pastor," Russ replied. "So . . . I may need it for a bit. That okay?"

"Sure thing, Russ. Keep it as long as you like!"

Next day in the late afternoon, Kip Quarfarth pulled up the church drive to the sight of Eddie Garrett and Russ at the pole barn. They were standing still as cornstalks, caught in the total absorption of thought. Their eyes were locked upward in suspense, as if waiting for a jet to fly over or an object to fall from the sky. When Russ spotted Kip over his shoulder, he nudged Eddie back to earth, and they contrived twin grins of ridiculous transparency.

But Kip had already followed their gaze to a telephone post, several yards back of the pole barn, and was studying its new ballast. Attached to the post were two large gray boxes that fanned out sharply from their mounts, twenty feet from the ground. Ringing the pole just above the boxes were four floodlights, pointing downward like suspicious pairs of eyes. Kip stared back at these with growing incredulity.

"What's goin' on here?" Kip asked. "Those what I think they are?"

"Uh, well . . . " Russ stammered.

"Those're loudspeakers!" broke in Eddie, unable to contain his excitement. "Some of Dad's old ones from work!" Russ had shot a hard stare in his direction, but it had been too late. "Those spotlights, too. Dad gives me all his old stuff to tinker with."

Ed Garrett, who owned The Little Big Top Shop in Nemo, worked his son hard in the family business, especially during the summer. Eddie installed loudspeakers on big-top set-ups when requested. As Ed upgraded equipment, anything old with wires attached went to Eddie.

"What's all this about, Russ?" Kip persisted.

"Well you see, that up there's actually a very *loud* loudspeaker," Russ said. With the lid off secrecy, he had little to lose. "Anybody tries to get into the barn again, we're gonna blast 'em across the countryside!"

"With what?" asked Kip, in building amusement. "Got an alarm on that thing? Let's hear it!"

"Oh, it's alarmin' all right!" replied Russ. "Sure you want to hear this, now?" With that, Russ stepped inside the barn and flipped a switch. Within seconds, a noise of unnerving ferocity erupted from the speaker and was volleyed across the countryside. So overpowering was the sound that one imagines it must have stunned birds in mid-flight and killed mosquitoes on contact. So deafening was it that the three figures cringing below had to shout in their urgency to be heard.

"Turn it off!" screamed Kip at the top of his lungs.

"Like the voice of God, ain't it?" cried Russ, as he slipped back into the barn to fiddle with the volume. But the voice of God it wasn't. Even Kip, a lifelong Baptist, knew that in an instant. It wasn't God at all. It was Luther . . .

*Did we in our own strength confide*
 *[rang out the second verse]*
*Our striving would be losing,*
*Were not the right man on our side,*
 *The man of God's own choosing.*

"How on earth did you do this?" Kip asked, still yelling despite the lowered volume.

"It's on tape," Eddie replied, "and the cassette player's wired into the motion lights. If . . . "

"You see," Russ took over, "when them lights come on—these thieves a' ours is goin' to church!" And Russ Ingersol stood straight, legs flared, hands on hips, in the proud repose of fated victory, as the triumphant text of Martin Luther hovered between earth and heaven like a song of the angels:

*The prince of darkness grim, We tremble not for him;*
*His rage we can endure, For lo, his doom is sure:*
*One little word shall fell him . . .*

All three were trembling, now—Kip in the shock of disbelief, Eddie at the prowess of technology, and Russ over nothing less than the awesome power of God.

Normally, word of Russ's and Eddie's latest foray into high technology would have spread around the church at twice the speed of sound. But Russ had pleaded with Kip to keep it secret. He knew that if members found out, some would begin to act on their impulse to turn up at dusk and trigger the alarm themselves. Soon the quiet grove would explode in shocking sonority on a nightly basis. The element of surprise would be lost, the chance of nabbing the thieves diminished.

"That's just the way folks are around here, Kip. You know it as well as anybody!"

Kip, still shaking, only nodded his head in agreement.

"'Course, that won't keep the stray squirrel or possum from triggering it now and then—but that'll be their funeral!" Russ chuckled.

"Lord help 'em," Kip concurred.

So the trio departed, their ears still ringing with late knowledge of the feebleness of "this mortal life" and the revelation that God's "kingdom is forever."

Russ called Eddie that same evening, just to reinforce his call for secrecy. "Now you haven't told anybody 'bout this, have yeh?"

"No! Nobody! I swear!"

"Good. And *please* don't go talkin' about it to your friends, Eddie! You *know* how kids are about this kind a' thing! Once they get a whiff a' the honey, they can't keep their paws out a' the jar!"

"Okay, Russ," Eddie said in a whisper. "I promise!"

With that, Eddie had hung up the phone. He was alone in his bedroom, but he walked to the door for a peek outside, just to confirm that no one was listening. Each of the Garrett children had a telephone set, Eddie's younger brother, Perry, included. Indeed, Perry was at that very moment lowering the receiver of his own unit. He was in the habit of eavesdropping on his brother and sisters whenever he could. It made him feel older than a mere eighth-grader and was great for blackmail. Lying on his bed, he tried to make his own sense of Russ's and Eddie's secret. Clearly it involved the new pole barn—and something about bright lights and loudspeakers. Whatever it was all about, it sounded exciting. There would be time to investigate, he thought to himself.

Perry Garrett's immediate preoccupation, however, was with surviving the summer alive. He possessed a sharp mind and an even sharper tongue. The combination often landed him in double-edged trouble. Only three weeks into summer vacation, he was already facing "death threats" from three neighbor boys. Like all the Garretts, Perry was on the small side, an easy mark for teenage boredom. These youths were devoting their summer to hunting Perry down on their dirt bikes. Whenever they spotted him, they would lay chase. But the Garrett boys owned the fastest minibikes money could buy. Perry had so far managed to outrun them. Safely out of reach, Perry would whoop it up to excess. This had only strengthened their resolve to keep the chase alive. It was shaping up to be the longest summer of Perry Garrett's life.

Perry closed his eyes and slipped into uneasy sleep. In his dreams, three large boys were chasing him. They were continuing to gain on him when from out of the sky came a blinding light and a mighty clap of thunder like a trumpet. While his pursuers cowered on their knees, Perry was carried up into the air by a blinding presence to safety.

Meanwhile, a mile down the road, Russ Ingersol lay awake, counting the days to Sunday. Their secret would hold momentarily, but once the first pair of eyes strayed upward of the pole barn to the speakers and lights above, the questions would commence. Then Kip Quarfarth would almost certainly spill the beans. Russ would face pressure to demonstrate his newfangled security system for an eager public. There would be ridicule if it failed. Russ felt besieged, assailed on all sides like Luther himself, left with none but God to deliver. "And he must win the victory," Russ repeated. "God must!" And the words had sung him to sleep.

That Saturday evening after supper, Perry Garrett gained permission to ride his minibike until dark. Dirt-bike trails crisscrossed several fields west of the airport. The area was mostly flat, but at its southernmost point, there were some hills and jumps. To these Perry headed as the sun sank lower in the sky. Along the way, he kept out a watchful eye for his assailants, but the coast was clear. Once around Devil's Loop, he told himself, then home.

The Devil's Loop was a series of sharp curves and ridges packed as tight as moguls, laid out in dense thicket. It was the most challenging course Perry had ever tried and, just lately, mastered. A surprise lay around every corner, making a clean run rare, but Perry had memorized them all. He was on the back circuit of a flawless attempt when he encountered the one nonnegotiable obstacle: bullies with grudges. Two of the boys had already been on the course and had heard him coming. They were idling their dirt bikes and blocking the trail when Perry swept around a bend at a furious pace. Perry's heart skipped a beat at the sight of them, but his speed so startled them that he was able to swerve around them. But now the chase was on. On through the course Perry sped, the two boys in hot pursuit. He was outdistancing them, he could feel it. On impulse he glanced over his shoulder, just to be certain. But as he faced back to the trail, Perry's luck changed. Riding toward him from the opposite direction was the third boy. Perry in his sights, he bore down hard, challenging Perry to a game of chicken. At the last possible instant, Perry had swerved left, off the path, and began a bumpy ride through the thicket, lashing legs and arms all the way. Darkness falling, he didn't see the boulder in time. On impact, the bike tipped upward, throwing Perry into the air. He fell hard back to the earth, scraping his face and shoulder. The bike, still idling on the ground, was damaged even more.

For a moment Perry lay in the dirt, aching. But the sound of bike motors hummed nearby. They would be on top of him in no time. Rising painfully to his feet, Perry cut the bike's engine, then got his bearings. Westward, a brilliant orange sun was slipping beneath the tree line. Fifty yards to the east ran a great fence, edging airport property mile after endless mile. On the horizon south, all was dim—all but a lone steeple, shooting heavenward, illuminated by floodlights on a timer set for 9 p.m. Perry knew it well. His father and brother, Eddie, had installed those lights the summer before. It was the proud steeple of the Ashgrove Baptist Church.

Leaving his bike, Perry crept fifty yards south into a scrubby ravine and awaited the stars. Once night fell, he would make a run for the church, find a way inside, and call home. Almost immediately the taunting began.

"Found your bike, sissy. It's about ruined, and we're gonna finish it off. Not so tough without your toy, are you! You can't hide forever, chicken. We're not leavin' until we find you, and when we do you're dead!"

For a long while, Perry shivered in the night air. The three boys had headed west, and their voices had grown more faint. But they were on foot. They would be back to get their bikes. Perry decided to make a break for the church. He gathered himself up, cuts, bruises, and all, and doddered toward the steeple. Next to the church was a long cornfield, its stalks still in their infancy. Once in this field, Perry became clearly visible on the horizon. Hearing the sound of dirt bikes, Perry immediately broke into a gallop. He had been spotted, and the boys were racing his way. By the time he reached the fence to church property, the three boys had closed the distance. They ditched their bikes and were running at him. Perry scampered up the fence, his heart pounding. Just before lunging over it onto church ground, however, he had chanced a glance to the far end of the yard, over to where the pole barn sat. Then, in a flash, it had all come back to him. The alarm, the lights, whatever it was Eddie and Russ had wired together, lay nearly within reach, waiting to be triggered by the simple motion of bodies. With a final surge of adrenaline, Perry darted across the lawn, the boys right on his tail.

From there, events unfolded quickly. Not fifteen feet from the pole barn, the fastest of the three had overtaken Perry and knocked him to the ground. Perry wriggled free but immediately was subdued by the others. They held him down in the grip of triumph, chiding him with fresh obscenities and slapping him about. Next they stood him up to take turns delivering body punches to his abdomen. All the while, Perry shrieked in terror and pain, with none to take notice but locusts and fireflies.

Then, from out of the darkness west of the pole barn, emerged two tallish figures. In slow strides, they made their way toward the scene. Parked behind them in the shadows was a long truck. In their hands were crowbars, which they patted ominously in the palms of their grizzled hands. The three boys froze at the sight of them.

"Don't fight fair, do yeh, boys," one of them said. "Why don't yeh let little shorty go—er we'll teach yeh a thing er two about a fair fight. Now, *get the h--- outta here!*" In an instant the boys let loose of Perry, who fell to his knees, grabbing his stomach. Then the trio backed away to a safe distance before commencing a familiar cant: "You can't tell us what to do! You can't make us leave!" and on it went.

Perry lay on his back with his knees pulled to his chest, squinting up at the two men towering above him. They were bearded and dressed in dark clothing and boots. As his pain slackened, Perry pieced together the obvious. These were none other than the pole-barn thieves, come back for the Kubota. But they had also just saved his neck. As the men pursued the jeering cowards, Perry lumbered to his feet and slowly backed away.

"Told you boys to scram! Now git!"

"We don't have ta if we don't . . . "

But they never finished. Instead, all voices were drowned out at once by a deafening burst of sound, swooping down upon them like holy judgment. Perry had unwittingly stepped into range of the motion lights. This had activated a line of current running into the barn to a cassette player, whose play button was already depressed. As the cassette tape rolled, the current had continued up through the roof to a telephone pole, into floodlights and speakers that swiftly transformed a tranquil country night into raucous day. Russ Ingersol's prayers had finally been answered in the timeless words of Martin Luther:

*A mighty fortress is our God, A bulwark never failing;*
*Our helper he, amid the flood Of mortal ills prevailing.*

Out across the fields it boomed. For one bewildering moment, all ears were constrained to take in the sound. In the next instant, six pairs of legs were scurrying in all directions, like cockroaches, caught in the open by the flick of a light switch. Perry disappeared behind the pole barn. The thieves retreated to their truck to attempt a hasty getaway. The boys jumped the church fence, started their bikes, and high-tailed it for the county line road.

*And tho' this world, with devils filled,*
*should threaten to undo us*

rang out the hymn, as three little devils on minibikes were apprehended by a deputy sheriff. He had been cruising the road south on patrol when the sky had lit up like the Fourth of July. When the boys spotted him, they had turned to flee but had given up at the entrance to the church. Climbing from his squad car, the deputy sheriff confronted both the awesome sound of the Reformation and two thieves in a truck, retreating the scene of a bungled crime.

*The prince of darkness grim, We tremble not for him;*
*His rage we can endure, For lo, his doom is sure . . .*

Sensing their peril, the thieves steered into the grass in hopes of busting out onto the road. But now two pick-up trucks had arrived and were blocking their flight—Ed Garrett, out in search of his truant son, and Russ Ingersol, come to collect a miracle. Both had seen the light. Now each heard the word:

*That word above all earthly pow'rs,*
*No thanks to them, abideth:*
*The Spirit and the gifts are ours*
*Thro' him who with us sideth.*

Two more sheriff's cars arrived. Beaten, the thieves abandoned their truck, hands in the air—not in surrender only but to shield their ears against the terrible noise. Meanwhile three bully boys sat in the ditch with their heads in their knees, likewise covering their ears. As Russ and Ed ran onto church property, a second sheriff's deputy greeted them with one loud, desperate plea: "Does anybody know how to shut that thing off?"

All the while Perry lay hidden in the scrub behind the pole barn, watching. Only after his father arrived, and he saw the deputies' drawn guns and the two fallen thieves spread eagled did he go limping to the site, calling to his father over the hymnic din, grimacing at his enemies in the grass . . .

*Let goods and kindred go, This mortal life also;*
*The body they may kill: God's truth abideth still,*
*His kingdom is forever.*

But toward the two thieves, sitting now forlornly in handcuffs, Perry felt another sentiment, and this he shared openly the moment Russ returned from pulling the plug on Luther for the evening.

"Dad, you gotta know!" Perry pleaded. "Those guys saved my life!" Perry then recounted to Ed, Russ, and two sheriff's deputies the harrowing events of the evening, culminating in his brief brush with death and uncanny deliverance at the hands of criminals. "I think God brought them to me," Perry ventured. "I even dreamed about it just last night!"

I arrived some time later, having been summoned by Winslow Cox, closest neighbor to the church. When Winslow had heard the hymn and seen the sky light up like sunrise from his back porch, he had feared Armageddon and called me for my opinion. As I pulled into the drive, all was quiet. The deputies were gone, the would-be thieves released with a warning, and three daunted delinquents delivered to their homes. Ed had whisked Perry away, torn by emotions of fatherly pride and consternation. Only Russ remained. He was sitting by the pole barn. His face carried the look of a man whose dearly held designs have been pried from his grasp. I joined him in the grass, waiting for his thoughts to speak.

"They let 'em go!" Russ began. Then he detailed the whole story, right up to the decision to release the two men, having no hard evidence to hold them and wishing not to, especially under the circumstances.

"Look on the bright side, Russ," I offered. "Wasn't it kind of nice to see some simple humanity, right from where you least expected it? You know," I continued, "if the Lutheran Reformation was about anything, it was that God's grace is available to anyone, at any time, period. Besides, after what they heard tonight, there is no way your thieves will ever be back—unless it's to Sunday church! Who knows . . . "

"Which reminds me, Preacher!" Russ broke in. "You haven't even heard this thing play yet, have yeh?"

"What do you mean?" I said. "It's my tape! I've been listening to 'A Mighty Fortress' all my life, Russ!"

"No, not like this you ain't!"

And with that, for a second time in one night, Luther awakened the sleepy countryside, and the earth around Ashgrove Church shook with the majesty of God.

## ♪ Hymn Notes ♪

It is difficult to overestimate the importance of Martin Luther (1483–1546) in Christian history. His reformation changed the Western church forever. This is nowhere truer than in the arena of sacred song. It has been said that Luther gave the common people the Bible because God speaks to us directly and that he gave us the hymnbook that we might answer God in the same manner.

Luther did not create congregational singing. Whenever and wherever reform has taken place, enthusiastic singing has not been far behind. But the Reformation in Germany liberated the heart and the imagination for vernacular hymnody on an unprecedented scale. While other centers of reform in Europe retreated to psalm singing only, Lutherans from the beginning composed hymns and spiritual songs in great number. The complete output of German hymns is thought to be as high as one hundred thousand.

Luther himself has been dubbed the first evangelical hymnist. He composed thirty-seven hymns of which we know. Only one has achieved a nearly universal acceptance: *Ein' feste Burg ist unser Gott* (1529)—"A Mighty Fortress Is Our God." It has to its credit at least fifty-three English translations from the German, the best known in America by Frederick Henry Hedge (1805–1890).

"A Mighty Fortress" was probably written at Coburg, at the height of conflict between Charles V of Spain and the German princes over the religious fate of their principalities. At the Diet of Spires (1529), Catholics resolved to soundly defeat the Lutheran movement. Inspired by Psalm 46 ("God is our refuge and strength") "A Mighty Fortress" was Luther's battle cry to defend the Lutheran cause. It was sung in the streets, at the gallows, and in battle. Lord Sabaoth, the victorious Christ, must win the day.

Whether in the face of entrenched religious power, countless social ills, or the plight of the individual soul, the same message applies: God's kingdom cannot fail.

The chorale tune to which the text is set is probably by Luther himself, perhaps adapted from an older Gregorian melody. It is a robust melody with considerable rhythmic interest, too often sacrificed to aid in congregational singing. It has been put to use musically in a variety of ways and by numerous composers.

# CHAPTER 5

# Brother Cat, Sister Mouse

## "All Creatures of Our God and King"

I T COULD ALL BE TRACED BACK TO HER ROOTS, BACK TO Crab Orchard, Kentucky, and the Hapness homestead, sitting by the banks of the Dix River. When Heidi's father died in a tractor accident, her mother had panicked. She began to slaughter the chickens, to sell off pigs and parcels of land, to whittle the Hapnesses down to two geese, a milking cow, and a vegetable patch. Before long, Heidi and her sisters were starving. Within months, they had lost their land and moved in with relatives at Berea.

By ceaseless begging, Heidi's eldest sister, Lou Ann, had won a spot on the pickup truck for the family dog, Blacky. The fate of Heidi's collection of scrawny cats was less favorable. "I want 'em all, Mama!" she'd cried. "They all need me the same!" Not about to be undemocratic, her mother had chosen to abandon all four. In a desperate act of compassion, Heidi had sneaked her favorite feline, Precious, into a chest of drawers. But on the edge of Madison

County, Precious had given in to a fit of frenzy. Once discovered, she had scratched Mrs. Hapness on the arms and was unceremoniously flung from the truck as Lou Ann restrained her hysterical sister.

Something in Heidi had died that day, though it seemed to have been more a loss of judgment than any decline in compassion. Here, on the west side of Indianapolis, Heidi Hapness exercised none of the former but an avalanche of the latter. On at least three occasions, she had been forced to vacate an apartment for violating the pet policy. Even

## *All Creatures of Our God and King*

Written by Francis of Assisi
Translated and paraphrased by William Draper
Copyright © 1927 (Renewed) J. Curwen & Sons Ltd.
International copyright secured. All rights reserved.
Reprinted by permission.

All creatures of our God and King,
   Lift up your voice and with us sing,
Alleluia, Alleluia!
Thou burning sun with golden beam,
   Thou silver moon with softer gleam:
O praise Him, O praise Him!
Alleluia, Alleluia! Alleluia!

Thou rushing wind that art so strong,
   Ye clouds that sail in heav'n along,
O praise Him! Alleluia!
Thou rising morn, in praise rejoice,
   Ye lights of evening, find a voice:
O praise Him, O praise Him!
Alleluia, Alleluia! Alleluia!

when pets were allowed, she had managed to stretch the rules, whether in quantity or class of animals kept. Things came to a head in a predictable pattern. The neighbors would grow suspicious. Heidi, a reluctant liar, would register half-hearted denials, leading to an eventual search by the management. Then would follow the screams, the slamming of doors, the animal control van, and Heidi's immediate expulsion.

"What was it this time?" people would ask her. "Another garter snake?"

Thou flowing water, pure and clear,
   Make music for thy Lord to hear,
Alleluia, Alleluia!
Thou fire so masterful and bright,
   That givest men both warmth and light,
O praise Him, O praise Him!
Alleluia, Alleluia! Alleluia!

And all ye men of tender heart,
   Forgiving others, take your part,
O sing ye! Alleluia!
Ye who long pain and sorrow bear,
   Praise God and on Him cast your care:
O praise Him, O praise Him!
Alleluia, Alleluia! Alleluia!

Let all things their Creator bless,
   And worship Him in humbleness,
O praise Him! Alleluia!
Praise, praise the Father, praise the Son,
   And praise the Spirit, Three in One:
O praise Him, O praise Him!
Alleluia, Alleluia! Alleluia!

"No, just a friendly squirrel couple," had been a recent reply. "They were comin' and goin' through the window. Hardly bothered with 'em most of the time. I was puttin' birdseed in a bowl—they looked so hungry, and I had all that seed mix left over from last winter with the hedgehog. I was only doin' what I had to do," she explained. "I mean, them squirrels needed me . . . " In a way, Heidi's spirit still lived in the family pickup truck, rolling down a lonely road to Berea.

"Dr. Doolittle!" exclaimed Hassie Longstreet one evening. The trustees were discussing Heidi's latest escapade—the adoption of a stray cat on church property. It was a gray tabby. It had appeared on a church-cleaning day at the feet of Russ Ingersol as he trimmed the hedge at the front of the building. It rubbed against his legs in an incessant figure eight and meowed until Russ gave it a swift kick in the ribs.

"Get outta here, cat!" he had bellowed, but Heidi had heard instead the "Yeoooowww!" of a startled feline. She had rushed to its aid, bringing it home to her heart to stay. "I'll call him Precious!" she had announced. "Precious II!"

Where Precious should reside in physical space was another problem. Recently evicted, Heidi was living in a rent-by-the-week motel. When asked about simply taking it home she had answered, "Wish I could, but I can't! Cat's aren't allowed where I'm livin', and I couldn't afford to lose another place just now."

Instead, Heidi had retrieved a plastic tub she'd used for her hibernating hedgehog, lined it with bedding, and set up kitty housekeeping under the eaves, backside of the pole barn. Once a day, she drove the six miles from her own temporary home to that of Precious, toting a can opener and a can of Little Friskies. She carried water from the church spigot and aired out the cat's bedding, especially after a rain. All this she had commenced without consulting a soul. While the trustees felt duty-bound to frown on any new initiative involving the building and grounds, those that had bypassed channels were especially suspect.

"That's it exactly!" Hassie reiterated insistently. "She's a female Dr. Doolittle!"

"Dr. Strangelove, more like it!" Phil Simpson smirked. "If she's talkin' to anything, it's to the bats in her belfry!" Phil was still stewing over Heidi's most recent plunge into irrationality. He was in charge of the interior of the building, an assignment that had really begun to smell after Heidi put up an injured skunk for the night in a storage closet off Fellowship Hall. The skunk had gotten loose, of course, and marked every inch of the building before he was discovered prior to the Sunday school hour. All services had been canceled.

"Well, we've got our share a' skunks in the church already!" Moderator Harold Hatch had quipped to defuse some of the tension. "They ought to have felt right at home . . . "

Phil had failed to be amused.

"I say first thing in the morning we drop it off right on her doorstep," he said, "cat, tub, and all!"

Others were taking a different tack. "Least it's a male cat," Sarge Grimshaw pointed out. "No kittens around the corner. That's one thing. And bein' a male, he'll wander away soon enough—you can bank on that! Stray males are drifters. I say leave it be for a bit, but just tell her it better keep its furry paws out of the church, or we'll have a kitty barbecue!" And all, even Phil Simpson, went along.

Typically such a discussion would have stretched out or even spilled over the banks of meaningful dialogue into the more gratifying arena of blatant gossip. But by now the hour was late, and board members were weary. They had shot their wad of enthusiasm for controversy on the other agenda item of the evening, the question of a food-pantry ministry. Several others and I had come to the conclusion that a quiet but growing problem of hunger existed in the rural communities dotting the countryside around the church. There were poor people living in dire conditions on the edges of Nebo, Plainville, and in various locales around Old US 40. Many were in makeshift mobile-home parks where children ran as free as the lifestyles that spawned them.

We proposed reallocating one side of the old supply closet for a food pantry. It had been emptied of cleaning and maintenance supplies since the construction of the pole barn. It cried out for a new purpose, and we were confident we had found it. We proposed a food-basket delivery program, getting names from neighboring agencies to target the most needy families.

"Who's gonna do all the work?" Kip Quarfarth had wanted to know. "Lotta work can go into a thing like that!"

We envisioned a pantry committee, I'd answered—representatives from boards and others who were interested in the project. We would divide into teams to handle food collection, storage, and delivery. Each board could appoint a representative to serve on the committee and then plans might proceed. There had been the requisite hemming and hawing, but then permission had been granted.

At the monthly deaconesses' meeting, chairwoman Addie Cox made the case for the pantry idea and asked for a volunteer to serve. "The very thought of hungry children out here all around us—why, it just breaks your heart!" she said.

Heads nodded the way they were supposed to whenever children in need came up, but no one volunteered. It was early September, a time of great distraction for the members of Ashgrove Church. Harvesting, canning, and freezing were crowding out spare time. What little remained was consumed by talk of last-minute getaways to favorite camp-sites or fishing holes. So it was that the most easily dis-tracted soul of all brought the greatest focus to the cause.

"I'll serve!" It was Heidi Hapness. She had slipped into the meeting late, fresh from a trip behind the pole barn to tend to Precious. "I'm out here every day—I mean, a lot, lately," Heidi caught herself, "—anyway, so I might as well do somethin' else while I'm at it, 'specially if it helps some-body . . . " But her decision had little to do with the logic of convenience. Heidi ran on the fuel of feeling alone. For all her tenderness toward poor, neglected animals, Heidi's heart beat just as strongly for children who were, as she was, acquainted with real hand-to-mouth living.

Only one uncharitable thought accompanied the grateful acceptance of Heidi's offer. It popped into several minds at once: "Better not let *her* give the food out! It'll all be gone in less than fifteen minutes. Why, she'll be givin' it away by the truckload!"

Late summer met up with early fall, and the food pantry now boasted shelves and a good stock of nonperishable foods. Cans of vegetables and fruits were arranged in neat rows by type. Canned soups, stews, and meats, donated in smaller quantities, sat together on one shelf. Rice, cere-als, pasta, and bread mixes were likewise grouped, and not far away were bags of sugar and flour for baking. Miscellaneous items included drink mixes and jars of peanut butter and jelly. Several members had elected to donate their own home-canned items. Madge Spires gave two cans of her pickle relish—"old family recipe!" she told me. Not to be outdone, Betty Mayes had brought three jars of her own homestyle ripe tomato relish and thrown in a jar of bread-and-butter pickles to boot. We had been very thankful to receive these and other home-made treasures but couldn't find the heart to tell the donors that the board of health had other ideas on the subject. They were placed on a separate shelf while the committee planned for their disposal in secret. (Author's note: The ripe tomato relish was excellent!) Soon everything was in place. Deliveries were due to begin the middle of October. They were to coincide with our first-ever harvest festival. It bore the title Nature Sunday.

Like most new initiatives at Ashgrove Baptist Church, Nature Sunday was regarded by a handful of members as a great inspiration and by everyone else as pure monkey business. It arose from my ongoing efforts to share the rich hymns of the distant past. In this endeavor, I had finally come around to my personal favorite. I had postponed its programming for many months for fear of ridicule. But the hymn aroused strong feelings in me. My wife, Donna, had even processed down the aisle to it at our wedding. The string of alleluias at the close of each verse still made my heart race each time I heard it.

My heart hadn't raced in months. Finally, when I could no longer bear the thought of another Sunday without the hymn, I had typed in its title at the top of the bulletin. It read "All Creatures of Our God and King."

"It ain't easy!" grumbled Harold Hatch.

"What's that?" I asked. We were sitting on the front row of the sanctuary between Sunday school and worship. Harold was staring at a hymnal, opened to a page never before exposed to the full light of day.

"Ain't easy being a good song leader in church when nobody's singing!"

"You don't like the hymn?" I asked, defensively.

"I don't *know* the hymn," Harold corrected. "Nobody does. It might be a swell hymn, a jim-dandy of a hymn, the spunkiest nature song to come along since 'Tiptoe Through the Tulips,' but nobody knows it, and nobody's gonna sing it except you and *maybe* me!"

"What do you want me to do?" I asked.

"I'd like you to think before you slip in these new hymns!"

"*Old* hymns!" I said.

"*You* call 'em old, but they're new around here. Back home, there's an old swap shop, a flea market," Harold continued. "Wanna know its name? New to You, they call it. If you've never laid eyes on it, then it's *new to you,* even if it's been around a couple hundred years."

"Seven hundred fifty!" I said.

"Whatever," Harold replied. "All I'm saying is, we need to prepare folks to sing the hymns they don't know. Help them along a bit. That way they may at least try to sing, and you and I might not feel like the Smothers Brothers up here week after week!" So I had relented, changing the opening hymn to "Heavenly Sunlight." *That* page in the book the morning sun shone down upon like an old friend . . .

In return Harold had agreed to work with me on Nature Sunday, a celebration of God's goodness in creation, which I had been contemplating in secret for some time. It would coincide with the fall harvest and the official opening of the food pantry. It also presented an ideal excuse to properly introduce my favorite hymn, "All Creatures of Our God and King."

That same morning, as Harold and I were bandying words and worship, another debate had been underway. In the new food-pantry closet, Phil Simpson and Heidi Hapness were wrangling over a problem of nature which, when food is around, is never far behind. Mice had invaded the food pantry. Heidi had been put in charge of food storage in the pantry. Now Phil was busy spelling out the unwritten addendum to her job description: rodent control.

"But what should I do about the mice?" Heidi asked.

"Well," explained Phil, in a word, "kill 'em!"

It had actually been two words, but they hit Heidi like an entire round of machine-gun fire. "Kill 'em? How? Why?"

"You got yer choices," Phil continued. "There's rat poison, but you gotta watch out that children don't get into it. Then you got glue traps, and, of course, there's nothin' like a good old-fashioned mousetrap! Some like cheese on it. I prefer peanut butter, 'cause they lick it right down to the trigger, then snap! splat!" Heidi scrunched her face into a painful expression, as if the trap had just sprung on her.

"Well, what about the poison? How does it work?" she asked, desperate for options.

"The poison," Phil began, "well, most kinds makes 'em thirsty, see, so they drink the water you leave out with the poison, which expands their little stomachs bigger and bigger, 'til they explode!"

"But I can't!" Heidi objected, "I can't be in charge a' that! Poor little things . . . "

"Well, too bad, Heidi,"—Phil had waited for this—"It's your job now. Lookie here at this bag a' flour here, all torn open. Look at them Kool-Aid packets, all bitten in the corners, ruined! Who's gonna make the kiddies Kool-Aid? Mercy sakes, Heidi, we're talkin' about mice here! Vermin!"

By now Heidi had fallen silent. To her, mice, cats, children—all were precious little creatures, things to love. Her mind could not register the difference. At last she managed to bring up the third option: glue traps.

"Well, what do you want to know?" Phil pressed.

"Does it hurt 'em, kill 'em?"

"Nope! Just traps 'em—'less they stick their dirty heads in it . . . "

"Oh," she said. And Heidi left the pantry much shaken and with a great deal to think about.

That week Harold, Shelly Higgins, and I sat down to plan the music for Nature Sunday. Every aspect of worship would focus on the theme of God in nature, I told them. A food-pantry dedication was planned at the close of the morning with a hearty potluck dinner to follow, and that afternoon the first baskets of food would be delivered to the needy. We wanted hymns that reflected the theme, I said. Then I sat back and braced myself for their ideas.

"'In the Garden'!" said Shelly.

"What about 'How Great Thou Art'?" Harold added.

"Better not leave out 'Lily of the Valley'!" added Shelly.

"And oh—'Beulah Land'!" cried Harold.

"No," said Shelly. "That's about heaven, not earth!"

"'Land of corn and wine'?" said Harold. "Sounds like harvest to me!"

"Why, Harold Hatch! Just what kind a' Baptist *are* you?" Shelly exclaimed.

"The happy kind in Beulah Land, I suspect!" he said.

"Well, what do *you* think?" Shelly asked at last, looking my way.

"You can sing 'His Eye Is on the Sparrow' as far as I'm concerned!" I answered. "Just give me 'All Creatures of Our God and King.'" And so our plans had been made.

On the Sunday morning before Nature Sunday, Phil Simpson had arrived at church early and immediately checked the pantry closet. Now he was standing by the door, awaiting Heidi's arrival. Fresh from her trip behind the pole barn, she skipped into the vestibule flush-faced until Phil marched her into the closet. There she turned a pale gray. Heidi had chosen glue traps. The back feet and tail of their first victim were stuck fast. The mouse lay on its side, frightened and exhausted from hours of struggle.

"What happens now?" Heidi asked innocently. "How do I get it unstuck?"

"Unstuck?" Phil cried out in amusement. "Oh, no, you can't get 'im free! He's stuck there, I'm afraid," said Phil. "Stuck there 'til he dies!"

Heidi appeared stunned. "But then what do I do? I can't just *leave* him there!"

As if on cue, Phil had paced to a corner of the closet where a few tools were still stacked against the wall, then returned with a shovel, placing it in Heidi's hands. "This'll do the trick," he said matter-of-factly. "It's all you'll need. First, you scoop up the mouse with the front side, then, out in the yard, you whack him to death with the back side, and finally, you dig a hole with the blade and bury him! One, two, three does the trick . . . " And with that, Phil had strolled out of the closet and into the sanctuary.

Moments before worship, audible from just beyond the walls, came the metallic clack of a shovel hitting concrete— once, twice, and again just for sure. Then followed a second unmistakable sound—that of a woman weeping.

Phil Simpson sat in the pew with his wife, Jeannie, his mouth gaping open, and he listened. He had hoped for the clack of the shovel, but he had not anticipated the hack of a breaking heart. It had come as a surprise to him, a great shock. Now he was slumped over, his head down, staring at the floor in remorse. For the first time in a long time, Philip Simpson was ashamed of himself.

During worship announcements, I attempted to pave the way for the coming week's festivities, including the singing of my favorite hymn, "All Creatures of Our God and King." Its author, St. Francis of Assisi, I began, was a lover of all God's creatures, from the highest to the humblest. There were many remarkable stories of his encounters with nature. There was the nightingale that harmonized with him in an oak grove at Le Carceri, and the raven that awakened him early each morning for prayer but, if Francis were ill, would wait an extra hour to let him sleep. And there were Francis's remarkable words to the herdsmen of Gubbio that they should feed the wolf that was attacking their flocks. "Brother Wolf" is hungry, he had told them. That is why he has done what he has done . . .

At that, Heidi had perked up for the first time since slinking in from the side yard. After her wretched deed, she had plopped down in the back of the sanctuary with the look of death in her eyes. Her face was blotchy, her eyelashes matted together, and her mouth tightly drawn as if barely holding at bay the sound of sadness. Now I was busy unveiling a large copy of a famous painting. In it, a man in a cassock was standing on a hill by a tree, bending over a flock of birds. One of his fingers was raised in the air, and his face carried a soft but serious expression. The birds were encircling his feet, and they gazed up attentively as he talked. "This is a Spanish painting of St. Francis of Assisi," I explained. "As you can see, he is preaching to the birds!"

There were a few chortles in the pews. Then, characteristically, Russ Ingersol blurted out an impromptu question: "What do yeh suppose he's sayin' to 'em?" A brief silence was followed by more snickers. At last, unable to suppress their amusement, several men began to supply the answer.

"'Don't eat the corn!'" someone threw out.

"How 'bout, 'Don't drop on my windshield!'" came another.

"'Wait right here—I left my buckshot in the trunk!'" And on it went, until the house of God was bathed in good humor.

As I put the picture aside, a woman's voice shot up from the back, silencing all the rest. "His eye is on the sparrow!" She shouted it aloud, and this time no one laughed. But Heidi wasn't finished. "His eye is on *all* a' his creatures, is what I mean!" she continued. "Even the ones nobody else cares about! That's what I'm sayin'," she said. "That's what I'm talkin' about . . . God loves all his creatures just the same, and that makes 'em *all* our brothers and sisters!"

After that, no one spoke another word on the subject, the preacher included. And just for a split second, as I put the picture away, it seemed to me that I had seen St. Francis smile.

The week whizzed along, busy with preparations for Nature Sunday and the maiden delivery of the Ashgrove Baptist Church food-pantry program. Packing lists were drawn up for forty baskets of food, to be packed according to family size. Ten delivery teams were prepared to make four stops each. Meanwhile Heidi carefully inventoried the pantry, to be sure of adequate food supplies.

She had other matters on her mind as well. A cold front hit central Indiana, and temperatures plummeted into the teens. Heidi had prevailed upon Russ to keep Precious in the pole barn at night. Russ had grudgingly agreed, even volunteering in the end to let the cat out again first thing each morning. Precious would wait at the metal doors as Russ undid the padlocks, then rub against his legs until Russ went crazy. "Get outta here! Yer nothin' but a dern nuisance, a pest!" he would say. But, secretly, he too was growing fond of Precious.

At long last, Nature Sunday arrived. Once again Phil Simpson had come early and entered the pantry closet, but this time he had exited again with a shovel and a plastic bag, which he carried behind the building out of sight. Soon the clanking of metal had commenced but ended again almost at once, long before Heidi ever arrived on the scene. Never before was a deathblow delivered in so tenderhearted a manner.

In worship I had revisited the story of St. Francis, but now I turned to the hymn text itself—not the version we would sing, but a literal translation by Matthew Arnold. It had been on my mind since Heidi's outburst the week before. I had realized in that whole awkward moment that she had a better grasp of my favorite hymn than I had myself. The mysticism of Arnold's translation seemed to capture her spirit, one I now felt compelled to share. In Francis's "Canticle to the Sun," as it was known, the sun and wind are brothers, the moon and water, sisters. From earth, our mother, to fire, our brother, the things of nature bring God home to us—all the way to "sister death," who brings us home to God.

The text of our hymn version was somewhat simpler, more straightforward. But it too captured the majesty of God in the world God wrought. All of creation, animate and inanimate alike, was made to sing to God. Whenever winds rush, clouds sail, sun burns golden, and moon gleams silver, God is praised. And wherever God's creatures are present, whether cat or mouse, squirrel or skunk—or hungry children in a trailer park—God can be found. All that is needed are eyes and ears, and, yes, noses, to notice, and voices to proclaim it so.

With that, we finally sang my favorite hymn, and my heart raced all over again. But this time around my sense of wonderment emanated from a different center. Heidi Hapness had moved up from the back pew and, remarkably, was sitting between Phil and Jeannie Simpson. Phil had apologized to Heidi for his insensitivity of the previous week, something Jeannie had wondered at aloud—particularly why such a thing didn't happen more often at home. Heidi, whose heart that day was too full for grudges, had been happy to forgive him. Now, together, forgiver and forgiven were endeavoring to sing:

*And all ye men of tender heart,*
  *forgiving others, take your part*
*O sing ye! Alleluia!*
*Ye who long pain and sorrow bear,*
  *praise God and on him cast your care!*
*O praise him, Alleluia!*

Then, at the last, all the creatures of Ashgrove Church had joined in a stirring rendition of a favorite of their own. It had not been my tongue-in-cheek offer to program it. Nor was it Harold's and Shelly's pressure to make good on the pledge. Instead, it had been Heidi's words, plain spoken and precise. "His Eye Is on the Sparrow," she had said, and after that there had been little choice. We sang simply of God's loving eye on sparrows and sinners alike, because, after all, it was simply true.

The church potluck dinner was a real feast. Heidi sat with the Simpsons and all passed amicably between them until the end of dessert. Then, out of the blue, as was her way, Heidi again stirred the pot of improbability.

"Well," she started, "I've made up my mind about somethin'."

"Yeah?" said Phil.

"It's about the mice," she continued. "I've been thinkin' about it since last Sunday, and since it's gotten so cold."

"Go on," Phil urged, already growing nervous.

"St. Francis gave me the idea, the way he told those people, 'Feed the wolf! He's hungry!' He was right, you know!"

"Hold on now, Heidi," Phil squawked, "you're not talkin' about *feedin'* the mice?"

"No," Heidi laughed. "Not the mice! The *cat!* I'm thinkin' I should move Precious into the pantry. It's gonna be real cold soon. The mice'll be wantin' to move in permanent for the winter, too. But Precious'll be here instead. He'll just kindly ask the mice to go find another home for the winter, and they'll tell him, 'Why sure!' And they'll pack their bags and leave!"

And Phil could feel his blood begin to boil. He raised himself up to protest. But he didn't. He caught himself and said, to his great surprise, "Well, all right, Heidi. Yer cat can be on night patrol in the pantry for the time bein'. But keep him locked up in there! Be sure he don't go wanderin' about the church gettin' into things, or I'll throw him to the wolves myself!" And Heidi agreed.

That Tuesday, late in the afternoon, Heidi arrived at the church. She entered the vestibule in midstream of a serious conversation, yet not another soul was in sight. It was only Heidi—and Precious. She was moving him into the pantry. She had his food and water dish, his blanket, a litter box, and the plastic tub, which for four weeks had served as his bed. This time the tub carried a lid, which had been stored in the trunk of her car. Heidi arranged things neatly on the pantry floor, all but the plastic tub. This she placed right beside the shelves of a now-bare pantry.

"You won't be needin' this any longer, Precious!" she said to him. "This whole room's your new bed," she explained, while opening a can of tuna fish and scraping it into his bowl.

"Meow!" he said.

"There you go, Precious. You talk to those mice now. Tell 'em to keep away—but be nice about it. 'Fact, give 'em a chance to find their own place. Besides, they won't be doin' any more harm here."

With that, Heidi placed the few remaining bags of flour, sugar, Kool-Aid, and other paper-wrapped items into the plastic tub and shut the lid down tight. Then, with a pat on the head, she bid the night watchman of Ashgrove Church farewell, pulled the door to the pantry closed, and left the building.

"St. Francis," I said to myself, recalling suddenly the words Hassie Longstreet had spoken of Heidi weeks before. Hassie had said Dr. Doolittle, but I thought, "No. Not so much Dr. Doolittle as another St. Francis." And in her own way just as crazy and confounding and captivating, too!

All this had happened as I sat in my study, still as a mouse. I had heard every word Heidi said, but it had not really qualified as eavesdropping. After all, my door had been standing ajar, my light was on, and my car was parked in the drive. And, frankly, I don't believe Heidi could have cared less who was listening in anyway. To her, we were all one big family. The family of God.

## ♪ Hymn Notes ♪

The life of Giovanni Bernardone, better known as St. Francis of Assisi (1182–1226) is one of the great riches-to-rags stories of all time. Born into wealth and privilege, Francis, at twenty-five, renounced a life of indulgence to wed Lady Poverty and live out the teachings of Jesus.

Many biographies tell the tale of his short life and preaching career and the swift spread of his movement: his conversion at the ruins of St. Damian; his tender care for lepers; the blessing and establishment of his order by Pope Innocent III; his simple message of repentance, reconciliation, and universal love; the stigmata—the five wounds of Christ—mystically burned into his flesh. Yet Francis is most celebrated for his wondrous connection with nature. From the inanimate sun, moon, and wind to mother earth and all the creatures that crawl upon it, Francis enjoyed a unique kinship with God's creation. Not only did he speak to it in personal terms. Francis sang to it.

Nowhere is his love of nature more vividly on display than in his "Canticle to the Sun," on which "All Creatures of Our God and King" is based. Blind and near death, Francis sat at a monastery table at St. Damian, where his faith journey had begun. Suddenly he was overcome by a feeling of ecstasy. After several minutes he cried "Praise be to God." His famous poem had just been written.

The most widely used English translation of the hymn is by William Draper (1855–1933), composed around 1910 for a children's festival. Simplified and contemporized, Draper's version contains little of the charming personification of nature present in the original: brother the sun, sister the moon, sister water, brother fire. Yet his text is lovely in its own right.

Rarely has a tune played better suitor to a text than *Lasst Uns Erfreuen* (Let us rejoice). It derives its name from the Easter hymn with which it appeared in the German collection *Geistliche Kirchengesang* (1623). Several other well-known hymns have been wed to this tune as well. The superb harmonization is by the famous English composer Ralph Vaughan Williams.

# CHAPTER 6

# Nearing Heaven's Gate

## "Jesus Loves Me"

*. . . whoever does not receive the kingdom of
God as a little child will never enter it.*
LUKE 18:17, NRSV

ENRIETTA LANGE WAS OLD. HOW OLD, NONE COULD SAY.
It might have been she had strayed too far from
her roots. Perhaps she had simply outlasted everyone who knew for certain. But my repeated inquiries into
the age of Henrietta Lange had yielded a unison response:

"Don't know. She's up there, though! Hennie's very,
very old . . . "

So old, in fact, that she had buried three husbands and
two grown children. So old that those who knew her had
lost interest in her age. All had given in to the extraordi-
nary opinion that Henrietta Lange would live forever.

Henrietta had chosen to spend eternity in a retirement
center on the edge of Marquette, Indiana. She had moved

there several months after having been diagnosed with an inoperable cancer—a fact she had kept to herself until shortly before the move. Secretly, she planned to settle in there and outlast the cancer. Eventually, she thought, it would simply give up and die, while she would go right on living. After all, she'd suffered nearly every ailment known to the human race already and outlived every one. Why should it be any different with cancer?

"Hennie, you've just got to give up the house!" her friends had pleaded upon learning of her condition. "You really must!" they kept on, just as she knew they would. But by then her bags were already packed. Not her friends' urgings, but a fresh realization of mortality, had made up

## Jesus Loves Me

**Written by Anna Bartlett Warner**

Jesus loves me! this I know, For the Bible tells me so;
Little ones to Him belong, They are weak but He is strong.
Yes, Jesus loves me! Yes, Jesus loves me!
Yes, Jesus loves me! The Bible tells me so.

Jesus loves me! He who died Heaven's gate to open wide;
He will wash away my sin, Let His little child come in.
Yes, Jesus loves me! Yes, Jesus loves me!
Yes, Jesus loves me! The Bible tells me so.

Jesus loves me! He will stay Close beside me all the way;
He's prepared a home for me,
    And some day His face I'll see.
Yes, Jesus loves me! Yes, Jesus loves me!
Yes, Jesus loves me! The Bible tells me so.

her mind. And not her own mortality—naturally—but that of someone else, someone dearer to her even than life itself.

Henrietta's old downtown home on the hill, just across from the university, had sold quickly. Buyers had come out in droves. Henrietta had no problem disposing of her many fine Victorian collectibles, either. Some of the best pieces had gone to their vocal admirers through the years whose names had ended up on scraps of paper, taped to their undersides. The rest were sold in parcels to dealers, thrilled to get their hands on some choice specimens from the dwindling supply of Victoriana.

In a twist of fate, one piece had even found its way down the road to our quiet grove and through the doors of Ashgrove Baptist Church. On a quiet Friday afternoon, Herb Chestnut's El Camino pulled into the gravel drive and backed up to the church entrance. Standing in the vestibule, I watched it slide off the edge of the tailgate and onto the grass: a mahogany library table in church Gothic. It was love at first sight. In a sudden impulse of generosity, I ran to Herb's aid, and together we hoisted it into the building.

"Where do you suppose it should go?" asked Herb, pulling to the right. "Fellowship Hall probably?"

"Let's think about this!" I suggested, heaving as best I could back the other way, back toward the pastor's study. "We mustn't be hasty. There are a lot of options, you know."

At last the table came to rest against the wall of the vestibule. I studied it eagerly, as Herb watched in amusement. Trefoils, threefold leaf designs, were deep carved into each corner. Elegant rectilinear shapes were incised down each table leg. And hanging down from the table top on three sides were inverted gables. Each one came to a point and was capped in a teardrop ball. On the front side was a single drawer with two brass pulls. The drawer was locked.

"Where's the key?" I asked.

"Hmmm," answered Herb. "Didn't notice that. Have to ask Hennie next time I see her!"

"Hennie who?" I asked.

"Why, Henrietta Lange, of course!"

"I didn't know," I told Harold Hatch. We were discussing my earlier conversation with Herb. "Not a soul ever told me about her!" I complained. "Why isn't she on the shut-in list?"

Harold smiled. "She's old," he said. "Very old. Why, I'd wager she's as old as that oak tree there," he said, pointing to a shady burr oak south of the building.

"But that's impossible!" I objected. "That tree's huge, way over a hundred years old!" Harold glanced at the tree again, then back at me, shrugging his shoulders as if in ironic assent to the opinion. "Hennie's old," he picked up again, "but she's no shut-in."

Harold then filled me in on the little he knew of Henrietta Lange's ties to Ashgrove Church. She had come from New Jersey in the mid-1920s, during the pastorate of Wilkes Cobb. After the death of her first husband, she had moved to Marquette, remarried, and reared her two sons. But Henrietta had kept in touch across the decades, attending the funerals of old-time friends, receiving in turn the mourners of the church at the deaths of her husbands and sons, and writing a nice check each December for the ongoing work of ministry.

"Why don't you go visit her sometime?" Harold suggested. "You could see for yourself, ask her about that missing key, maybe even learn a thing or two—Hennie's full of surprises."

The Forest Green Retirement Center sat on the northern edge of the city of Marquette, surrounded by open field earmarked for a new housing development. Bulldozers dotted the landscape. Except for a few old hardwoods on facility grounds, there was scarcely a tree in sight. A large sign identified the facility. It shot up from a giant mound of impatiens, slated to die in the approaching autumn. The setting itself spoke a heavy message of the impermanence of things. But as if to remove every last doubt, a smaller sign sat next to the larger one. It read Heaven's Gate—Hospice Care.

I parked, entered a large new atrium, and approached a woman at the information center.

"I'm looking for a Mrs. Lange," I said. "Henrietta Lange."

"Ah, Dr. Lange! Straight down that hall," the woman pointed, "then the first right. Room 128. You can try her there, but she may already be on rounds."

"No, there must be a mistake," I said. "I'm looking for a resident, not a doctor. She only moved here recently."

"Well, Dr. Lange has only *lived* here for a brief time, but she's been *working* here as long as I can remember. Henrietta Lange is one of our staff physicians."

Room 128 lay along a freshly carpeted corridor of the facility's Williamsburg Wing. Wall sconces lit the way and reproduction paintings hung over striped wallpaper above chair-rail and wainscoting. Up and down the hallway, doors with brass nameplates were tightly shut. The door to one room only stood open. It was 128, and as I approached it, I heard humming. I stopped and peeked around the corner into a room, spacious yet cluttered with oversized furniture. Everywhere, on tables, chairs, an ottoman, the floor itself, were open journals and books.

Henrietta was poring over one of these with thick spectacles and a look of immense concentration, while still the refrain of a familiar tune escaped from her taut lips. It was a melody I might well have recognized, had I not been casting about for a way to announce my presence. But Henrietta had saved me the trouble.

"Come on in, young man!" she said, not even looking up. "Lost, are you?"

I told her who I was and of the Ashgrove connection. Then I thanked her for the library table.

"That old thing!" she said. "Been in the family forever."

We visited briefly, speaking of old times at the church and of my current ministry there. I was poised to broach the subject of the missing key when Henrietta's grandfather clock struck the hour, and Henrietta rose up with the fury of a jack-in-a-box. Firmly grabbing hold of her walker on wheels, she said, "Ten o'clock! Gotta go! Time for morning rounds."

"Mmmm," I said.

"Otherwise I'd stay and visit some more."

"Maybe I'll tag along a bit if that's all right."

"Suit yourself," she said.

With that, Henrietta lumbered down the hall, out of the Williamsburg Wing and into a plainer one dubbed Jamestown, stopping in at several rooms to see elderly patients in various stages of wellness and illness. She greeted each one with soft words of cheer and comfort. She studied charts, took vital signs, listened to chests. Her stethoscope hung from the top bar of her walker, its diaphragm dangling down nearly to the floor. She would insert the earpiece and press the diaphragm to her patient's chest, and say, "Cough!" and her patient would cough. And when the effort didn't pass muster, she would add, "Now, cough like you mean business!" Occasionally she would turn the end over to the bell side and listen awhile with it. "That's for deep tones," she explained.

At the close of each visit, Henrietta opened a pouch, fastened to the walker, and pulled out a handful of bite-size candy bars. "Milky Way, Butterfinger, or Snickers?" she would ask. With a smile, sometimes even a giggle of guilt, they would make their choice. And when patients said, "None, thank you," then Dr. Henrietta Lange would choose one for them, adding, "Here. Give it away to visitors. They'll come back sooner that way!"

"I'm the candy lady!" she cackled, maneuvering left toward a different wing of the facility. Newly installed automatic doors opened upon our approach. A young cry was audible from a room halfway down the hall. Above the entrance was the same discomfiting sign I had noted upon arrival: Heaven's Gate, it said. Hospice Care.

Henrietta followed that cry to the exclusion of all else. We bypassed several rooms where pairs of young, wide eyes stared out anxiously for the source of the sound of feet and wheels that had come to mean one unmistakable thing: chocolate. But Henrietta continued on. Her ancient face strained now for the first time, not with her own pain but with that of a newborn anguish. At last she stopped at a door, slightly ajar. At eye level, in place of a brass nameplate, was the metal track for a less permanent kind—the sort that can be slid easily in and out again. A strip of white cardboard had been inserted there, bearing a name in black ink. It read Banks, William.

Henrietta lowered her head and rapped her bony knuckles on wood. Moments later a nurse peeped her head out.

"Oh, Dr. Lange!" she said. "Just a moment!" The nurse disappeared back into the dark room, and after a pause, a woman in her mid-thirties emerged from out of the shadows. Her face was long and drawn, and her hair was disheveled. Her eyes were deep-set and encircled by streaks of gray like a raccoon's. But she broke into an easy smile at the sight of Henrietta.

"Hi, Hennie!" she said sleepily.

"Oh, child! You and Willie have been on my mind all night! I won't disturb you further now, but just know that I'm with you!"

"No, it's all right. Really. I think he'd like to see you."

With that, the door opened wide. Henrietta introduced me to Teresa Banks, William Banks's mother, as two nurses left the room. Inside, all was dark and, finally, still. "Just like the night before," whispered Teresa. "He finally slept good somewhere in the middle of the night but woke up this morning all hurting and distressed. We changed his bed and 'jamas and just now he's calmed down again." Henrietta nodded her understanding. Then, taking my hand, she led me to the bedside.

There I beheld a small boy, no older than five. He was smothered in blankets. His face was gaunt, bloodless. His eyes were tightly shut, but the moment Henrietta called his name, they opened alertly.

"Hi, my little one!" she said, "Hi, my sweet!" I watched her study him, check his chart, take his pulse, feel his swollen glands. She asked him simple questions to which he nodded yes or shook no, his bloodshot eyes never once abandoning their plaintive gaze into hers. And when she put the stethoscope to his bare chest, it was more the bell, less the diaphragm. It was deep tones she sought. There was something more here, something well beyond any doctor-patient relation. A kind of energy passed between them, bridging the chasm of years, naming them together, here and now and always. Then, all at once, I recognized it. It was clear as her bell. It was love.

"This is Willie," she said. "And he's my boy!"

"Glad to meet you, Willie!" I said. And I smiled through the sadness of it.

Back in room 128, Henrietta told me Willie's story. The Banks family were long-time patients of hers. She had delivered Teresa and her brothers, as she had their mother before them, not to mention "half the town of Marquette," as the joke went. But there was a further connection between them. Henrietta's second husband had been Teresa's great-uncle. Having no grandchildren of her own, Henrietta had welcomed each of the Bankses permanently into her heart, even beyond the deaths of her second and third husbands. When Willie was stricken ill, she had ached as if he had proceeded right from her own womb.

"Nobody knows this but me—and now you," Henrietta confided. "I gave up my house and moved here for one reason: to be near Willie and his mother and father. Willie has a rare form of leukemia. We've battled it since just after he was born. There's nothing more to be done. If and when he dies, I intend to be close beside him—all the way," she said. And the words had a strange but familiar ring to them. "Just as I hope to be here for *all* my patients," she continued, "and I can't count on that anymore—short of living here myself."

Then Henrietta made tea. She boiled water, prepared the tea bags, and set out cream and sugar. As she worked, Dr. Henrietta Lange had begun once again to hum, and this time I had listened. Soon her tune evoked words well-known, words that I realized had been stealing into my consciousness all morning long, through talk of little ones and staying close beside, all the way, and, of course, the ominous Heaven's Gate sign.

"You like that hymn, don't you?" I said.

"'Jesus Loves Me'? Why, it's my favorite, can't you tell?"

"I thought of it when I saw the name of the hospice unit: Heaven's Gate."

"Chose the name myself," Henrietta replied. "Elder's prerogative, you know!"

"But isn't it a little," I started, "I mean, doesn't it . . . Don't people get a bit, you know, put off by it," I managed, "a little scared?"

"Oh, I don't know," she mused. "Something scary about heaven? . . . When I was quite young," Henrietta continued, "I read the book! It was a poem first, you know. A man in the story recited it to a little boy named Johnny. Johnny was dying. The man spoke these words:

*Jesus loves me! loves me still, tho I'm very weak and ill,*
*that I might from sin be free,*
*bled and died upon the tree . . .*

"Don't recall hearing *that* verse before," I commented.

"*Say and Seal* was the title, I believe. It was a gift of my Uncle Frank's. He was a West Pointer. Brought it to me on my tenth birthday, signed by Anna Warner and all! Of course, we grew up singing it, too!"

Suddenly the grandfather clock struck noon. It was time for me to go. I finished my tea and thanked Henrietta again for her hospitality. I was nearly out the door when Henrietta called me back. "Wait a minute," she said, reaching into her pouch. "Milky Way, Butterfinger, or Snickers?"

"Snickers! It's my favorite!" And I said it with all the feeling of a beloved patient—even a son.

Willie Banks hung on only a pair of months longer. Word of his death came to us early on a Sunday morning, and so we broke our worship routine to accommodate a time of prayer. We prayed for Willie's family, for their strength and understanding. We thanked God for the blessing of life while we have it and the end of pain when it is gone; we extolled the spirit of an ageless aunt of endless love; and we concluded worship with a hymn, a word of sweet consolation—Hennie's hymn, "Jesus Loves Me."

The day of Willie's funeral, the Hatches, the Chestnuts, and I drove the hour north to celebrate the love of Jesus in Willie's life one last time. At the memorial service, confined to a wheelchair, was a now frail Henrietta Lange. She had given up her apartment in the Williamsburg Wing and moved quietly down the hall into Heaven's Gate. Her pain of body and spirit was of double strength that day, but her eyes had lost none of their penetrating intensity. Holding fast Teresa's hand, she followed every spoken word, nodding often. With her free hand she dabbed the tears from her eyes, reaching over now and then to do the same for Teresa. And she sang all the words to all three hymns, saving up her best for the last of them, chosen again of seeming necessity:

*Jesus loves me, this I know, for the Bible tells me so;*
*Little ones to him belong, they are weak but he is strong.*
*Yes, Jesus loves me! Yes, Jesus loves me!*
   *Yes, Jesus loves me!*
*The Bible tells me so.*

At the end of the service, we stood in a long line to greet her. At my approach, Henrietta threw up her arms to offer me an embrace. "Hello again, young man!" she said. She gazed intently into my eyes. "A little child's gone in!" she reflected, still quoting from her favorite hymn. "I think I'm next!" But she didn't utter this. Her eyes had said it for her. Anyone could see it: she would not last long, now. Old Henrietta Lange was due to embark on one last journey.

Once again I had intended to bring up the key, to inquire whether Henrietta knew its whereabouts. Once again it slipped my mind. Instead, I just squeezed Henrietta's hands, smiled, and said good-bye, persuaded it was for the last time.

Arriving again at the church, I retreated to my study, exhausted from the strain of sadness. Under the window where I'd made room was the library table, appearing more magnificent than ever. I had lobbied shamelessly to bring it there, to claim it for my personal sanctum. Yet it was more than just a pretty piece now. It was a symbol of a loving journey, a link both to a dying past and a promised future. It could not stay there. It was meant to be given, to be shared, admired by all, like the very love it bespoke.

Back through the vestibule and down into Fellowship Hall I heaved it, grabbing it in the middle, endeavoring not to drag its legs over the tile floor. Frustrated, I turned the table on its side, thinking to hoist it up and bear it with the edge of the tabletop resting against my thighs. It was then, by chance, that I had brushed up against it: a faded envelope, wedged and taped into the table's underbracing. The paper tore in the act of freeing it, and onto the floor clanked a metal object with teeth and a loop at the top. It was the missing skeleton key.

I returned the table to its upright position and knelt before it. Reverently, like an act of worship, I inserted the key into the keyhole and gave it one full clockwise turn. The lock let out one crisp click, sweet music in my ears, and then the drawer pulled open. There to one side was a single book, its cover disfigured, its binding coming apart. I opened it to the title page. *Say and Seal*, it read, *by Anna B. Warner.* And on the facing page was a note:

*For Henrietta, on the occasion of her tenth birthday.*
*All fond thoughts, Uncle Franklin*

And then, a date, too magnificent to fathom: It read June 21, 1889.

"But that's impossible!" I cried. "That can't be!" And I peered out at the burr oak tree, standing proud on the south lawn, shedding its calico leaves again for the hundredth time. "Young!" I thought. "A mere child of a tree!" For I knew a mighty oak of a woman, a Lazarus of a soul. And now she was heading for a home beyond heaven's gate, which opens wide to children of all ages, there to live henceforth and evermore.

## ♪ Hymn Notes ♪

It is the first song we learned to sing in Sunday school. We memorized it before we could recite a single word from Scripture. We sang it before roomfuls of admiring adults on Promotion Sundays around America. "Jesus Loves Me" was the earliest and the essential word of the gospel we heard and believed as children in the church.

Anna Warner (1820–1915) lived a charmed life on Constitution Island, upstream of New York City on the Hudson River. She and her sister, Susan, took up writing after their father lost a fortune in the panic of 1837, which had caused the family to move permanently from the city to their island home. Susan had the bigger career, publishing several successful novels. Anna's first love was hymn writing. She edited two hymnbooks, and the second collection, *Original Hymns,* contained the hymn for which she is best remembered.

"Jesus Loves Me," written in 1859, was adapted from a poem spoken by a character in her novel Say and Seal. In the story, Mr. Linden recites it to a dying child, Johnny Fax, as a source of ultimate comfort and assurance. So it has remained to this day.

Perhaps the most widely sung hymn in the Christian world, "Jesus Loves Me" has been a consistent choice of missionaries wishing to convey the simple message of faith to children and adults alike. Over the years, many inspiring stories have resulted. In the People's Republic of China, for instance, during days of little contact with Chinese Christians, a message got through the censors to friends in America. It read, "The 'This I Know' people are well."

When once he was asked to summarize the Christian gospel, the eminent theologian Karl Barth, replied, "'Jesus loves me, this I know.'" The rest is commentary.

The tune long associated with "Jesus Loves Me" is by William Bradbury from his collection *The Golden Sower* (1862). It is a simple melody, ideally suited to the plain, heartfelt text. Bradbury composed the chorus appending each verse.

For years the Warner sisters conducted Bible studies on Constitution Island for cadets at West Point. They would ferry over on Sunday afternoons for tea, gingerbread, and gospel truth. Upon their deaths, the Warner sisters were granted full military honors, and their home became a national historic site.

Anna Warner lived to the ripe old age of ninety-five.

Source: Jane Stewart Smith, *Favorite Women Hymn Writers* (Wheaton, Ill.: Crossway Books, 1990).

# CHAPTER 7

# Sweet March of Surrender

## "Onward, Christian Soldiers"

MRS. MILLIE GRIMSHAW, CHAIRWOMAN OF THE BOARD OF Christian education at the Ashgrove Baptist Church, was caught in the clutches of dread, the kind that follows you into your dreams. Each spring the feeling was back, choking out Easter joy like jimson weed in a bean patch. Once again Millie had avoided the whole bothersome business until the last minute. Now the crushing weight of obligation pressed upon her frail frame like hundred-pound barbells.

"But why," Millie queried herself aloud, "why, if Jesus' yoke was said to be so easy, did the Holy Spirit dream up Vacation Bible School in the first place?"

Millie had her own theory about this, but that something as widely hallowed as this annual pilgrimage of children to the lap of Jesus might be devil's work in disguise was a thought best kept to herself.

All the planning books recommended a church start preparations for Bible school as far back as January. There

# Onward, Christian Soldiers

### Written by Sabine Baring-Gould

Onward, Christian soldiers, Marching as to war,
With the cross of Jesus Going on before!
Christ, the royal Master, Leads against the foe;
Forward into battle See His banners go!
Onward, Christian soldiers, Marching as to war,
With the cross of Jesus Going on before!

At the sign of triumph Satan's host doth flee;
On, then, Christian soldiers, On to victory!
Hell's foundations quiver At the shout of praise;
Brothers, lift your voices, Loud your anthems raise!
Onward, Christian soldiers, Marching as to war,
With the cross of Jesus Going on before.

Like a mighty army Moves the Church of God;
Brothers, we are treading Where the saints have trod.
We are not divided, All one body we—
One in hope and doctrine, One in charity.
Onward, Christian soldiers, Marching as to war,
With the cross of Jesus Going on before.

Onward, then, ye people, Join our happy throng;
Blend with ours your voices In the triumph song.
Glory, laud and honor Unto Christ the King—
This thru countless ages Men and angels sing.
Onward, Christian soldiers, Marching as to war,
With the cross of Jesus Going on before.

were numerous reasons for this, not the least of which was the ever-knotty predicament of teacher recruitment. It all came down to human nature, specifically the widespread distaste for the word *no* in the mouth. To avoid the guilt of saying no, people will agree to almost anything, provided it is scheduled far enough into the future. The key is to strike early. Talk of July in the dead of winter has the feel of a brief eternity. Sad for Millie, it was now already late May. The no's were in full bloom. There was one remarkable exception.

"Yes, yes, I will!" replied Pat Keltch. "Thanks for asking me!" Millie was on the phone with her, a relative newcomer to the church. Had she been addressing Pat in person, Millie might have conjured a smile at such an enthusiastic response. But it was late on an evening of frowns up in Millie's sewing room. The church directory lay open next to the phone on her worktable. An onlooker would have been mistaken to imagine Millie was meeting with success already at the Ks of the alphabet. In reality, Pat had not been on Millie's A list for Vacation Bible School recruitment. Truth be told, she had been passed over for the B list, as well. This was her third, desperate trip through the pages of the church family roster.

"Well, that's just . . . real nice, Pat," Millie managed. "Maybe then you wouldn't mind helping Madge Spires with the little ones—you know, toddler-age and such, up to kindergartners?"

"Wherever you want me, Mrs. Grimshaw, will be just fine! And I'll just plan to take my week's vacation from work then—you know, Bible school being during the day and all . . . "

"Oh, well, that's awful nice, Pat, awful nice . . . We'll be see'n' you then at the meetin' Monday night, seven sharp?"

"I'll be there! Bye—and thanks!"

Millie lowered the receiver. She lifted her pencil and placed a check by the line on her worksheet that read Toddlers, but this Millie did with a decidedly tentative stroke of the lead. Pat's eagerness worried her. It was this brand of enthusiasm in newcomers that could lead to far-fetched ideas, the kind that made regular church people tired just to think about. This was something to keep an eye on. Next, Millie dialed Madge Spires. Madge had been stalwart custodian of the Sunday school toddler department for upwards of thirty-five years. She had stuck to her post through the administrations of four pastors, five Sunday school superintendents, and six United States presidents. Madge had been willing, once again, to take on the toddlers for the five days of Vacation Bible School. Alerting Madge early as to the identity of her class helper was a simple courtesy.

"I hope Pat's gonna work out for you, Madge. Don't know her too well, but seems nice enough . . . "

Then, in that confounding way of grace to shape our thoughts in spite of us, Millie had heard herself announce to Madge a marvel she had yet to confide even to herself: " . . . and Madge—Pat Keltch is gonna give up her week's vacation from work to be at Bible school! Now isn't that just somethin'?"

"'Spect so!" Madge had agreed.

"Yes, it *was* somethin'," Millie mused as she hung up the phone and closed the directory for the day. But her mind strayed quickly from the thought when she noticed the time: 8:45 p.m. It was an unspoken rule of her generation not to phone a friend after 8:30 of an evening. No one in her acquaintance any longer actually kept farmers' hours. Most stayed up at least for the ten o'clock news. But old rules were still rules, and Millie hoped Madge had not thought her rude. The whole business was a darn shame,

Millie ruminated. "Merciful Lord, I've got to stop all this 'fore it kills me!" The words had been directed not so much to God as to her husband, Seymour. He was downstairs in the den polishing off an apple crumb cake and watching a rerun of *Bonanza*.

"Took yeh a while, Millie! What'd yeh do, dial up the whole *county?*"

"Pert' near, and I'm still shy three teachers!"

"Well, stop *askin'* everybody and start *tellin'!*" Seymour barked. He knew perfectly well the church didn't work that way, but Seymour, better known as Sarge, did his best to bring to each life situation at least a little taste of Marine boot camp.

"*You'd* best be prayin'," Millie inflected in that way of hers that never failed to flaunt her rank in this corps, "best be prayin' I find some teachers soon, or I'll be a'tellin' you a week's worth, as my assistant in the primary department!"

"That'll be the day!" Sarge retorted, but they both knew from long experience that if drafted Sarge would serve.

"Oh, merciful Lord!" Millie chanted again, this time in place of formal prayers, "I have got to stop all this 'fore it kills me!" Then she went to bed.

Yet, amid all the stress of a day in the life of the chairwoman of the board of Christian education at the Ashgrove Baptist Church, it was another thought that came to rest in Millie's mind in the final moments before sleep. "She's giv'n' up her week's vacation to help out at Vacation Bible School!"

And Millie Grimshaw smiled in her dreams.

At the Monday Vacation Bible School meeting, plans stuck to the pattern like planets to their courses. Miraculously, every line on Millie's volunteer worksheet now carried the name of a teacher or an assistant. Each was a woman, of course. Vacation Bible School leadership was always women only. This was not theory; it was pure practice. Here, if anywhere, the paradigms of the past held sway.

The Bible school theme, Adventure with Jesus, covered the stories of five journeys in the Savior's life, concluding at the cross and resurrection. Lesson material for each class was distributed, including thirty-five student take-home sheets for each day. Instructions and supply lists for the corresponding crafts were handed out. The best of the best snack ideas were floated as every year, and, like every year, the same five were chosen: popcorn, pretzels, mini pizzas, peanut butter in celery sticks and, as a special Friday treat, worms (molded Jell-O) in dirt (Oreo cookie crumbs).

"Now *how* many children should we plan on?" asked a very scatterbrained kitchen crew of one. Cynthia Spittler had assisted her sister, Claudia, in the past. But Claudia had died in December, leaving Cynthia to fend for herself. The fact that she was asking now for the third time seemed to augur trouble in the kitchen.

"*Thirty-five!*" an impatient Millie repeated. "Like I said before, there's never more than *thirty-five* children at our Bible school!" Millie declared it like an edict, and next to no one doubted that it was.

There remained one matter to settle. Each Bible school culminated in a closing exercise, a Friday evening celebration showcasing the week's accomplishments for the gratification of children and parents alike. Children recited Scripture, sang songs with little hand motions, and showed off their craftwork. Who would be in charge of this? Millie wanted to know. The pastor always brought a word of welcome and an opening prayer, but someone else needed to plan the order, introduce the different classes and the songs, and so forth. Millie had taken on this burden the last three years in a row. "It's someone else's turn!" she ended.

Indeed, Millie Grimshaw wanted desperately not to be in charge. It had been a hard year for her physically. There had been death in her family. She was tired. Millie confessed none of this openly, but the strain of it was visible to the watchful eye. Unfortunately for her, everyone was looking down. Not a soul volunteered. All knew well that peculiar feeling of aching bones and frayed nerves by Friday evening of a Vacation Bible School. Moreover, to a person, those present could coach, coddle, or boss a group of children in their sleep, but standing up before a roomful of adults caused them to wilt like lettuce. There was one notable exception.

"Um—" a demure Pat Keltch suddenly broke the awkward silence, "I suppose I could try that—if, that is, you all don't mind . . . " Her eyes alone had been peering deeply into Millie's pain. "We feel it, too!" they seemed to say, but Millie did not respond.

"Have you ever done that kind of thing before?" Millie wanted to know.

"Well, no, not quite," Pat admitted. "But I'd be glad to try, if it would be all right."

Around the room, all other pairs of eyes looked relieved.

"Well . . . " Millie responded haltingly, "thank you, Pat . . . are all agreed?" She was scanning the table as if trolling for dissension, but all heads were nodding in the affirmative. The job was Pat's.

"I can help you with that now, Pat." Millie offered after the meeting. "All you've got to do is just let me know!"

"And if I can *ever* help *you* in any way, Mrs. Grimshaw, *you let me know!*" Pat had rejoined.

That night Millie lay in bed awake, thinking thoughts that would not go away. How would Pat Keltch manage her closing program? Should Millie simply have handled it after all? And what had Pat meant by her offer of help?

What had Millie allowed Pat to see in her to prompt such sympathy? What, at any rate, could Pat Keltch possibly do for her, Millie Grimshaw, that she could not do perfectly well for herself? And the questions gnawed at her like bedbugs through the night and into the dawn.

On the Sunday morning after Independence Day, which was the Sunday morning before Vacation Bible School week at Ashgrove Baptist Church, I preached from Ephesians 6, on the whole armor of God. "Finally, be strong," the passage began, "put on the whole armor of God"—the belt of truth, the breastplate of righteousness, the shield of faith, the helmet of salvation, the sword of the Spirit. These images of Roman warfare were so outmoded as to be almost comical, I had begun. A disciple of Paul today would have to draw spiritual analogies from semiautomatic rifles and rocket grenade launchers, gas masks and radiation suits. But these images weren't finally about mortal combat. Their real purpose was to gird Christians with courage for that other struggle, the inward struggle for the human heart and spirit.

To illustrate the point, I turned to a favorite hymn of the church, "Onward, Christian Soldiers." The hymn could conjure countless mental pictures, depending upon the mind at work. Veterans had been known to grow teary-eyed as they sang it. Sarge Grimshaw once confided that it always made him want to salute. As children, we would march in time to the refrain without even thinking. Others found its militaristic edge offensive. They wished to strike it from the hymnal once and for all along with the whole ancient hymn category Christian Warfare.

It helped to remember that its author, Sabine Baring-Gould, had written the piece for children to sing in a procession between two English villages. He was curate for a small parish in the needy and neglected mining town of Horbury in Yorkshire. The poor children of Horbury and the children of the mother church on the hill, St. Peter's, were to unite and march together the mile distance between them. Baring-Gould could find nothing appropriate for the two groups to sing, so he had scratched out "Onward, Christian Soldiers" in all of fifteen minutes. It seemed clear that he had played upon that timeless and innocent fascination of children with war, but one would be hard-pressed to fault the direction he took it: one "happy throng" with a "triumph song," a "shout of praise" as their "anthems raise," singing "all one body, we," in "hope and . . . charity," guided by the "cross of Jesus, going on before"!

The hymn's truest vision is of God's children from divided worlds, marching as one army into the loving arms of Christ. Likewise, I concluded, the purpose of God's armor is not to vanquish our enemies of "flesh and blood" (Ephesians 6:12) but, in the spirit of righteousness and peace, to extend to all the invitation to gird ourselves for the loving work of the gospel in the world.

The first in line to greet me at the close of worship was a nearly giddy Pat Keltch. She rushed to my side as if drawn by a magnet.

"Pastor," she cried, "I want to do that!"

"Do what, Pat?" I asked.

Pat did not reply. Instead, grabbing my arm, she dragged me to the Vacation Bible School preregistration table where Millie sat discussing the week's final arrangements with her assistant director, Pauline Jones. At last, Millie had just announced, everything was coming together.

"I know what I want to do!" Pat interrupted Millie in midsentence.

"What you want to do about *what?*" we asked almost in unison.

"The parade! The march! You know—what the man did in the song in Pastor's story!"

Our lips were frozen in hard and fast confusion

"In Bible school!" Pat pleaded. "For the closing—I want to have a parade!"

It was a blessing that Millie simply retreated without a word. She collected Sarge and swiftly departed the church for the day.

"A parade!" she fumed. Now the true colors of things were flying! Unknown to her, it was only the beginning.

For years the thirty-five children of the Ashgrove Baptist Church Vacation Bible School had been divided by age into four classes, each led by a teacher and her assistant. Volunteers on a schedule managed snack and craft time. Each morning session began promptly at 9:00 and concluded at 11:30 on the money. Following a traditional opening exercise with children's songs, pledges of allegiance to the flags and the Bible, basket offering competition that pitted the girls against the boys—the girls *always* won—and a closing prayer, children filed out of the sanctuary by class and rotated through a Bible lesson, craft time, snack time, and song time. It was a plan of elegant simplicity, a sturdy vessel on a placid sea. Millie thrived on predictability. For her, familiar ground and paradise were the same place.

Nothing in life escapes change forever. From the moment the registration table opened on Monday morning, it was clear this would be a Bible school like no other. Most children of the church had preregistered as usual, but soon carloads of unknown children began to wash in like a tidal wave. Each had followed a similar path, traceable to a rundown neighborhood deep in the city, back to the exemplary recruiting of Pat Keltch. This was Pat's old neighborhood, and she had kept in touch. She had spoken personally to the parents of each child and arranged for transportation. That morning and every one to follow, Pat and her son, Jed, arrived at 8 a.m. with the first carload of children. Then Jed doubled back to pick up a second load. Not long after, a rusty Rambler wagon pulled into the drive, packing enough children for a Chinese fire drill. Its violent knocking of engine lifters drew every eye, then repelled every ear. As the car rolled to a stop, its doors opened long enough for chaos to disembark, and then it sputtered away. This pattern would be repeated daily through the week.

Monday enrollment was a record-breaking forty-five children. The numbers swelled each morning until, by Thursday, the student-teacher ratio was ten to one. Beyond the sheer numbers were the students themselves. As a group, they could be summed up in a word, and that word was wild. They were dirty, knew nothing of country manners, and had no fear of any living thing. The boys were particularly unruly, especially three brothers with the last name of Jameson. It was difficult to stand out in this chaotic crowd, but somehow the Jamesons managed. They were known in their neighborhood as "them Jameson boys," and they milked the reputation for all it was worth. They also happened to be Pat's old next-door neighbors. Her invitation to them to attend Bible school was something of a double mission, she had confided: to give their mother a much-needed break and to "help them learn about Jesus." Success in the first category seemed a safe bet. Attainment of the second goal would be more difficult to measure, I had thought. What about Jesus did she want them to learn? I had wondered. "Just that he loves 'em, I guess," had been her reply. "All of us need his love, you know." It was certainly the place to start, I had agreed.

Millie Grimshaw had not been party to this conversation. By the end of the first morning, she was repenting of having ever approached Pat Keltch about Bible school. Already she was bracing for embarrassment at the closing program. Now children none of them knew the first thing about were overwhelming her teachers. She feared mass mutiny by midweek. This was no longer Millie's Bible school; it was disaster. On Tuesday Millie had made good on her threat to enlist the help of her husband, Sarge. His assignment was not to teach but to intimidate. He floated from class to class and glowered at the most fidgety of the lot. But even his worst scowl was virtually without effect. Sarge's Marine training assumed a prior order of discipline. He knew nothing, short of physical force, about how to bring order to a beardless anarchy. The Jameson boys began to grimace back at Sarge, as if completely taken by this new way to look mean. It was all he could do not to hurt them. Secretly, though, Sarge was developing a fondness for the Jamesons. Their fearlessness appealed to him, but their hidden vulnerability resonated with something even deeper down within. At some point he had stopped scowling and started speaking, and they had begun to respond. Soon he was teaching them his repertoire of rope tricks and other sleights of hand.

"Show us that again!" they would exhort him—irresistible words to a born ham.

All the while, Pat was having the time of her life. Since her arrival at the church with her teenage son, Jed, and their baptisms into a fresh start, she had been seeking a cause, some purposeful expression of her newly found faith. Millie's invitation had spoken to her yearning at unexpected depth. Her exuberance for the mission of Bible school was catching. Even the teachers began to respond to it. By Wednesday they had found their rhythm, and the children were settling in as well. There was energy in all this turmoil and, miraculously, it was being harnessed for the benefit of all. There was one sad exception.

Millie Grimshaw remained in misery. As difficult as it had been to distance herself from the ruinous course of this Bible school, harder still was to have it succeed in spite of her. A part of Millie wanted desperately to board this train of excitement, but she feared it was already moving too fast, and she did not know how to grab hold. Millie was being left behind. "Where's the joy?" she wondered privately—the joy she once had felt as she put her shoulder to the wheel of Christian work. "How will I ever get back the joy?"

Friday morning commenced with a fresh flurry of activity. Opening exercises were canceled, and all the children were lining up together in the vestibule. It was the dress rehearsal of the big parade. Pat had done her best to choreograph the movement, but getting eighty children to go anywhere in the same direction was, according to Madge Spires, "like trying to sweep up chicken feathers."

Jed Keltch was to lead the procession, carrying the cross of Jesus. Next, singing "Onward, Christian Soldiers," students and teachers alike were to file out the front doors and around the church to the left, past the old oak tree and on to the corner of the pet cemetery. From there they would skirt the edge of the ball diamond, swing back left, and then proceed around the other side of the building, coming to rest again at the front entrance. There the processional cross would be posted. Closing exercises would continue outdoors. Folding chairs had been placed in neat rows just for the occasion.

Pat rehearsed the maneuver twice as a mortified Millie looked on. She had informed Pat and everyone else that it was entirely too much to manage, but Pat was in earnest. She had painstakingly cultivated the participation of every teacher. I had been recruited to teach the words of the hymn to the children. I had chosen verses 1, 3, and 5 only, plus the refrain. References in the others to "Satan's host" and "the gates of hell" seemed a bit much for children, not to mention most adults. Trustee Ed Garrett had wired up speakers at the church entrance. These were connected to a microphone on the sanctuary piano, so Shelly Higgins' accompaniment might follow the children along their merry way.

Naturally, it didn't work. At the pet cemetery, the hymn had already turned into a round. Once the procession wound back to the building, no one was singing at all. It brought to my mind Baring-Gould's own second-floor storefront chapel in Horbury. Hymn singing would "bump down the stairs," he wrote, and then come up "irregularly through the chinks in the floor." He had taken it all in good humor, and we were attempting to do the same. Only Millie scoffed and sulked with her arms crossed like a child's.

It was at this point that Sarge made his own private determination about the parade. He shared none of his thoughts to Millie or Pat. Instead, he pulled aside the Jamesons and a few of the other boys and spoke until their faces lit up like sparklers.

"Now you all be sure to be good little soldiers for Christ and come back tonight!" Sarge was overheard to plead, as their old Rambler wagon pulled away down the drive, "'cause tonight we've got some marchin' to do!" And his words worked mightily upon them Jameson boys.

On Friday evening at 6:30 sharp, the rusty Rambler wagon was back. It creaked into the gravel drive of Ashgrove Church, just as it had twice a morning throughout the week. But on this occasion, it had pulled over to park. The motor gasped a terrible gasp and then cut off. At last the awful engine clanking ceased. Nine children disembarked, including three Jamesons. Climbing from the driver's seat was Mrs. Jeannie Jameson, worn, haggard, and extinguishing a cigarette. The boys heaved a duffel bag around the back of the church, then disappeared inside.

By seven o'clock, the children were lining up in the vestibule in costume. Most wore robes of various shapes, sizes, and colors. Their heads were bedecked with mortarboards fashioned out of construction paper. Nearly all 160 little feet were clad in sandals or thongs, a sign of the journey each of the eighty children had taken through the week with Jesus, all the way to the cross. Each girl held a bouquet of plastic flowers, each boy a small stick with an American flag attached. Standing next to the cross that was planted in the ground was Jed Keltch. He wore a long white robe and was prepared on cue to hoist the cross up over his shoulder. Jed was Jesus, leader of the Ashgrove Vacation Bible School parade.

By now the gravel drive was filled with cars, and the deacons were putting up additional rows of chairs. Half the congregation had turned out to see this spectacle that had been the talk of the church all week. They sat intermingled with strangers from many miles down into the city. All were gathered to witness whether sheep of different folds could flock together.

At 7:15, I opened the evening with a welcome and prayer. Then, on cue from Pat, Shelly Higgins began to play and sound to bellow forth from four loudspeakers— Ed had added a pair, running wire out fifty feet on either side of the building. The church doors flung wide and out marched the children. "Onward, Christian Soldiers" was underway.

Suddenly everyone turned in the direction of loud howling, emanating from the south corner of the building. A lone, proud figure, attired in a National Guard uniform, was stepping in place and barking out marching commands to the music.

"Left, left, left-right-left!" boomed Sarge Grimshaw, self-appointed drill sergeant in the Ashgrove Bible school parade. Even against the amperage of four speakers and one hundred human voices, Sarge held his own. The result was a garble of hymn text and tune and verbal command:

> *Onward* - left! - *ian sol* - right! - *diers,*
>   *marching* - left! - *to war* - right! left!
> *With the* - left! - *of Je* - right! - *sus,*
>   *going* - left! - *before* - right! left!

Millie, meanwhile, had been hovering in the background. When she saw her husband, Sarge, in full dress uniform, her first reaction had been one of great shock. But the shock had soon given way to awe, and the awe, to wonder, and the wonder, to profound satisfaction. This was her Sarge, keeping step for these aimless, wandering children. For the first time all week, Millie had cracked a smile.

Pat Keltch saw that smile. As the last class rounded the bend and headed out into the churchyard, she had come to Millie with a plastic bouquet and pressed it in her hands. Then she gave Millie a deep embrace. "Thank you!" Pat said. And she said it trembling with emotion. "Thank you for this!" And she took Millie's hand and led her down the aisle, into the route of the parade. And Millie followed.

Everyone was marching now—everyone but the Jameson boys, that is. When the music began, they and some others had sneaked out a side door and around to the back of the church. There they had opened their duffel. When all the parade had marched past, Sarge fell in line, with Pat and Millie just behind. As they cleared the back corner of the building, out popped them Jameson boys and company, dressed in combat fatigues and outfitted with canteens, ammo belts, and army helmets—the whole armor of God! This had been per arrangement with Sarge, who was welcoming them into the line with a

*Like a might - y ar* - right! left!
  *moves the church of God* - right! left!

This had been their special secret. This was a soldiers' march for Christ and, together, they were bringing it home.

But then Sarge's eyes had settled hard on unexpected trouble. Over the boys' shoulders were the emblems of runaway enthusiasm: rifles! Just of what sort was hard to tell. The status of their chambers, whether designed for bullets, BBs, or blanks, was likewise impossible to know.

"What the . . . ?" said Sarge.

"Oh, my goodness!" exclaimed Pat.

Millie just shrieked.

But the Jameson boys were beaming. They had devoted their afternoon to the procurement and concealment of these parade trophies, and they were marching now in full crusade fervor. Sarge did all he knew to do. He drilled on, as all the marchers sang:

*we are not di - vid* - right! left!
  *all one bo - dy* - left! right! left!
*one in hope and* - left! right! left!
  *one in char - i - ty* - right! left!

The parade progressed along in tight step. Three times through the verses brought the cross home to its hole in the ground and the first marchers home to the cross. These were the girls of the toddler class. Coming to a halt before the cross, they looked around as if uncertain what to do next. Finally, a little girl, stepping right to the very foot of it, laid down her plastic bouquet and moved to the side. Another girl followed her example. And so the plastic flowers piled up as subsequent waves of marchers finished their course. When boys with little flags began to arrive, they naturally followed suit. Down the flags went, onto the pile. In no time, there were flowers and flags strewn all over the ground. All that anyone carried was surrendered to the cross of Christ. When at last the Jameson boys arrived, guns in tow under Sarge's watchful gaze, the path of fate was well trodden and irresistible. The guns came off their shoulders and fell clanking in a heap, right at the foot of the cross atop flags and flowers. The soldiers of Christ cast their weapons down on the plowed earth, as if they knew the prophecy of Micah by heart:

*and they shall beat their swords into plowshares,*
*and their spears into pruning hooks.*

And Seymour Grimshaw, sergeant, United States Marine Corps, saluted the cross of Jesus Christ.

At the end of the line marched Millie. When she saw all the flowers and the flags and the guns all stacked up at the cross, then at long last she, Millie Grimshaw, caught up. There was one thing only missing from this great mass of offerings to Jesus. Millie let her flowers fall to the earth, and then she herself knelt down on the ground. And Pat knelt at her side, her arm about Millie's shoulder. And Millie's soul wept with the joy of long-delayed release.

*Onward, then, ye people [all sang for the last time]*
*join our happy throng,*
*blend with ours your voices in the triumph song . . .*

And there were no lefts and rights any longer. All were together now, all of one strong voice. There were no exceptions.

And Mrs. Millie Grimshaw, chairwoman of the board of Christian education at Ashgrove Baptist Church, dreamed sweeter dreams that night than she had dreamed in years.

## ♪ Hymn Notes ♪

Sabine Baring-Gould (1834–1924) lived and wrote through the whole span of the Victorian era in England. Born into wealth, Baring-Gould nevertheless spent several years of his ministry among the lower classes. It was during his curacy in the poor mining community of Horbury that he penned "Onward, Christian Soldiers," his best-known hymn. He later served a parish in Dalton and then inherited a large estate in north Devon, where he became rector of the parish and spent the remainder of his ninety years.

"Onward, Christian Soldiers" was written in less than fifteen minutes for a Whitmonday school festival in Yorkshire. Children from two villages sang the hymn as they marched the mile distance between them. While the words of the hymn aren't quite down to the child's level, its warlike imagery has tapped into children's enduring fascination with playing soldier.

Baring-Gould was a high-church Anglican, which is clear from the hymn text. Allusions to the Apostles' Creed are numerous ("Hell's foundations quiver"; "where the saints have trod"; "all one body . . . in hope and doctrine"). But the effect of the hymn transcends denominational affiliation. The cross of Jesus guides the mission of all Christians.

The traditional setting of the text, by Arthur Seymour Sullivan (1842–1900), has a marchlike quality all its own.

Especially the moving bass of the refrain picks the feet off the floor. The melody builds in intensity, as in a battle. The melodic high point is always struck, appropriately, on the words "with the cross of Jesus."

Baring-Gould's other well-known hymn, "Now the Day Is Over" (1865), was also written with children in mind. Based on Proverbs 3:24, it is an evening prayer, perhaps still suited for any child who has ever fretted in the dark.

## CHAPTER 8

# Second Surrender

## "Just as I Am"

Him that cometh to me I will in no wise cast out.
JOHN 6:37, KJV

THE SECURITY GATE SWUNG OPEN IN ONE SLOW, SWEEPING motion. A crisp autumn breeze brushed against his face, air from the outside, the first oxygen of freedom in five long years. He remembered the words his father used to speak whenever they crossed the border back into his home state: "Smell the air, boys! Michigan air! Ain't it sweet!" He would nearly hyperventilate in compliance with those words. Now, after so much time, he finally understood their meaning.

Jason Lane was a convicted felon. He had served out his sentence in the Missouri City Correctional Facility nearly without incident. There was the single episode of misconduct. He and an inmate nicknamed Skink were jumped by three prison rowdies, out for fun and for their smokes. Though badly beaten, they had delivered a few licks themselves, and all were disciplined alike. As in other matters, Jason had shrugged and forgotten it. He was not prone to spite. While most inmates worshiped their own innocence like a religion, Jason had come to view every bad rap as more or less his just deserts. Even the clearest injustice Jason supposed to be rightful by some larger measure of guilt.

# Just as I Am

### Written by Charlotte Elliott

Just as I am, without one plea
　　But that Thy blood was shed for me,
And that Thou bidd'st me come to Thee,
　　O Lamb of God, I come! I come!

Just as I am, and waiting not
　　To rid my soul of one dark blot,
To Thee whose blood can cleanse each spot,
　　O Lamb of God, I come! I come!

Just as I am, tho tossed about
　　With many a conflict, many a doubt,
Fightings and fears within, without,
　　O Lamb of God, I come! I come!

Just as I am, poor, wretched, blind—
　　Sight, riches, healing of the mind,
Yea, all I need in Thee to find—
　　O Lamb of God, I come! I come!

Just as I am, Thou wilt receive,
　　Wilt welcome, pardon, cleanse, relieve;
Because Thy promise I believe,
　　O Lamb of God, I come! I come!

Jason wore straight-legged jeans and an Eagles T-shirt beneath an army surplus jacket. He carried a single grocery bag, folded over twice at the top to make a grip and bearing all his earthly possessions. These included a Timex wristwatch with a broken band, a monogrammed cigarette lighter he had crafted in high school shop class, a pearl-handled pocket knife, his wallet, still containing the three one-dollar bills from the night of his arrest, and a sheath of letters, neatly pressed in a stack the thickness of an unabridged dictionary. All other belongings Jason had written off years before. Upon learning of the charges and his likely conviction, he had phoned a buddy collect, revealed the location of a hidden apartment key, and invited him to empty its contents. What he asked in return was a periodic deposit in his account for the purchase of cigarettes and personal effects. His buddy's parting words, "I'll come see you soon, Jase!" were the last he ever heard him speak. No deposits were ever made, and his subsequent collect calls were denied. When Jason was moved to the state facility, he abandoned all hope of contact.

In his other hand, Jason carried a half sheet of paper with directions to the nearest bus station—about a three-mile walk. Paper-clipped to it was a one-way ticket, which had arrived in the prison mail the month before. Jason walked down a country road for half an hour before arriving at the outskirts of a small town. Just past the welcome plaque was an A & W Root Beer. Jason entered and studied the menu hopefully. Five minutes later, he emerged with a barbecue sandwich, a small root beer in a frosty mug, and 38 cents change. Jason Lane, ex-convict, free man, sat at a picnic bench and savored the moment. Finished, he opened his bag of belongings and brought out the stack of letters, unbound them, and began to pore over them idly. After some time, Jason stacked and rebound them and returned them to the sack.

Next he grabbed for his wristwatch, thinking to check the time. Of course it had stopped, its long-life battery long since drained to impotency. He shook it hard and placed the crystal to his ear, more by habit than with any firm hope in the resurrection of the dead. Then, with the adrenaline of anxiety, he picked up and started down the street in a gallop.

An hour later, Jason stood in a short line to board a Swallow Lines coach. With no luggage to store, he was the first one up the steps.

"Destination?" asked the driver, as he took the ticket from Jason's outstretched hand.

"Plainville," Jason replied, "Indiana."

Of all the beloved hymns of the Ashgrove Baptist Church, the one most adored was "Just as I Am." The congregation had been alarmed to learn it was a hymn I'd never sung. Indeed, I had barely heard it, except on those chance occasions I was baby-sat by an elderly neighbor on the night of a televised Billy Graham crusade. Part of the Graham legacy was the opinion of some that "Just as I Am" should be sung at the end of every Christian worship service held on American soil. This view had spread over the airwaves out to our little grove, and this made me nervous. My quarrel was not with the hymn's sentiment. Goodness knows we all needed to hear the invitation to come as we are "without one plea," and weekly was not too often for most. But worship was more than a revival meeting. Sometimes we should depart worship with a discipleship challenge, or a mission challenge, or a call to work for justice. Each of us had a single pair of eyes, hands, and legs. If we sought Jesus only on our knees with hands clasped and eyes shut, we might miss him in the faces of the poor and downtrodden. We might fail to share him with the blind or lame or captive. Surely we weren't to keep the Lamb of God to ourselves . . .

At first worshipers chalked up my wide-spanning hymn selections to ignorance. After failing to guide me back along the narrow way, they became testier. When I had the audacity to close worship on All Saints' Day with "For All the Saints," I was accused of committing grievous error. In most instances, I would have dismissed the opinion as misguided, but it came from the lips of the closest thing to a saint our church could boast. Her name was Penny Jones.

Penny Jones was Mother Teresa in bib overalls. Some believe pure altruism is a fiction. We do what we do only through some motive of gain, even if the incentive is hidden. People arrive at this conclusion by different routes. Maybe they have lived around much selfishness and greed, or they have been burned once too often by shameful deceit, or they have never met a soul who wasn't a sore loser at Monopoly. Or perhaps they've simply never rubbed shoulders with the likes of Penny Jones.

By the time I came to the church, folks no longer scratched or shook their heads over her startling acts of charity. Instead, the mere mention of her name elicited a warm tingle of well-being, a spark of hope that all in the world was not lost. Now, after raising a dozen adoptive children, tirelessly championing scores of causes, and taking in hundreds of stray or injured dogs, cats, birds, and varmints, Penny had embraced a new mission. No one had understood just what it was all about, but most everyone was certain only good could come from it. After all, with Penny it always had.

I told Penny that "For All the Saints" was a special hymn to me, written by the English pastor William How. She would have approved of him, I said, because he passed up money and prestige to work among the poor in London. I continued that this hymn helped me offer thanks to God for saints like her own husband, Ed, recently deceased, that this was why I had chosen it for All Saints' Day.

Well, Ed was no saint, she informed me, but she missed him every day and she thanked me for the sentiment. Still, she maintained, "Just as I Am" was the truly best hymn to have after preaching "'cause none of us ever knows what poor soul might be knockin' on salvation's door . . . See, most folks are scared," she said. "They don't feel worthy, 'cause they've done so much they're ashamed of. Unless they hear they can come to God just as they are, most likely they'll never make it at all."

And her words and the tone of them broke my will, so that without thinking I had promised Penny I would program "Just as I Am" sooner rather than later, and more often, too.

"Good, then," she had said matter-of-factly, as if my response were preordained. "That'll be a real good thing, Pastor! Real good!"

Late in the afternoon, Jason's bus crossed from Vigo into Putnam County and made a short stopover at Brazil. Jason got off and paced the sidewalk in front of the station. By then his anxiety had grown so acute that his legs had tingled in his seat. He had gritted his teeth until they ached and tapped his palms on his knees so vigorously that the man in the seat next to his had finally begged him to stop. When Jason reboarded, the man had moved farther back in the coach. This had only fueled Jason's deep suspicion he was unworthy of the opportunity that lay before him, that it was doomed to end badly like everything always did. But then the bus pulled out of the station, drawing Jason ever nearer to untold destiny in the sleepy town of Plainville.

As the sun began to set, Jason gave in one last time to his longing for assurance in the form of words, pressed flat and bound in the bottom of his bag of worldly possessions. He reached for the sheath of letters, opened the last one, and drank down its message like wine. Every sentence had become a mantra, quieting his spirit, restoring his hope. It started on the envelope itself:

*Mr. Jason Lane, 00057987*
*Missouri City Correctional Facility*
*Missouri City, MO*

*Dear Jason,*

He was Mr. Jason Lane—not Lane, or Loser, or the many crude appellations Jason hoped in time to erase from memory. Yes, there had been the identification number. For five years, he had been more a number than a name—but no longer. Now 57987 would be assigned to some other poor fool . . . And more, he was Dear—Dear Jason—dear to somebody, worthy of a kind address from another human being . . .

Jason read on:

*I am writing after much prayer to make you an offer.*
*I don't have much, but what is mine I am willing to*
*share with you after you get out. Since you have*
*written of having no people to help you or place to go,*
*you are welcome to come stay with me while you get*
*on your feet. My children are grown, and it's mostly*
*just my pets and me. We can hunt you up a job and*
*get you started back in life. In case you don't believe*
*me because as you said it's hard sometimes knowing*
*who to trust, I'm sending you a bus ticket here. It'll*
*get you all the way. If you decide not to come, you can*

*just cash it in and you're welcome to it. But I wish
you'd try, because I felt God's leading in this. Let me
know what you decide.*

And the letter was signed

*Your true friend,
Mrs. Penny Jones
134 Cherry Street
Plainville, Indiana
317-849-1216*

"True friend," Jason repeated in his mind, "true friend,"
as if trying it on for size. But a sudden flash of outside
lights cut the exercise short. Hurriedly he stuffed the letter
back into its envelope and stuffed it in his jacket pocket.

"Coming up to Plainville, Indiana," announced the driver.

Soon the bus pulled into a small station. Jason waited
nervously for passengers to disembark. At last he stepped off
the bus and slipped quietly into the terminal building. To his
left upon entering was a little wishing well with a chubby
cherub, spitting water that rolled down its fat tummy into a
pool bathed in coins. Jason pitched in three pennies for good
luck. Then, locating a pay phone, he inserted his last quarter
and dime, took a deep breath, and began to dial.

"Yer just plain crazy is what! Yer completely out of your
blessed gourd!"

"Well, that may be, Gib. I guess we're gonna find out—
*'cause he stays!*"

"That last mangy-lookin' dog you found wandering over
at White Lick Creek was about bad enough. Puttin' it
down would've been a blessing. Now you're pickin' up
prison trash! Next you'll be harborin' drug addicts!"

"I used to think you had a heart, Gibson Mayes! Now I see it's just a cold slab a' hardened meat."

"Least it ain't bleedin' over everybody!"

"Why don't you come meet him? Who knows, you might even like him!"

"I don't want to meet him! I don't want to *like* him! I just want him out, so I can stop worrying about you for at least a night and catch up on my sleep!"

Penny Jones and Gibson Mayes shared a long and argumentative history. The controversy at hand was over Jason Lane, who had arrived at Penny's a week earlier. She had made up her mind he wouldn't come. He hadn't committed either way. Then, at 9 p.m. on the Monday of his release, Jason had phoned from the Plainville bus depot. Penny had hopped into the station wagon with her dogs, Jumbo and Pete, and burned rubber, collecting him faster than her parakeet could say, "Praise Jesus!"

Their first meeting might have been a study in awkwardness and doubt, but such an encounter with Penny was out of the question. She had rushed into the station, matched Jason up immediately with his picture in her mind's eye, and embraced him warmly, as a mother hugs a son fresh back from fighting a war. Her every kind word, every quaint gesture, every sigh of joy so overwhelmed him that all his fears and misgivings evaporated into the night. Like nearly every object of her affections, he was putty in her hands.

Only a bovine few remained unaffected by her charm. Chief among these was Gibson Mayes, who considered her the most sorely self-deceived soul he had ever known. From the time she was little, nursing injured birds and bunny rabbits back to health, and then wailing aloud as the men went out with rifles and hounds to hunt their next of kin, Gibson had considered her an awful nuisance of a female.

But this was not entirely surprising, given their ties. Gibson and Penny Mayes Jones were brother and sister.

"So, did yeh ask him yet what he *did?*" Gibson continued.

"Not goin' to," she answered.

"Why?"

"Because! It doesn't matter! It's in the past. Jason is a nice young man. I'm not gonna embarrass him about what was . . ."

"Then *I* will!" Gibson said defiantly. "I'll call up the sheriff. Have him run a background check. And I'll go tell your jailbird what I found out, too!"

"Why, in the holy name of God, are you bein' so mean-spirited?"

"Sis, fer mercy's sake he's a criminal! Once a criminal, always a criminal! Folks don't change . . ."

When congregants heard of my promise to Penny to program "Just as I Am" with greater frequency, they moved to seal the pledge in practice without delay. Harold Hatch found an opportunity to bring it up almost every time we were together.

"Now, about hymns this week," he would start out, "there are lots of good ones that go real well with 'Just as I Am'! You've got 'Only Trust Him,' 'All Your Anxiety' [he was counting them out on his fingers] and of course there's always another one by a woman: 'Pass Me Not'—Fanny Crosby. You know *her*, don't you, Pastor?"

"I do now, Harold," I said proudly. But I realized I knew nothing of the man who penned "Just as I Am," certainly not that *he* was after all a *she*. So I decided to look into the author whose simple words were complicating my life on a weekly basis.

Charlotte Elliott lived in nineteenth-century England during the Age of Romanticism, when wealthy Anglicans began to join the evangelical wing of the state church for the first time. She was born to privilege in a family of prominent preachers, but due to early illness she was frail and prone to depression much of her life. As often in the annals of hymn writers, she seemed to have played a weakness off as a strength, publishing successful collections of poems for others likewise afflicted. But Elliott's emotional struggles continued. She had been particularly plagued, it seemed, by a stubborn sense of her own uselessness. This is most evident from the many stories that grew up about the writing of "Just as I Am." One of these described a visit from a Swiss evangelist, Cesar Malan, who observed her distress and admonished her to "come just as you are—a sinner—to the Lamb of God, who takes away the sins of the world." More widely attested was the account of her clergyman brother's fund-raising bazaar for a school to educate the children of poor ministers. Charlotte was too ill to attend, and, lost in a feeling of worthlessness, she "gathered up in her soul the great certainties . . . of her salvation" and "set down for her own comfort the formula of her faith." The result was "Just as I Am," which went on to make more money for the cause than any bazaar ever could have.

It was a moving story, I had to admit. It suited the hymn text well. Being a "poor minister" myself, and prone to similar emotions of self-doubt, I developed an unexpected feeling of kinship with Charlotte, her story, and her words. I was very glad for this and just a little sorry . . .

On the third Tuesday of November it drizzled rain through the morning. Eight quilters were busily at work in Fellowship Hall, thumbing their noses at the approach of winter, conjuring a warmth all their own. A crazy quilt of blues, greens, and browns over a cream background was in its second week on the frame. There could be little doubt—from hem to heart it was a man's quilt. Once a year, the ladies prepared one special for the Salvation Army men's shelter. This one Gladys Hatch had patched together from the quilters' scrap trunk. This made for a patchwork of great recollection, calling forth much tender feeling around the frame as the ladies stitched.

It did not, however, stop Alberta Rump from her own thoughts of a less charitable nature. Bert sat on the far side of the frame in the middle, directly across from Penny Jones. She glanced up at Penny from time to time with an inquiring expression.

"Somethin' on your mind, Bert?" Penny asked at last.

Bert, a stranger to diplomacy, tried her hardest to practice it anyway. "Well, I was just wonderin' how your . . . boy was doin'. . . ."

"Which one?" Penny knew which one, but chose to let Bert sweat it out a bit anyway.

"Yer *new* one, a' course—the convict!" With Bert, subtlety melted away like snowflakes.

"*Ex*-convict!" Gladys corrected.

"So," Bert continued, "he found a *job* yet?"

"No, not yet. That's where he is today again. Lookin'. Not everyone'll hire him, as you might imagine." Silence fell over the group. "Part of the problem," Penny continued, "is gettin' him suitable clothes for goin' out and findin' work! He came out a' prison with practically nothin'. As winter comes on he's gonna need a lot of things . . . "

Soon the subject of Jason had played out as far as it safely could. Even the quilters, models of charity, questioned Penny's judgment at committing to such a thing as the reform of Jason Lane. But at dinner, replenished by the last and best of the summer harvest, their spirits had softened somewhat, and the subject of Jason resurfaced.

"So . . . how long you reckon Jason might be stayin' with you, Penny?" Gladys Hatch wanted to know, "—through the winter anyway, you 'spect?"

"Well, most likely," Penny answered.

"Quite a winter is comin', too, ladies!" Gladys continued. "The almanac is callin' for a mighty nippin' January and February . . . "

"My word, yes," echoed Millie Grimshaw. "Supposed to be about the chilliest we've seen in over ten years!"

"Nah, I heard *five* years!" corrected Bert. "Can't be as bad as '83!"

"*Ten* years!" insisted Millie. "I'll show yeh myself!"

"Still won't believe it!" said Bert. "I won't!"

"Either way," broke in Gladys, "it's gonna be cold!" And Gladys proceeded to share a brainstorm that, after a little coaxing, every quilter had agreed to.

I had a standing invitation from the quilters to Tuesday dinner, and I rarely missed. With both satisfaction and regret I had listened to their conversation about Jason. Since his arrival, I had neither paid Jason a visit nor offered any support besides a greeting and a handshake, tendered the single Sunday he had attended worship in jeans and his Eagles T-shirt. Penny had relayed Jason's unease that day. He had reported the sensation of having been stared at. I presumed it to have been more than a sensation. Jason was overdue a pastoral visit, that much was clear.

Later in the week, Penny greeted me warmly at her home in a quaint Plainville subdivision with streets named after fruit-bearing trees. For Sale signs were posted as usual in the front lawns on either side of her. Also on hand for my welcoming reception were her dogs, Pete and Jumbo, five cats, darting about at the speed of improbability, and numerous birds of the air, flitting freely from perch to perch but never lower than Penny's shoulder. She directed me down the hall to a room with the door ajar. It was now Jason's room, though through the years it had been home to dozens of strays of various species.

"How'd you ever fit everybody into this house, Penny?" I asked.

"Oh . . . there's more to this house than meets the eye!" she answered wryly.

Penny knocked once and called his name: "Jason, honey! Pastor's here to see yeh!" Jason gave the go-ahead to enter, and then Penny retreated, leaving us alone.

Jason was lying on his bed watching television after a frustrating day of watching television. The phone had not rung. Three weeks and dozens of job applications on the far side of incarceration, Jason was feeling as caged as ever. "Her birds are freer than me!" he joked. We talked for some time about his past. His parents were long divorced. His mother was remarried and living in Hawaii, while his father drifted from place to place. He had phoned Jason on Christmas day of his first year at Missouri City, but that was the last Jason had heard from him. Jason had often dreamed of turning things around, then showing up again in their lives a new man, someone they could be proud of. Now, once more, the dream was fading. Our conversation turned to faith. Penny of course had been at him like fleas on a dog to give over his burdens to Christ, but something in Jason resisted.

"She tells me I need Jesus. Heck, I know that already. What I can't figure out is who in this world needs *me!*" Jason expressed gratitude for Penny and all she had done for him. "Wish I could do something back for her, something to really thank her, but, right now I've got nothin' . . . nothin'!"

"Well, I'm sure you'll find the right way to say 'thank you,' Jason!" I offered, not knowing what else to say.

Then an unlikely parallel of circumstance began to gnaw at me. She had been a darling of the religious elite, he an ex-con and social pariah, yet they shared the same spiritual self-doubt, the same suspicion of unworthiness to receive grace. Life circumstance and 150 years of history separated Charlotte Elliott and Jason Lane, but they were first cousins of uncertainty. Their lives cried out in chorus for the unmerited favor of God. At last I understood Penny's concern that the Jasons of the world be thrown a line to pull them from oblivion. I also realized that one of the very best lines had come from the pen of Charlotte Elliott herself:

*Just as I am, thou wilt receive,*
  *wilt welcome, pardon, cleanse, relieve;*
*Because thy promise I believe,*
  *O Lamb of God, I come! I come!*

I left Jason with an invitation to attend worship during Advent—those four expectant Sundays before Christmas. "We could all use a little hope!" I added hopefully. But already I had bigger plans in store. From the living room, Penny turned and smiled as I made my way up the hallway, dodging paws and wings. A simple glance into her eyes told me she already understood what had passed between us and what I intended to do about it. With barely a word spoken, we each seemed to grasp that our plans coincided. With brief parting words, I was on my way.

On the first Sunday morning in Advent, the church was aswirl with gossip. People hardly noticed the Christmas decorations that Anna Quarfarth and helpers had painstakingly displayed that Friday. Phones had rung nonstop all day Saturday, and many ears were still red with the imprint of receivers. One face was red as well, flush with triumph.

Gibson Mayes had paid good money to have Jason tailed for several days. Five mornings in a row, as he told it, Jason had walked to a shady corner of the sunny town of Plainville, disappearing down an alley between a tavern and an abandoned warehouse. Each afternoon through Thursday, he had emerged again with nothing in hand, but on Friday he was carrying a black case the size of a Bible. On Mulberry Street, two blocks from Penny's home, he had tucked it suspiciously into the back waist of his pants and pulled his coat down over it. The surveillant called Gibson, and within minutes Penny's home was surrounded by squad cars. Jason was wanted for questioning. Penny had come defiantly to the door, insisting he was not there. A thorough search turned up no trace of him. But Gibson, who was on the scene, had lit into her hard.

"Folks get in big trouble for harboring fugitives, Sis! This ain't one a' yer injured birds! This is criminal activity!"

"Criminal for sure, Gibson! Wherever Jason is, he's innocent, and I stand by him!"

All that Saturday, Penny had refused to answer the phone or the door. No one had been observed coming or going, but as Penny had said, there was often more to things than met the eye. Meanwhile imaginations ran wild. What was that criminal planning to do with the gun in that black case? Was Penny his hostage? Would Jason Lane invade one of their homes next? Would it all end in a bloodbath? I had been away for the day and heard nothing of the disturbing news until Sunday. It was too near worship to take any action. Better to stay the course of the morning, I thought, and look into it later.

I sat in the sanctuary as people gathered. Shelly Higgins stroked the ivories with some old-time favorites. To distract myself from all the noise, I eyed the day's bulletin. The cover featured an Advent wreath with one candle lighted. Inside, the order of worship was typical for the occasion: the lighting of the Advent candle of hope, a reading from Isaiah the prophet, two Advent hymns not well-known to the congregation, a sermon called "As You Were," and, at the bottom of the page, the heart of my plan, printed in bold type. Each Sunday of Advent, our worship would end with the same hymn. Jason Lane or any so inclined could heed its tender call and march up the aisle, just as they were—except now it seemed Jason would not be coming . . .

Then a hush fell over the gathering. I had been staring at the floor, sulking, when silence caught hold of every tongue and held fast. Shelly's fingers froze on the piano keys. Looking up, I witnessed what resembled the onset of a wedding. Heads were crooked over shoulders, staring up the aisle like the mother of the bride. Coming up from the back was Jason, flanked by Penny and Gladys Hatch. Jason wore a suit that many recognized as Penny's husband's. Since Ed's death the year before, his three suits had hung in the closet unused. But that Saturday, Gladys and Penny had taken down his blue pinstripe and altered it in the privacy of Penny's basement. At its north end, a sofa had been scooted aside and a large picture removed from the wall. In their place, a metal door had stood open, revealing a hidden room Ed Jones had dug out in secret, just for such occasions as this. The room was a safe place, a stop on a modern Underground Railroad. Through the years, numerous runaways had found shelter there, including battered wives and youth in trouble. Not another soul knew of it until, in desperation, Penny had turned to Gladys for help.

"I just don't think I can keep facin' this kinda thing without Ed!" she told her.

"Well, don't you worry yourself, Penny," comforted Gladys. "You know I'm glad to help, and your secret's safe with me! I always wondered where all those piles a' dirt in your yard came from!" Gladys added good-naturedly. "Now I know!"

The pair had pinned and stitched their way through the day, calling Jason over for a periodic modeling. Then Gladys had departed as she had come, up a steep flight of stairs leading directly into the backyard tool shed, and out. Now they were walking the aisle of a church sanctuary—another safe place in which all should find refuge in time of crisis and need.

As they drew nearer, my eyes settled on a bulge in Jason's right suit-coat pocket. It pouched out in a firm shape not unlike the one described in the police report. The women and Jason walked all the way to the second pew, then sat down. All sat stiff in their seats, all but one deacon, who made a hurried exit from the sanctuary and ran straight for a telephone as fast as his legs would carry him. Not knowing what else to do, I motioned for Harold Hatch to commence the congregational singing, and our Advent worship was underway.

Ten minutes later, the sanctuary doors opened and three men entered. Gibson Mayes had called the police and awaited their arrival. Now they were standing in the back, arms folded, stern-faced, posting sentry. Penny turned and saw, then faced the front again with a look of fresh resolve. She linked arms with Jason, who seemed unaware of anything.

Worship unfolded awkwardly. The Bundy family lit the Advent candle, with little Paula Bundy's eyes darting back and forth the whole time between the police officers and Jason Lane. He and the ladies remained seated, hand in hand, through the singing of "O Come, O Come Emmanuel" and "Come, Thou Long-Expected Jesus." And when Harold read the passage from Isaiah 61, his booming bass lent such emphasis to the phrase "to proclaim liberty to the captives and release to the prisoners" that the entire congregation squirmed at once.

My sermon began with a passage from the sixth chapter of the Gospel of John. Jesus proclaims himself the "true bread from heaven" that comes down and "gives life to the world." The One denied hospitality in Bethlehem is God's hospitable love offered to all! This very chapter, I continued, was often linked to the hymn and hymn writer so much on my mind over recent weeks: "Anyone who comes to me, I will never drive away" . . . "that I should lose nothing of all that he has given me." These were the words that had spoken to Charlotte Elliott, I said, author of the hymn we would be singing in worship through Advent. She sought a truer acceptance than others could supply, than she could offer herself. Plagued by poor health and feelings of uselessness, she had written "Just as I Am" as an expression of her own surrender into the loving arms of Christ. We all needed such acceptance, I continued. In order to believe in ourselves, we each sought one whose faith in us was stronger even than our own doubts. That one was the Lamb of God. It was not that we were worthy of such love but that God was merciful to offer it. Nothing more was required than, in humility, to *come.*

"There he goes!" rose a voice from the back. "He's movin'!" It was one of the officers, and what he said was true. As Shelly had led in with the refrain of the invitational hymn, Jason had risen to his feet and begun moving out of the pew. His head was bent low. Right behind him were Penny, now in tears, and Gladys, taking pains to steady her. Yet both sang out with full-toned strength:

*Just as I am, without one plea*
  *but that thy blood was shed for me,*
*and that thou bidd'st me come to thee,*
  *O Lamb of God, I come! I come!*

From the back, meanwhile, a private conversation was growing more public. Gibson had been exchanging whispers with the two officers, but now his voice ratcheted up to audibility.

"Go!" Gibson was insisting. "Get him—or he'll get away or maybe take us all hostage!" The officers moved into the aisle now, hands on their holsters. Gasps of alarm broke out like a fresh descant to the hymn. But Jason continued forward. As he approached the chancel, he carried the peaceful expression of a man who has made up his mind. Gone was the strain of anxiety. The prison gates of his life were opening. Here, in a little country church, Jason was breathing the air of freedom for the first time.

"I finally figured it out," he whispered in my ear a moment later, "I mean, what I've got to give, and who wants it!" The rest he didn't need to say. I knew already. "I'm giving all I've got to give to God—I'm giving myself!"

I moved to give Jason an embrace but stopped short. He had turned to Penny, who was weeping openly. Then, reaching into his coat pocket, he took out the black box.

"There it is!" Gibson was pointing now, nudging an officer. "That's the box. What's in it's hot fer sure!"

Now Jason was opening it slowly, aiming it down toward Penny. Two guns were lifting from their holsters, the safeties coming off. "Hold it!" came a command from the back, as every head turned to the sight of pistols, pointed our way. But the hymn rolled on:

*Just as I am, though tossed about*
  *with many a conflict, many a doubt,*
*fightings and fears, within, without,*
  *O Lamb of God, I come! I come!*

The lid of the box was fully open now, and Penny's mouth gaping wide along with it. She reached in and lifted out a chain and, dangling from it, a large, polished chrome pendant.

For five days in a row, Jason had done odd jobs in a small-time metal shop housed at one end of a worn-down industrial complex. In exchange he had been invited to brush up on his shop skills. Stamped out by hand on an oval were two faces, side by side, smiling. Beneath them were the words *True Friends.* Penny, tears still streaming, fastened the chain proudly around her neck.

"It's all I had to give," Jason explained, overcome with emotion, "but it's my way of saying 'thank you' for being my true friend."

*Just as I am, poor, wretched, blind;*
  *sight, riches, healing of the mind,*
*yea, all I need in thee to find,*
  *O Lamb of God, I come! I come!*

By now others had come forward to join them, six quilters led by Alberta Rump, who carried a package and a sheepish grin. In Bertlike fashion, she shoved her bundle into the unsuspecting arms of Jason Lane, who tore away the wrapping from a crazy quilt of blues, greens, and browns. Stitched in the corner were the words

To Mr. Jason Lane—our brother in Christ
The Ashgrove Baptist Church Quilters
Christmas 1988

"For winter warmth," Bert said. "Supposed to be the coldest winter in more than *ten years!*" And every quilter laughed. But Jason was sobbing like a baby.

*Just as I am, thou wilt receive,*
  *wilt welcome, pardon, cleanse, relieve;*
*because thy promise I believe,*
  *O Lamb of God, I come! I come!*

Then pandemonium broke out as worshipers streamed to the front to add their own benedictions to the unlikeliest of events, on a Sunday in Advent when Christmas sneaked in early. They came as they were, brought what they had, and left a little richer.

Alone in the back, two guns were again safely in their holsters as two grimacing officers shook their heads at Gibson Mayes, whose mouth stuck open like a fish on a string.

But in the midst of all the noise and carrying on, a saint stood perfectly still. Penny Jones stored up all these things in her heart, the fuel of joy and conviction to burn another day. And undoubtedly that day would come. For that was Penny—just as she was.

## ♪ Hymn Notes ♪

Charlotte Elliott (1789–1871) was in her own time a remarkably successful hymn writer whose output related to her lifelong battle with ill health and depression. In the English Age of Romanticism, when emotions reigned supreme, she became a popular purveyor of the hymns of heart religion. Born into a family of prominent evangelical preachers, she was also a stalwart defender of the evangelical cause.

As a young woman, Elliott had been a well-known artist as well as an author of humorous poetry. A serious illness at the age of thirty left her an invalid and "acquainted with grief" for the rest of her life. Her collections of poems were both personal therapy and mission outreach to those similarly afflicted. *The Invalid's Hymn Book* (1834) or *Hours of Sorrow Cheered and Comforted* (1836) might not sell well today under those titles, but considering today's market for self-help books, Elliott may have been ahead of her time. Her hymns number nearly 150.

"Just as I Am" gained its current popularity through its prominent use in the Billy Graham crusades. It was during the singing of this hymn that Graham himself first responded to the invitation of faith.

The familiar tune, *Woodworth,* by William Bradbury (1816–1868) did not find its home with this text until 1860, when they appeared together in his *Eclectic Tune Book*. Since then all other settings of the text have fallen by the wayside. Bradbury added the concluding "I come" to accommodate the tune, in long meter.

Elliott spent her entire life in the two English towns of Clapham and Brighton. At the time of her death, more than a thousand letters were discovered expressing gratitude to Elliott for the hymn "Just as I Am."

Source: Jane Stewart Smith, *Favorite Women Hymn Writers* (Wheaton, Ill.: Crossway Books, 1990).

# CHAPTER 9

# Back in the Arms of Father-Mother God

## "This Is My Father's World"

I T WAS TIME TO GO CAMPING. I HAD DELAYED THE INEVITABLE like a long-cocooned caterpillar. But my excuses had all played out. The spring cold snap was ended, April showers had performed their duty, and now Easter had come and gone. The butterflies were flying. It was time to go camping.

Since I'd first let on of my considerable skills in the great outdoors, congregants at Ashgrove Church had been eager to test them. My life began to crawl with the invitations of members to camp, fish, and even hunt. Secretly I feared they were placing bets on the likelihood I would embarrass myself badly. But against sound judgment I agreed to a mid-May outing with the chairman of the deacons, Herb Chestnut. We were to camp on the outskirts of his old family farm, a hundred-acre spread twenty miles south of Plainville. We would depart on a Friday afternoon and return late Saturday, but "in time fer the preacher to rest up before his one day a' work!" Herb joked.

The Chestnut property was a hodgepodge of open field and scrubby wood. Herb farmed a portion of it with his sister, Reba. She lived there alone in a trailer, the family home being little more than a broken-down shotgun shack. I knew little of Reba, except that she had married and divorced once and attended church twice a year, on Easter Sunday and Mother's Day. Easter morning, she had slipped

## This Is My Father's World
### Written by Maltbie Davenport Babcock

This is my Father's world, And to my list'ning ears
All nature sings, and round me rings
   The music of the spheres.
This is my Father's world! I rest me in the thought
Of rocks and trees, of skies and seas—
   His hand the wonders wrought.

This is my Father's world—The birds their carols raise;
The morning light, the lily white,
   Declare their Maker's praise.
This is my Father's world! He shines in all that's fair;
In the rustling grass I hear him pass—
   He speaks to me ev'rywhere.

This is my Father's world—O let me ne'er forget
That tho the wrong seems oft so strong
   God is the Ruler yet.
This is my Father's world! The battle is not done;
Jesus who died shall be satisfied,
   And earth and heav'n be one.

in late and left early—right in the middle of the sermon.

"She's a strange one all right," Gladys Hatch had confided at the close of the service. She had marked Reba's abrupt departure and felt obliged to offer me some consolation. "But her mother, God love her, was a dear woman. Reba worshiped the ground she walked on. We'll see her back on Mother's Day, I'll wager—you watch!"

Mrs. Alvera Chestnut, Reba's mother, had died unexpectedly some years earlier—just at the time of Reba's divorce. None but her brother, Herb, had seen much of Reba since, and he seldom spoke of her.

"She's not too strong on the faith side a' things," he had offered in a rare moment of candor. It was partly my curiosity over Reba that tipped the scales in favor of an overnighter on the Chestnut farm.

On a mild May afternoon, Herb pulled into the church drive, his truck laden with camping gear. It was Friday, the thirteenth day of the month—an ominous choice for my Ashgrove camping debut. I threw down a bedroll and duffel bag in the truck bed. Into the cab I carried a satchel bearing a Bible and sermon outline, and my banjo. Herb eyed the latter with a grin.

"Thought I might strum a few tunes," I explained self-consciously.

"All right, Preacher," he said. "If it's too bad, though, I'll make yeh walk home!"

The trip down to the farm lasted thirty minutes. Conversation came in small clumps, tucked between long silences. Herb had us tuned to his favorite country and western radio station, a source for me of both irritation and consolation. But as we turned west from the state road onto a gravel one, Herb switched off the radio and his words took on a serious tone.

"You know, Preacher, she may drop in on us—she knows

yer comin'!"

"Reba, you mean," I clarified.

"She's a good gal, just a little rough around the edges. She's kept herself cooped up alone out here for years now. People are not her favorite thing. Don't take anything she says the wrong way . . . "

We reached another, smaller gravel road, this one rife with ruts and bespeckled with wildflowers and weeds. Up this, on the left, lay the old Chestnut family home, a study in mistaken architectural style and failed construction technique rolled into one. Behind it, compassed by abandoned farm implements and overgrowth, was a twenty-by-ten mobile home. Nearby were several old beater trucks, stuck in a slow-motion rust competition.

"Hmmm. Where's her new truck? ["new" meant running, little more] Guess she's gone! I'm sure she'll be along soon, though," Herb warned.

We followed the road into a wood, then uphill through a clearing, reaching at last an overlook with a clump of trees on one side. From this summit there opened up a lovely vista, stretching to farms and small towns across the horizon.

"Well, this here's the spot. Can see into three counties from up here, Preacher. And yeh can really see the stars! Why, you'll get yer nickel's worth tonight . . . "

"I can't wait!" I said, a bit a-tingle. Since moving to the city, I'd grown homesick for the brightness of stars against the black curtain of night. Summers, growing up, I would drive with friends out a country road and lie in the grass for hours, hunting constellations and watching shooting stars light across the sky.

"There's where we'll sleep." Herb pointed to a lean-to, nailed up between the trunks of two trees. It was completely open on one side, like the stable of a church nativity scene. "Got some straw in the pick-up we'll lay down, and a tarp. Makes it nice and soft for bedrolls."

"Well, that'll do for me!" I blustered, unwilling to show the first signs of concern for bodily comfort. Privately I contemplated how soft I had grown since youth. As a Boy Scout, I had once camped in an ice blockhouse in the dead of winter with snow on the ground. In summer, I'd laughed off mosquitoes and ticks as benign emissaries of God's warped sense of humor. Primitive campsites had been second homes to me. Now, a decade later, I'd come to feel like an alien to the natural world.

"So, how 'bout *you* get goin' on a fire," Herb pressed, "'n' *I'll* fetch the makings for stew. Know how to use one a' these, don't yeh?" Herb pressed an ax in my hands, while tossing another grin my way.

Ten yards from the lean-to was a pit bearing the charred remains of many campfires. Ample firewood lay in the nearby growth. The ground was dry, as were pine needles, fallen and brown. Tinder for the fire. I gathered some of these, along with kindling and fuel. Next I used the ax head to chip wood splinters from a log. All of this I arranged into a neat fire stick-fire lay—an old technique remembered from my Boy Scouting days. I lit the tinder in three places and let it catch. Soon the kindling was aflame. With more twigs and wood chips, the fire began to take. After several minutes, I flattened out the larger sticks and began to lay on logs at angles, letting plenty of oxygen through to the flames. Squatting, I blew long, steady puffs of air between the logs, further fanning the flames. Now it was a fire for keeps.

"Not bad—but gasoline's quicker!"

The voice was not Herb's. Startled, I looked up to see Reba, standing over me. She was dressed in bib overalls and work boots, her graying hair pulled in a ponytail beneath a floppy gray gardening hat. Hanging down from the side of her mouth like a statement of defiance was a cigarette. It was the long, filterless variety, delivering its deadly toxins into lungs and surrounding air unrestrained. Flanking her were two hefty German shepherds, Reba's constant companions on the farm. They sniffed at me, a stranger to their land, and I sensed that had she commanded they would have gladly chawed a chunk out of my backside.

"Thought I'd come see if you two men were still alive up here!" she announced.

"Long as yer here, Sis, stay for supper—'fact, how 'bout yeh fix it!"

"Like . . . *heck!*" Reba said.

When the fire was hot for cooking, Herb threw on a pot of water. While he dredged beef cubes in seasoned flour, Reba and I diced potatoes, carrots, onions, and turnips. After browning the meat in salt pork fat, we boiled it for half an hour before adding the vegetables. Then we sat back and let it stew.

By the time the sun began to set, I had offered thanks to God for a hearty meal in a spot of heavenly beauty. We sat on logs around the fire as the temperature dropped. A pie iron baked in the coals. Herb's wife had prepared it that afternoon.

"Betty's not much for campin'," Herb remarked. "But she loves to see me go, I think!"

"Now there's a big surprise!" Reba quipped.

"So, Preacher," Herb began, slapping large portions of pie on clean plates, "when you gettin' out that banjo? Better be soon, 'cause I'm turnin' in at nightfall!"

After dessert, I retrieved the banjo from the truck and opened the case. Reba studied it intently as I tuned.

"Now, bear in mind," I disclaimed, "I'm self-taught!" Then, feeling a terrible fool, I broke into a folk song I had committed to memory:

*I'll sing you a song and it ain't very long,*
*'bout a young man who wouldn't hoe corn,*
*the reason why I cannot tell.*
*This young man was always well, this young man*
*was always well . . .*

The old tale of a man's failed courtship and life due to laziness spun out in five verses. Both Chestnuts seemed bemused, but Herb's words were more pensive.

"Makes me think a bit a' Pop . . . man who wouldn't hoe corn . . . shucks!"

"Don't go bringin' *him* up, Herbie, ruinin' a perfectly fine evenin'!"

"Dad was—well, guess you'd say he wasn't a happy man," Herb explained. "He was a rough one . . . hard on us kids and real hard on Mom, especially when he was drinkin'. But he was a . . . "

"He was an ass!" Reba put it plainly.

"Now, Sis . . . "

"How about you do us a *church* song, *Wyatt?*" She quickly changed the subject.

"You mean a hymn, Reba?" I asked, cracking a smile. She had called me by my first name: Wyatt. This was music of a kind all its own. It had come out in one syllable—wite—as so often people pronounced it at Ashgrove Church. Yet she had said it. That was the point. "Well, I can't play one on the banjo, but I suppose we could all sing one."

"Oh, you go ahead!" Reba insisted.

In an instant I had settled on a hymn I knew by heart, one that was cheerful and themed to our setting as well as any I could imagine.

"Here's one," I said. "Sing along if you know it."

*This is my Father's world, and to my list'ning ears,*
*All nature sings, and round me rings the music of the*
*spheres.*
*This is my Father's world, I rest me in the thought*
*Of rocks and trees, of skies and seas—his hand the*
*wonders wrought.*

Verse 2 I could likewise remember—more about nature's praise to God, in "birds," and "grass, morning light," and "lily white." And God, the Father, whispering back to us through them all. But then memory failed. I stopped and shrugged.

"Yeah, everybody knows that one," commented Herb.

"Not me," corrected Reba. "Never heard it before. Who wrote it?"

I told Reba I couldn't remember but would be glad to find out if she wanted.

"No need," she had said. "I didn't say I liked it. The world's not all 'lily white,' you know . . . and whoever God is, he's not *my Father!*"

And her brother rolled his eyes at me and shook his head as if to say, "Leave it be!"

Herb was true to his word. As the sun sank beneath the horizon and the stars popped out like studded diamonds, he retired to his lean-to. And with a "Herbie" and a "Wite!" Reba too set out with her dogs down the gravel road, guided only by a crescent moon and her own practiced feet.

I sat alone at the fire, reviewing sermon notes by flashlight, distracted by the night chill and the twinkling of a billion stars. *This* was the music of the spheres, I had proclaimed to myself. If God shined anywhere, it must be here.

Back home in the city, I had felt a strange compulsion to answer Reba's question—even absent encouragement from her. Out under the stars that chilly night, "This Is My Father's World" had stuck with me. It had likewise clung to my mind during the day that followed, even through my difficulty catching a fish at the pond down the road from the farm. Herb and Reba, who had rejoined us, caught a dozen bass and bluegill between them. They had found it all quite amusing, so that Reba had chuckled long and loud between puffs on an endless stream of cigarettes. Finally, having had enough of ridicule and secondhand smoke, I had traded in "This Is My Father's World" and begun to hum another tune: "Chestnuts Roasting on an Open Fire." This had put me in a better mood, but by the end of the day the hymn tune was back on my mind again.

I was certain it had to do with Reba. She was strong and self-reliant, out there in the solitude of nature. But her quiet country life not only lacked company, it seemed sadly devoid of God. More than once that day she had made a scornful comment about men and their appalling weaknesses. Reba had little use for fathers or men in general, and no use at all for a God who was either. "If God's a man," she quipped, "then I'm headin' to hell for sure. What's more," she added, "if I was God, the way this world is I'm not sure I'd want credit for it . . . " In truth, it was a hard point to dispute.

All this had directed me back in earnest to that sweet hymn I loved but which seemed to rub Reba the wrong way. Was it just so much naive dribble, or did it utter something true after all? I reacquainted myself with the last verse, the one I had been unable to recall. To my embarrassment, it began "This is my Father's world, O let me ne'er forget"! In addition, I read up on the remarkable life of its author, Maltbie Davenport Babcock. These things I stored up to await the knock of opportunity.

At Ashgrove Church, each Mother's Day began the same. Ushers were supplied boxes of corsages with instructions to pin them on the blouses of every mother who came to worship. Gladys Hatch was conducting a refresher course in corsage pinning when I popped my head into the vestibule in search of Reba Chestnut.

"The idea is not to draw any blood," Gladys was saying, as she pinned a fresh boutonniere to each usher's lapel.

"Wait a minute! How do we know for sure if someone's a mother?" Jimmy Grimshaw asked, half in jest, which was his way.

"How long you been comin' to this church, Jimmy?" Gladys snapped. "You ought to know by now who the moms are, but if you don't, then *ask!*"

"Sure would be easier just to pin 'em on *all* the ladies!"

I found myself in agreement with Jimmy. Motherhood was more than a thing to admire—it was a universal grace, a common link between us. A pity, then, once a year to divide women according to whether or not they had borne a life in the womb. Instead, why not lift up the generous love of motherhood as something to which we might each aspire?

"Uh . . . Gladys?" Phil Simpson followed up in a bit of a whisper. "What should we do about Brandy Carns?"

Brandy was the newest mother in the church. Her parents, Clarence and Brenda, had a spotty attendance record to begin with, but since the turn of events in their daughter's life it had slackened even further. Brandy, then seventeen, had become pregnant out of wedlock. In March, near her eighteenth birthday, she had delivered a healthy baby boy. Now it was rumored she was bringing her child to church on Mother's Day.

"Well, you give her a flower, of course!" Gladys answered. "She's a mom, isn't she!"

There were those, naturally, who avoided Mother's Day. Anna Quarfarth, dolefully childless, hadn't attended on that day for years. Others found the sting over a mother's loss still so acute that they kept away for fear of sobbing through the morning unabated.

"Has anyone seen Reba Chestnut?" I asked.

Heads shook in the negative. "Just wait," said Gladys. "She'll be here." After Easter, Gladys had dropped Reba a line, reminding her to be sure to come on Mother's Day. Acquainted as I was with Gladys's frankness, I imagined her adding something along the lines of "It sure would have made your mother happy to know you were coming to church now and then!"

"She's not comin'," Herb broke in. "Saw her yesterday evenin'. Said she probably wouldn't make it."

"Did she say why?" I asked.

"Best ask her yourself."

In Mother's Day worship, moms sat in the pews, their veins coursing with pride. Thanks to Gladys's coaching, not a drop of blood was spilled. Even Brandy Carns sat pleased as peach fuzz with her new baby throughout the hour. But one wounded heart was noticeably absent—one who did not merit a corsage but whose love of a mother was as strong as a mighty oak.

That next week I performed an irrational act. Unable to reach her by telephone, I drove the distance to Reba Chestnut's farm. Pulling up to the trailer, I spotted a floppy garden hat tucked in a patch of weeds. Reba was on all fours, getting a jump on the long summer battle with burdock and crab grass. Though she must have heard me coming, she didn't budge until I was standing next to her in a wild carrot patch.

"Hello, Reba!" No answer. "We missed you at church on Sunday! . . . Everything okay?"

"Fine!" she spoke at last. Then, "Well, not really—I . . . " Now Reba was up on her feet and facing me. She struck a match and lit the last cigarette of a pack. "I couldn't come."

"Why, what happened?"

"I . . . " Reba hesitated. Then it all spilled out. "Well, I was *just too mad* at her!"

"Uh oh!" I reacted. "What did Gladys write to you?"

"Who? Oh—no, not *her!*" Reba corrected. "At Mom! I was mad at my mother . . . "

Reba went on to describe a kind of delayed hostility toward the one she had most adored. "I've been so angry at Dad all these years, guess I never got around to Mom—'til now."

"But why? What did she do?"

"Not what she did. It's what she never did. Never stood up to him. Never stood up for any of us. Never cared a lick for her own self-respect!"

The Chestnut household had been a restless, raging place. Her father had robbed the cradle and taken his sixteen-year-old bride, Alvera, from her Kentucky home up to the outskirts of Indianapolis. There he had tried his hand at farming. Three children had followed quickly. But Herb Sr. was not a good farmer. As his drinking picked up, family life became increasingly cast down. Things escalated into abuse. Herb and his younger brother fled the home at the earliest opportunity. Reba had remained, bound to her mother as a buffer against her father until his death. By the time Reba had married, she was already a hardened woman, unable to abide much from a man, too fearful of appearing weak to adopt a lifestyle of compromise. The marriage had ended badly. Then her mother had died. Reba had returned to the family farm a rock and an island.

"I just can't tolerate that kind of weakness. I've learned to be strong. But Mom was soft."

Why all of this had erupted in her now was a mystery. But Reba had wrath to spare. Much of it was directed at her father and mother, but the balance had gone to God. "That's why I walked out a' worship, Easter!" she continued. "All that talk about victory in the cross began to get to me. Dying, sacrifice, surrender—I just can't go for all that! You gotta be tough and hard in this world to survive it. No one else is gonna do it for you." Not even God, she had continued. Least of all God—a Father. No, never that . . .

Yet there was almost a questioning in her tone, I thought. It was as if she was certain of what she said—but not really. Perhaps she was herself like a long-cocooned caterpillar, it occurred to me, struggling free from a long and lonely bondage.

After a silence, I spoke. "You know, Reba, you were right last week about God. God isn't a man. God isn't a woman, either. God is just God. But God is something no man or woman can ever be. God is *always* loving, and that is the greatest strength we have. Because of God's love, we don't have to hate our mothers or fathers or anyone who hurts us. We can come to honor whatever there may be to honor in everyone . . . we can learn to forgive."

Then I relayed to her what I'd learned about the author of the hymn we had shared around a warm campfire—Maltbie Davenport Babcock. I told her of his renowned physical might but gentle bearing, of his love of nature, and of his untimely death at the young age of forty-three, the same year "This Is My Father's World" had first been published. "He knew the world for what it was," I said. "It took him young, but he had still given thanks for its beauty. He didn't give up on it—or on God."

Reba thought for a moment. "How did he die?" she asked at last.

"I don't know," I said. "But I'll try to find out."

We spoke for a while longer, and then I left. "See you later," I said. It seemed better than good-bye, and I was already nursing hopes that it might even be rather soon.

I sat back in my chair at a cubicle in the central library. Spread out before me were most of the public collection of books on the subject of hymn writers and hymnody. Several weeks had passed since my surprise visit down to the Chestnut farm.

How did the mighty Babcock die? That was the question assigned. I now knew he had been on a tour of the Holy Land, shortly after being chosen to succeed Dr. Henry van Dyke at the Brick Church, New York City. I had learned that he met his demise in a hospital in Naples, Italy, as the trip ended. But beyond that I had come up short, failed the exam. As to what precipitated the untimely death of a man of iron I could not discover.

And so I was left with his life instead. Especially I'd been taken with a simple story from it, a humorous account that spoke volumes about our options in the dangerous world God made. It concerned a young man being bullied by an older one. Physically and verbally he had him in a corner. Coming upon the scene, Babcock had calmly grabbed the bully by the waist and the collar, picked him up, and heaved him over a fence.

I had laughed when I read it. But then I'd begun to reflect. We have all needed a Babcock on the scene of our lives. But a Babcock isn't always there. Sometimes the defender of the weak dies. It doesn't matter how. What matters is where we stand when we seem to stand alone.

Babcock's answer came to me in the third stanza of his hymn, the verse I had forgotten:

*This is my Father's world, O let me ne'er forget*
*That though the wrong seems oft so strong,*
  *God is the Ruler yet.*
*This is my Father's world, The battle is not done,*
*Jesus who died shall be satisfied,*
  *And earth and heav'n be one.*

Now I was writing all of this down in a letter to Reba— the humorous account of Babcock's life, the missing verse of the hymn, all of it.

"In this beautiful, terrible world God made," I meditated, "we cannot count on much. But we may always count on God to be loving as a father should be, as a mother should be. This is the truest thing in life, and the truest thing in death."

"Please join us in worship on Father's Day, Reba!" I concluded. Then I signed the letter, licked shut the envelope, and dropped it in the mail.

Father's Day Sunday was a bustle of activity. The sky had cleared after a night of steady rain. As a hazy sun worked to dry the ground, busy arms and legs were assembling chairs in neat rows looking west. Only the lectern was placed facing eastward, right in the path of the sun's rays. But this was small price for the pastor to pay. I had asked the deacons for permission to hold morning worship outside on the lawn, and they had agreed. My reunion with nature at the Chestnut farm had worked a desire in me to combine praise of God with a celebration of earthly beauty. Father's Day seemed the ideal opportunity and "This Is My Father's World" the perfect theme.

Following the Sunday school hour, worshipers streamed from the building into the midmorning heat. Each picked up a hymnal from the stack on a table next to the center aisle. Women in dresses tested the hot metal seats before sitting in them. Young children in shorts or skirts who sat down without care were letting out little yelps up and down the rows. Female ushers were stocked with father appreciation kits bearing disposable razors, aftershave lotion, and the like. These they were handing out to all men indiscriminately. It was a double standard, a breach of protocol to be sure, but as usher Heidi Hapness said, "What the matter? There's plenty enough to go around. And, mercy sakes, don't we want *all* the men to smell good?"

I sat in a folding chair pulled up alongside the lectern and followed with amusement the high jinks of one seven-year-old, pretending to shave with the blade guard still in place, then drenching his face in Max Factor. Thus distracted, I missed a lone figure, hurrying to a seat in the back, just as Harold Hatch had us stand to sing the opening hymn, "Faith of Our Fathers." Shelly Higgins played from an old upright piano lugged outside just for the occasion. Only when congregants were again seated and a hush fell over the ceremony did I spy it, on the extreme end of the very back row of chairs—a floppy gray gardening hat, pushed down in the front to hide the face. I thought I could make out a faint trail of cigarette smoke, climbing up its sides, though it might have been the glare of the sun instead. But I had no need to see more. I knew its wearer and why she had come. She was there to honor her father, and mother, and God.

In the sermon I spoke of God's sheltering love as the model of all fatherhood. God performs this faithfully, unremittingly. Real fathers founder. But we were all encouraged to strive at such protective love, just as God's mothering love adjured us to nurture others. Both were habits worth forming. When they were practiced, they added immeasurable beauty to the intricate world God made. Together, such fatherhood and motherhood formed a sturdy floor and ceiling for a child, a safe beginning in a dangerous world.

Next I segued to the story of a hymn writer whose best-known hymn we would soon be singing. The life of Maltbie Davenport Babcock, American Presbyterian minister, mingled tenderness with toughness to rare effect. He was a star athlete, a tall hulk of a man with muscles of steel, who excelled at swimming and baseball—but also music, drama, and singing. Though superior in strength, he was a defender of the defenseless who would tolerate no coercion of the weak. Then I told a story only one other worshiper that day had ever heard. It was the account of how Babcock, champion of the weak, had once grabbed a bully who was badgering a smaller boy by the scruff of his neck and the seat of his pants and pitched him gently but decisively over a fence! And from the back, beneath a floppy gray hat, came a cackle of recognition. It was better music than any *Amen.*

Maltbie Babcock, I concluded—lover of nature, enthusiast of all God had made—understood the world's fallenness and brokenness. He knew all was not well on earth. But God is still in our midst, creating. God is not finished yet. Gently but decisively God is pitching the scourge of sin and death over the fence. That was why Babcock's hymn expressed confidence in the ultimate satisfaction of Christ. And why Christians have presumed to pray "thy kingdom come, thy will be done on earth, as it is in heaven." And why, however our spirits have been marred along life's jagged way, we remain people of hope and daring, prone to love, destined to grace.

Then all stood for three stanzas of Babcock's best-loved hymn, from the heavily perfumed baby face in the front to the floppy, smoky gardening hat in the very back. We sang out as children of the Father under azure sky, cradled in the arms of green mother earth.

## ♪ Hymn Notes ♪

Maltbie Davenport Babcock (1858–1901) was a brightly burning candle, too soon extinguished. Born in Syracuse, New York, and educated at its university, he excelled at athletics, the arts, and scholarship alike. An Auburn Theological Seminary graduate, Babcock pastored Presbyterian churches in Lockport near Lake Ontario, in Baltimore, and, briefly, the Brick Church in New York City. His Renaissance breadth of accomplishment included proficiency as an organist, pianist, violinist, baseball pitcher, swimmer, public speaker, teacher, and poet. The text to "This Is My Father's World" first appeared as a sixteen-stanza poem in Babcock's collection *Thoughts for Everyday Living*, published the year of his death.

While the contemporary church debates the concept of God as Father, the hymn's title turns on the notion of God as companion and friend, as opposed to some remote cosmic force. Likewise, the beauty of nature, far from evoking belief of some impersonal pantheistic sort (God in nature), is here a window to faith in a creative and personal God. In verse 3, found in modern hymnals in at least two versions, Babcock addresses the world's discord, whether understood to be a conflict given in the very nature of things or a product of fallenness. Either way, the hymn concludes with the hopeful expectation of a final unity: "And earth and heaven be one."

The authorship of the hymn tune, *Terra Beata* (blessed earth), also known as *Terra Patris* (Father's earth), is in dispute. It derives either from a traditional English melody or is an original creation of Franklin L. Sheppard (1852-1930), an organist, editor, and Presbyterian churchman. The tune itself consists of a pair of two-bar phrases, each followed by one identical four-bar phrase. The sense of drama and closure this provides, all in a cheery, stairstep line, reinforces the optimistic theology of God's creative work, still coming to final fruit.

# CHAPTER 10

# The Baptist Nun

## "Jesus Is All the World to Me"

VERA CRAMER WAS WASTING THE CHURCH'S MONEY.
Each Sunday she strode into the Pathfinders Sunday school class toting her large-print King James Scofield Reference Bible, made her way to the far corner of the room, and sat down. If there were no chair in the vicinity, she moved one to the spot. She would sit directly left of the Christian flag so that the edge of her blouse brushed against its tasseled fringes. Vera Cramer would then scoot the chair quietly, almost Ouija-board fashion, into the flag until, halfway through the hour, she had all but disappeared behind its delicate folds. There, for the remainder of the class, sat a left shoulder, arm, waist and leg, and half a head of graying hair, pulled back in a tight bun. Always, open in Vera's lap, shone the gold-edged pages of her giant-print Bible.

The class would be engrossed in some uniform Bible lesson of a minor prophet, an epistle of Paul, or the life of

Jesus. Participants took their student books home during the week, and sometimes they even studied them. Almost without fail they remembered to bring them back on Sunday. Vera's copy, offered to her with a hopeful smile at the outset of each new quarter, would never be seen or heard from again. The extra copy, slipped into her hands each

## Jesus Is All the World to Me

### Written by Will L. Thompson

Jesus is all the world to me, My life, my joy, my all;
He is my strength from day to day,
　Without Him I would fall.
When I am sad to Him I go, No other one can cheer me so;
When I am sad He makes me glad—He's my friend.

Jesus is all the world to me, My friend in trials sore;
I go to Him for blessings, and He gives them o'er and o'er.
He sends the sunshine and the rain,
　He sends the harvest's golden grain;
Sunshine and rain, harvest of grain—He's my friend.

Jesus is all the world to me, And true to Him I'll be;
O how could I this friend deny, When He's so true to me?
Following Him I know I' right,
　He watches o'er me day and night;
Following Him by day and night—He's my friend.

Jesus is all the world to me, I want no better friend;
I trust Him now, I'll trust Him when
　Life's fleeting days shall end.
Beautiful life with such a friend,
　Beautiful life that has no end;
Eternal life, eternal joy—He's my friend.

week, remained unopened. It lay smothered in her lap beneath the great weight of Vera's Bible. Vera cared little for the words of others, whether classmates, commentators, or clerics. She spent each class period craned contemplatively over her Bible, oblivious to all truth but that lifted from God's pages, up through thick-lensed, horn-rimmed glasses, into her own weak eyes.

Meanwhile two copies of the lesson book sat unused. Books had been purchased at three dollars a copy from scant church coffers expressly for the students enrolled. After just thirteen short weeks, the books were obsolete. I, Vera's pastor, was diverting attention from other duties to prepare the weekly lesson. This use of my limited time was as valuable as students chose to make it. The truth was painfully obvious. Vera Cramer was wasting the church's money.

Vera lived alone on the second floor of a storefront facing out to Old US 40. Through the years various establishments had occupied the space below her—a diner in the 1960s, a variety store in the 1970s, and now a coin laundry. Not long after moving there, Vera had gone to work at the laundry part-time. She sat at a small desk and changed bills into quarters, nickels, and dimes. Country-western music rained down from a single speaker placed high on a shelf immediately behind her, while from across the room a television trumpeted the gushy verbiage and background slush of daytime soaps. Vera noticed neither. Her head remained buried as if ducking the crossfire. Vera's real business was an ardent pursuit of the gospel truth, whispering softly to her from the Bible, where it lay sprawled out across the little table. Her concentration was so profound that often customers had to wave dollar bills in her face just to get her attention. Grudgingly, she would pause to count change or break a fresh roll of coinage from its wrap, banging it against the edge of the table. This she did with such force that it took on the character of protest. It was as if Vera was the one moneychanger Jesus at the Jerusalem temple had managed to convince. Dollar bills and coin rolls were kept in a cigar box held fast by a large red rubber band. The box itself resided beneath Vera's arm. It served as a prop for her prompting finger that guided her poor eyes through the verses of the open Bible. Everything, even money, had its sublimated place beneath the all-important power of the Word.

Each Sunday morning, come rain, shine, snow, or sleet, Vera made the mile-and-a-half trek from the town of Bridgeport up to County Line Road, then north to the doors of Ashgrove Church. Out in the country there were no sidewalks. Vera walked on the road and only moved to the grassy shoulder when vehicles passed from both directions at once, and then reluctantly. Rides were offered her from time to time, but she invariably declined them. Vera was just on the skinny side of obese, so her choice to walk was a good one. But it was hard on her feet. She had taken to jogging shoes and sweat socks. These she wore over pantyhose, covered to the knee with a skirt or dress. Vera never wore slacks to church or anywhere else.

At her side she carried the Bible. Its cover was in black pebble-grain cowhide, an expensive piece of work, undoubtedly the priciest thing she owned. But it was old now. Its spine was worn smooth from toting mile after mile across the years. A closer look would even have revealed the outline of palm and fingers, the very handprint of Vera's pious devotion. Here was one cover by which to judge the value within. Once at church, Vera would sit motionless on a corner bench in the vestibule until the Sunday school hour. She would never speak unless spoken to, and not always then. Instead, she stared out a window onto the gravel drive and marked the arrival of worshipers.

With a wry expression she watched them vying for spaces in the grass to park the cars she methodically shunned.

After Sunday school, Vera would bypass coffee and fellowship to secure her seat in the back sanctuary pew. She would open the Scofield and begin to read. This continued through the prelude. It lasted through the call to worship and invocation. It persisted through hymns, anthem, and offertory alike. It even outlasted the sermon, the invitation, and the final benediction. Only when the pastor had greeted the last worshiper at the threshold to the world did the Bible close. Then Vera would quietly glide through the vestibule and out again to County Line Road and home. On an average Sunday, Vera managed to converse with no one, exchange reluctant greetings with no more than two parishioners, and make accidental eye contact with only half a dozen others. She had handled no bulletins, passed no offering plates, and neither stood for nor opened her mouth to sing any hymns. During my years with Vera, there was one exception only to this, and when it occurred, it left the pastor breathless.

Once, at the tail end of Sunday school, Vera had heeded nature's impromptu call to the ladies' room and had absentmindedly left the Scofield Bible behind in her seat. Moments later, the second bell rang and the class broke up for the fellowship hour. I was left alone with her Bible, and I sat staring at it, lying there as if it were someone's secret diary. I waited, but Vera did not return. Then, thinking to pass off curiosity as kindness, I picked it up to deliver it into her hands personally. But the Bible fell open instead. It opened willingly, dutifully even, right to John's Gospel. These pages were well worn. Most of the Bible appeared pristine, without smudge. But John's Gospel was ragged, marked over, lived in. Pages were creased. Words and phrases had been circled and underlined.

There was even writing in the margins. Unable to help themselves, my eyes strained to make sense of Vera's scribble. Immediately they shrank from the page with embarrassment, as though having glimpsed nakedness. These marginal notes were in reality love letters. Vera had been writing letters of love to Jesus. I returned the Bible to the seat and hastily left the room. Later on in worship, Vera sat tranquilly in the pew, oblivious to my transgression. But I could not forget.

Soon it was time for the next quarter of Sunday school lessons. The new theme was, of all things, the Gospel according to John! At last we were singing Vera's song. Even she would be unable to resist this subject, I predicted. I was wrong. During the first class session, I lavished every enthusiastic tone of voice, pitched every question, and directed every key insight to the lady wrapped in the folds of the Christian flag. I strained to spy out which chapter of John she was living in that morning. In desperation, I even directed one question to her by name.

"So, Vera," I started, "what does it mean to you when John says here that God's Word became flesh and dwelt among us?"

Vera started, as if an icy wave had just slapped over her beach chair by the sea. But then she looked straight at me for the first and only time in memory and uttered simply, "Everything!" That was all she said, and no one else had anything to add.

That same morning in worship, I glared at Vera from the chancel, out to her remote pew, where her head was buried as always in the Book. I had the strong sensation that she and I alone were in worship. It was the self-conscious discomfort pastors are prone to when a close friend or family member or some person of prominence turns up in worship unannounced. I remained at a loss to understand her. I had failed even to rouse her at her point of highest passion. But without my irksome preoccupation with her that morning, I might have missed it.

It was time for our second hymn, one of my least favorites. "Jesus Is All the World to Me" had always smacked of the worst kind of sentimentality, so I believed. The words gushed, the trite melody grated. Worst of all, it was a study in religious self-absorption, employing the personal pronouns *I, me,* and *my* nineteen different times. But I had never experienced it as I did that day, in the life of Vera Cramer.

From the first introductory strains, the difference was visible. Vera perked up. She reached for her bulletin, then for her hymnal. She flipped right to the page, as I had dreamed she might one day turn to a weekly Sunday school lesson. Next, Vera Cramer did what none had ever witnessed. She began to sing! The words were halting at first, but soon they grew clear and strong. "Jesus is *all* the world to me!" she intoned. And when we came to the refrain, Vera delivered, "He's my friend!" with such force it caused heads to turn. But Vera didn't notice. Now she began to rock to the music, to swing and sway and reel. Soon all timidity dissolved into sweet abandon. She might have been a Hasid, caught in the ecstasy of prayer, or a Gypsy, dancing through the night by the light of the moon. But it was only Vera. Vera Cramer—unapproachable, impenetrable Vera—was dancing with her one true love: Jesus.

We assume that those who live to themselves have something to hide, that they are running from a dark past, harboring many secrets. Surely this is the case at times. But not always. There are people who simply yearn to be alone, who revel in solitude, who seek the face of God. In our struggle over what to do with them, we assign names. Catholics have mystics and contemplatives; Buddhists have monks. Baptists, for lack of a spiritual term, have tended to label them nuts. But Vera Cramer was far too sane to fret over easy labels. And while I would never learn the secrets of her past, I came that day to take at face value what Vera's life had been crying out for months: Jesus was all the world to her.

When I had seen off the last worshipers to their cars and Vera had finally shut her Bible for the morning and was preparing to go, I mustered the courage to ask about her enthusiasm for the morning's middle hymn.

"Well, I just like it a lot," she responded. That was all she said. But for Vera, it rated a thick volume.

Months later, Vera arrived at church carrying two armfuls instead of one. On one side was her Scofield Bible, by now a veritable appendage to her right arm. On the other, Vera bore a bundle of books, crisscrossed with two sturdy red rubber bands. Vera was returning every student quarterly she had ever not used in Sunday school. She marched right up to her pastor and placed the bundle in my hands. She wore a rare smile on her face, though I could not discern if it answered more to a feeling of satisfaction or embarrassment. But I was certain it did not matter.

"Here," she said. "Thanks."

"You're welcome," I said.

And that was all.

## ♪ Hymn Notes ♪

Christian testimony comes in many forms in order to penetrate many different pairs of ears. Sometimes a simple song, direct and unadorned, touches a heart more deeply than all the eloquence ever put to the page. This without a doubt has been the case with "Jesus Is All the World to Me," a hymn of profound immediacy and simplicity that has reached count-less souls with the message of Christian consolation.

Will L. Thompson (1847–1909) was a composer, editor, and publisher of many hymns and songs, both sacred and secular. Remembered as the Bard of Ohio, Thompson reaped his greatest satisfaction from the simple rendering of sweet gospel texts and tunes. His two best-known works are "Jesus Is All the World to Me" and "Softly and Ten-derly." He composed the words and the music to both.

"Softly and Tenderly," an invitational hymn, was a favorite of Dwight L. Moody, used often on his evangelistic tours. Moody is reported to have said on his deathbed, "I would rather have written [it] than anything I have ever been able to do in my whole life!"

"Jesus Is All the World to Me" was first published in Thompson's hymn collection of 1904. The words are per-sonal and capitalize on the power of repetition. The notion of Jesus as "my friend," the persistent theme of "Jesus Is All the World to Me," is both applauded and shunned in Christian circles. Christian theology in fact asserts both the transcen-dent otherness of God and God's nearness, God's immanence. There is room in Christian hymnody for expressions of each.

The tune, in triple meter, has a lilting quality, reminiscent of much popular music of the era. One can almost hear a banjo strum along on beats 2 and 3 of each measure. It is a fitting accompaniment to words of such tender sentiment.

## CHAPTER 11

# Second Rest

## "Love Divine"

THE OLDS NINETY-EIGHT TURNED UP THE DRIVE TO ASHGROVE Church, pulling in between two cars in a tight-fitting row. For at least a minute, it backed out, then in again, in a lame attempt to straighten itself, nearly scraping the cars on either side. Soon it was more crooked than ever, at which point it stopped, satisfied. After another long moment, an elderly man climbed leisurely from the driver's seat and stretched his arms high in the air, as if having just arisen from a nap.

"Earl's here," announced Jimmy Grimshaw, staring out the kitchen window toward the road. "Right on time."

"Yeah," Kip Quarfarth agreed, "a half-hour late!"

In fact, Earl Norris, Ashgrove Church's eldest member, was forty-five minutes tardy. He had been scheduled to cook pancakes for the men's prayer breakfast, but by now the task was already well underway. Done stretching, Earl had turned as always to regard his limited-edition, canary-

# Love Divine

### Written by Charles Wesley

Love divine, all loves excelling,
   Joy of heav'n, to earth come down;
Fix in us Thy humble dwelling,
   All Thy faithful mercies crown.
Jesus, Thou art all compassion,
   Pure, unbounded love Thou art;
Visit us with Thy salvation, Enter ev'ry trembling heart.

Breathe, O breathe Thy loving Spirit
   Into ev'ry troubled breast!
Let us all in Thee inherit, Let us find that promised rest.
Take away our bent to sinning, Alpha and Omega be;
End of faith, as its beginning, Set our hearts at liberty.

Come, almighty to deliver, Let us all Thy life receive;
Suddenly return, and never, Nevermore Thy temples leave.
Thee we would be always blessing,
   Serve Thee as Thy hosts above,
Pray and praise Thee without ceasing,
   Glory in Thy perfect love.

Finish then Thy new creation, Pure and spotless let us be;
Let us see Thy great salvation Perfectly restored in Thee:
Changed from glory into glory,
   Till in heav'n we take our place,
Till we cast our crowns before Thee,
   Lost in wonder, love and praise!

yellow Oldsmobile, for more than twenty years his single mode of transportation. "Yeah, you're a honey!" he said for the thousandth time. He reached into his back pocket and drew out a clean white handkerchief, folded over three times and creased flat. Leaning over the car as though to give it a kiss, he spit shined a smudge on the driver's side door. Then he returned the hanky to his back pocket and sauntered into the church.

"Mornin', Earl," several of the men had called as he came up to the church kitchen. They said it in loud voices, because Earl was certifiably deaf and rarely wore his hearing aids. When he did wear them, he never turned them on. For the most part, Earl preferred his world that way—namely, silent.

"Boys," he replied, and "Pastor," nodding my way. "Smells good, but—aren't I cookin'?"

"It's after 8:30, Earl," Kip Quarfarth replied. "We started without yeh."

"Oh," he said off-handedly. "'Spect I overslept."

"Anyway," Kip continued, "did you remember the pancake mix?"

"Well, no," said Earl. "Must've forgot it in my sleep! Ol' memory's not what it used to be."

"It's all right," said Jimmy Grimshaw. "We're covered."

"Oh, then, whatta I owe yeh?"

"Nothin'," Jimmy replied.

"Three dollars," Kip muttered, but Earl didn't hear him.

Soon stacks of piping hot pancakes were on the table, and I was offering grace. We ate quietly until Jimmy broke the silence. "So, how's it runnin' these days, Earl?" He had meant Earl's Olds. Jimmy loved old cars. He'd as soon talk about them as drive them.

"What's that?" asked Earl.

"How's the car runnin'?" Jimmy repeated.

Earl thought. Then his eyes glazed over and his mouth fell open. This was Earl's posture of utter incomprehension. It was nearly catatonic and generally led to unconsciousness if left unattended.

"How's Ginger getting along?" It was Harold Hatch to the rescue.

"Oh, Ginger!" Earl answered, his face a sudden flush of recognition. "Why, she's been purrin' like a kitten, Harold!" he said.

Harold had a knack for speaking loudly to the hard of hearing without giving the appearance of shouting. Moreover, he had long understood Earl's peculiar relationship to his car. Such a reference to Ginger as "it" left Earl completely baffled. "How's it runnin'" might as well mean "How's the water runnin' out of the faucet?" or "How's the country runnin' with a new president?" It might refer to many things, but not to Earl's car. His car was not an it; it was a she. It was Ginger. Naming a car was not an unprecedented act, yet no one had done so with quite the implication Earl Norris had. Ginger was more to him than an automobile; Ginger was a companion.

Actually, Ginger had not been purring at all that morning. Ginger had been knocking badly, but to deaf Earl Norris it had sounded like a purr. For several days it had seemed noticeably louder to everyone but him. To Earl, Ginger remained as always: peerless, impeccable, supreme.

"We're practically the same age," Earl liked to joke. "She's a Ninety-Eight, but I'm only ninety-four!" Remarkably, Earl's Olds looked brand new. This was astonishing given the fact that he had totaled her twice. In neither accident had Earl suffered so much as a scratch. In gratitude, Earl had twice paid the difference between Ginger's blue-book value and the cost to restore her. "What else could I do?" Earl reasoned. "She saved my life!" Now much of Ginger's body was brand spanking new. It was tantamount to cloning a person. Certainly Earl would not have disagreed.

It hadn't worked that way with Earl's wives. "Three times at the altar," he would muse, "and all alone. All three of 'em gone on to heaven." Earl had once again become a widower just four years earlier. "Last wife, Wilma, was only seventy-five when we married," he said. "Pretty little thing—bit young, but I brought her along." But Wilma had died of a heart attack. "Died sudden," Earl explained, "right there in Ginger, there in the passenger seat. Just up and died, just like that . . . " After the untimely death of his third wife, Earl had vowed never again to marry. "I've decided just to stick with Ginger," he explained. "Even when she gets in a little trouble, why, she always bounces back. A car's a man's best friend," Earl had amended the old saying.

Breakfast ended and a Bible study commenced. We were completing the third and final chapter of 2 Peter. "The day of the Lord will come like a thief," we read. "What sort of persons ought you to be in lives of holiness and godliness . . . ? . . . while you are waiting . . . strive to be found . . . at peace, without spot or blemish . . . "

"Sounds like 'Be ye perfect' in different words," Harold pondered.

"Sounds like a tall order to me!" Jessie Calhoun said.

I pointed out that striving for perfection was one way in which early Christians waited with expectancy for Christ's return. Commitment to Christian growth, not the attainment of perfection, was the idea. Self-satisfaction was a recipe for complacency and a good way to get caught napping at the appointed hour.

"Where's the *peace* in that?" Harold asked.

"Good question," was my response.

Meanwhile Earl had slept through the whole discussion, the embodiment of perfect peace and contentment.

"Earl!" Harold called. "Wake up, Earl! Time to go!"

"Oh, okay," answered Earl sluggishly. "Must've dozed off there for a minute."

"For an hour, more like," Kip muttered again.

"Wait a minute," Earl said. "Aren't we gonna sing?" It was a curious thing. He was nearly stone-cold deaf, but Earl Norris loved to sing. He had a miserable voice, even making allowances for age and deafness. But Earl loved singing deep down in his bones. He had insisted upon it at the men's prayer breakfast from the start, and whenever the other men objected, Earl would pull rank.

"Come on now, boys," he would say. Then he would lament the state of society in which the young no longer honored their elders. "Why, Moses brought down a law against that kinda thing!" he would remind us. "Now sit back down and let's sing a thing or two!" And that's how it would go more often than not.

There wasn't a pianist in the group, so everything was sung strictly a cappella. This suited Earl fine. He wouldn't have heard the accompaniment anyway. As a consequence, though, the men were forced to sing out loud and strong. Otherwise Earl would venture off on his own both in tempo and pitch, exacting torture on every good ear within hearing range. I enjoyed all this considerably. Hearing a group of men bellow out a tune was a rare pleasure. It helped that the hymn most frequently sung was one I loved greatly. Earl himself described it as his favorite, and we sang it to his good pleasure at least every other week. This had been one of those weeks.

Harold would lead us off, swinging his hymnal back and forth in time, just in case Earl might be watching. Earl usually had his eyes shut instead, transported by the grandeur of every word, from the opening line to the final cadence. By the last verse, Earl often would be visibly shaking, as if some foreign presence had gradually taken possession of his being. It might have been fatigue, old age palsy, or, just maybe, it answered to the title of the hymn itself: "Love Divine."

The meeting ended and the clean-up crew began to scrub the griddle and wash up. The rest of us made a hasty exit.

"Well, see yeh boys!" Earl said, shuffling back out to the gravel drive. Before climbing into his old Olds Ninety-Eight, Earl had once more removed the handkerchief from his back pocket and added a little more spit shine, this time to Ginger's hood. When at last he pulled out and turned left onto County Line Road, Earl failed as always to look either way. A truck, coming up fast in the opposite direction, slammed on its brakes just in the nick of time. The irate driver had honked half a dozen times and volleyed obscenities out the window while Earl, still blocking his path, adjusted his rear-view mirror. He never heard the first word of it.

"Yowee!" shrieked Sarge Grimshaw. "That was close!" He was standing with the others, just outside the front door. Earl's departures from church had grown into something of a spectator sport.

"You say he took his driver's test last month, Harold?" Kip asked.

"Yep. That's what he said."

"These bureau of motor vehicles people need their heads examined," Sarge protested. "That man's a danger to himself and every last one of us on the road!"

And away Ginger clanked—a perfect purr in her engine, Earl would have said.

Earl Norris hailed from the little town of Carefree, Indiana, down at the bottom of the state, where the Ohio

River takes a sudden sharp bend to the north. His father, Alfred Norris, had been one of the few local tobacco growers in the only region of Indiana that harvested it. The family had attended a Methodist church there—a "second blessing" church, Earl had described it to me once, during a visit to his home.

"You know what that is?" he asked me, convinced no one under seventy had had time to learn much of anything.

"I guess not," I confessed, but Earl didn't hear me. He was busy forging ahead.

"Received the second blessing myself back in '36. It was at a revival meetin'. People prayed something furious to be sanctified. Then it just came over me."

"What did?" I asked.

"Why, the blessing!" he said.

"But what is it?" I pressed, "What does it mean?"

"Didn't I just tell yeh? Means yeh get sanctified, get the second rest—means yeh don't sin!"

When his father died in the 1940s, Earl had inherited the family farm. But, according to the teachings of the pastor of the Methodist church, smoking was incompatible with perfection. It polluted the body, God's temple, which in the sanctified person the Holy Spirit had come to indwell. The pastor had pointed up the hypocrisy of raising a crop for a use you could not sanction. He had proposed to Earl that he try his hand at growing something else. But this had left Earl in a quandary. His father, Alfred, had settled decisively on tobacco after failing miserably with corn and beans. "This patch a' land just refuses to grow anything else," he'd told his son. Who was Earl to imagine himself wiser in these matters than his own father? And so Earl had elected instead to join the Baptist church in Carefree. There, he'd heard, the pastor himself smoked two packs a day.

When later Earl came to the west side of Indianapolis, he brought along his new Baptist identity. But he was still a second-blessing Methodist at heart. "God's made me a new creation!" Earl explained. "Guess you could say I'm pure and spotless—just like ol' Ginger there!" he said, pointing to his immaculate automobile.

At that moment, something had clicked. These were words I had recognized. Indeed, they went back to the Saturday men's group and our weekly rendition of the hymn "Love Divine." These were the words of the second rest.

Of the 6,500 hymns Charles Wesley penned, "Love Divine" had ascended over the centuries to a place of pre-eminence. Its spirited tune, *Beecher,* certainly was responsible in part. But the hymn text itself must also have played a role. "Love Divine" is a prayer for complete sanctification, for the indwelling Spirit to perfect us. Who would not wish to become one with the grace of God? But behind such sentiment is the curious Wesleyan doctrine of entire sanctification, the idea that it is possible to grow in faith to the point of perfection—in effect, to no longer sin.

"Love Divine" was Charles Wesley's poetic rendering of his brother John's hard-boiled belief in perfectionism. The "second rest" was the peace of perfection; the "Alpha and Omega" stood for justification and sanctification—where faith began and was completed; and the "finished creation," "pure and spotless" was the sanctified Christian, changed "from glory into glory." All this answered to Earl's blissful assessment of his own sanctified state. He deemed himself the very embodiment of the hymn he loved best.

"To sin, from the Latin, means to 'miss the mark,'" I said, "to aim wide of the target. If Earl swerved off the road and totaled Ginger twice, it seems like that would qualify!" I was sitting across from Harold Hatch at the

Dairy Queen, a mile from Ashgrove Church. My words were garbled by a mouthful of Dilly Bar, and some of the ice cream was dripping down my tie. The fact that *I* qualified a sinner by this definition was not in dispute.

"But did Earl tell you *how* they happened, *how* he got in those wrecks?"

"No."

Harold made a snoring sound, and let his head fall onto the table with a thud.

"You mean he fell asleep at the wheel?" I exclaimed.

Harold nodded.

Suddenly I understood: the doctrine specified *conscious* sinning! "If he was asleep at the time," Harold explained, "then he didn't consciously do it. And if he didn't consciously do it, then it wasn't sinning. That's how Earl believes. As far as he's concerned, he's still no longer a sinner."

"It must be nice to work things out like that," I commented. "Maybe I'll fall asleep in the pulpit and preach the perfect sermon."

"Or, you might just preach the way you always do," Harold countered, "and leave it to us to keep on being the perfect listeners!"

As Harold said this, the rest of the Dilly Bar fell from the stick and landed in my lap.

Two days later, the sad news came that Ginger, the canary-yellow Olds, had died. A week before, at a routine oil change, the automotive shop had forgotten to add the oil. This had explained the knocking noise that Earl had mistaken for purring. Ginger had put up a noble fight, but on the seventh day there was a terrible grinding, audible even to Earl, followed by one ear-splitting thonk. Then she had coasted to a stop for good. Ginger had thrown a rod, the equivalent in human beings to a massive myocardial infarction. As in the case of his third wife's demise, there in Ginger's front passenger seat, Earl had known almost immediately that Ginger had expired. Had it been just one more collision with a tree or a lamppost, Earl might have considered another costly repair. But it was the engine, an automobile's soulful center. He could have thrown in another motor, but that, he realized, would not have been she. Sweet Ginger, the canary-yellow Olds Ninety-Eight of Earl's heart, was gone.

Earl Norris wept bitterly. He wept more than at the deaths of his second and third wives combined. They had lived out their lives. Nothing had been withheld them. They had gone home to God at their appointed hour. But not Ginger. She had been stripped of her perfect condition for no other reason than shameful neglect. It was exasperating, it was criminal, and it was breaking his heart.

As the tears ebbed, Earl had a strange sensation, a sudden surge of adrenaline he had not known in years. Anger! White-hot anger, and right on its heels, unconscionable thoughts began to form in his mind, thoughts he would never have dreamed possible. He wanted to kill the lunkhead who had forgotten to add the oil. The man was a murderer. Earl wanted to string him up by his toes, to pluck out his eyebrows, to tie his neglectful fingers in knots. Earl hadn't felt such enmity toward another human being in decades. He knew in his heart that this was sin, but he couldn't help himself. Earl was wretched, and in this unspeakable state, the awful truth had sent shivers up his spine. He, Earl Norris, was yet a sinner! He had gone immediately home, clasped his hands tightly together, and prayed to God almighty for deliverance.

Sunday came, as Sunday always does. Usher Jimmy Grimshaw was standing outside the vestibule at the front entrance to the church. He was looking out toward County Line Road when a golden-yellow, late-model Buick pulled reverently into the drive. It chose a spot near the road and cut off. Soon, up the gravel drive tramped Earl Norris, his head down in that reflective posture of a mourner.

"Hey, Earl!" Jimmy yelled. "Whose yer . . .new *friend?*"

"It's a loaner," Earl answered. "I may not buy again," he added. "Been lookin' into bus schedules."

Jimmy nodded, not knowing what to say.

In worship, Earl sat quietly. For three days he had undergone a thorough self-examination. "I'm too old for this!" he had thought, but he'd continued anyway. Earl had been living under an illusion. He realized he had been grasping at things he could not hold. In truth he was far from perfect, just as his Ginger was far from eternal. She was just a car. He was just a sinner. But there was one thing more . . .

After the sermon, I had given Harold a nod. Then, as we had prearranged, Harold had walked down the aisle to where Earl sat and announced in his best loud voice that wasn't screaming, "Now let's all turn to hymn number 45, and sing everyone's favorite hymn: 'Love Divine'!"

Earl looked up in surprise. He had slipped into his normal Sunday stupor, somewhere between sleep and catatonia. But those two words had wrested him free. "Love Divine." Earl knew why this was being done, this inclusion of his favorite hymn. After all, there was no funeral this time, no proper opportunity for the public grieving of such personal loss as man's best friend. Instead, the congregation sang the hymn dearest to Earl's heart, offering it up for God's good pleasure and his own. We fell back on Wesley—on the "joy of heav'n," the "faithful mercies" of God and "pure, unbounded love." This was the better message of the hymn: not a prayer to be made perfect but a prayer for Christ to dwell perfectly within us—sinners.

And as he sang out loud, clear, and sinfully out of tune, Earl Norris, eldest member of Ashgrove Church, finally found his second rest.

*Finish, then, thy new creation;*
  *pure and spotless let us be;*
*let us see thy new creation perfectly restored in thee.*
*Changed from glory into glory,*
  *till in heav'n we take our place,*
*Till we cast our crowns before thee,*
  *lost in wonder, love, and praise.*

## ♪ Hymn Notes ♪

Charles Wesley (1707–1788) the eighteenth child of Samuel and Susanna Wesley, was born into a long line of pastors and poets. He wrote hymns on countless scriptural texts and about every possible aspect of the Christian faith. Charles was the younger brother of John Wesley and his "brilliant cavalry leader" in the Methodist cause. It is not surprising, then, that another prominent subject of his hymns was Methodist theology. An example of this is his extensive hymnbook titled *A Collection of Hymns for the Use of the People Called Methodists* (1780). Among its stated purposes was to provide "clear directions for making our calling and election sure: for perfecting holiness in the fear of God."

"Love Divine" first appeared in a separate collection, *Hymns for Those That Seek and Those That Have Redemption* (1747). In Wesleyan theology, as in most Christian thought, redemption is seen as involving more than our justification by grace. It involves equally our sanctification, the process of our being made holy. This happens not by our own effort but through Christ's incarnation in us. The difference for the Wesleys was the possibility of attaining complete sanctification. The "second rest," a reference to the "sabbath rest" of Hebrews 4:9, is the fulfillment of that blessing. The net effect is a life without sin.

For his ability to combine subtle doctrine and tender poetic expression, Charles Wesley has been dubbed the sweet bard of Methodism. For his breadth of verse, committed to every conceivable aspect of Christian experience, he has often been referred to as the greatest hymn writer of all time in terms of quantity and quality.

The tune, *Beecher*, to which the text is set, was composed by John Zundel (1815–1882). A German-born church musician and composer, Zundel served as organist at Plymouth Church in Brooklyn. There he collaborated with the brothers Henry Ward Beecher and Charles Beecher on the *Plymouth Collection of Hymns and Tunes* (1855).

## CHAPTER 12

# Invitation to a Miracle

## "Amazing Grace"

I T WAS MORE THAN IMPLAUSIBLE. IT BORDERED ON COLD, factual impossibility. Yet there was the letter, speaking for itself on fancy, ragged-edged paper stock. Ashgrove Baptist Church, Cinderella of the westside church music scene, had been invited to participate in the annual Amazing Grace Songfest.

"What's this?" Harold Hatch asked. He had strolled into the pastor's study before the Wednesday evening prayer service. As he peered over my shoulder, the bold type of the letterhead had caught his eye. He stared down at it incredulously, until he could contain himself no longer.

"Well, I'll be a wretch like me!" he exclaimed at last.

"I know," I said. "It's big. This is very, very big!"

"Bigger than the Plainville-Nebo Association Thanksgiving choir!" Harold added.

"We should think this through carefully," I counseled. "Make the most of it. It should be a great experience for everyone involved."

"Well, 'everyone' is an awful big word!" Harold cautioned. "But oh, are there ever some folks who'll be tickled pink over this!"

And glancing down once more at the gilded message of the fancy letterhead, Harold intoned loud and strong: "Grace Deliverance Chapel—Let Grace Lead You Home!"

Grace Deliverance Chapel sat at the corner of Mumford and Underwood, just southeast of the interstate bypass. Mumford and Underwood were small side streets in a

## Amazing Grace

**Verses 1-4 written by John Newton**
**Verse 5 found in A Collection of Sacred Ballads, 1790**

Amazing grace—how sweet the sound—
   That saved a wretch like me!
I once was lost but now am found, Was blind but now I see.

'Twas grace that taught my heart to fear,
   And grace my fears relieved;
How precious did that grace appear
   The hour I first believed!

Thru many dangers, toils and snares I have already come;
'Tis grace hath brought me safe thus far,
   And grace will lead me home.

When we've been there ten thousand years,
   Bright shining as the sun,
We've no less days to sing God's praise
   Than when we'd first begun.

neighborhood hemmed in by highway, heavy industry, and, as viewed from the inside, decades of prejudice.

Deliverance, as it was commonly known, was the former Mt. Olive AME Church. This, however, predated the mysterious outbreak of revival in July 1976. Through a remarkable kindling of energy and spirit, no fewer than five hundred African Americans from all sides of the city and beyond were baptized in the name of Jesus and set free from the power of bondage. "Emancipated," they called it, released from sin, death, and human fear.

Emancipated from more than these, in fact. That this had occurred in the bicentennial year of American freedom had not gone unnoticed. Exactly two hundred years before, the founders of the nation had signed the Declaration of Independence, establishing the incontrovertible equality of all men. But "all," it turned out, was a big word, too. For the next ninety years, a word like "most" or even "some" might better have captured it in practice. Some men were created equal. Others had been born slaves.

And so it was highly significant that in our nation's bicentennial year, the congregation now known as Deliverance finally emancipated itself from its long-standing difference with Chirb Industries, a manufacturer of cigarette lighters and accessories, which lay adjacent to the church building. Between the two was a parking lot, the ownership rights to which had been in dispute for thirty years. Mr. Chirb held a deed of title to the land, while the church maintained it had been issued illegally. Church records from the 1930s documented the property's donation by a couple named Farling. While the Farlings had willed two parcels to the congregation, in the estate settlement the title to the land had been sold to cover undisclosed expenses. Unaware of this, the church had cleared the land for parking. When John Chirb later acquired the deed, he took possession of the lot, paved it, and began to charge the church members to park there on Sundays.

But Chirb Industries had fallen on hard times. Faced with bankruptcy, Mr. Chirb had been willing to sell the lot back to the church for a hefty price. With the outbreak of revival, parking had become more critical than ever. The church had embarked upon an ambitious plan not only to buy the lot but to purchase the Chirb factory as well and level it to the ground. While this more than anything was a matter of necessity, it soon came to symbolize the deeper purpose of such dizzying numerical success. In this unlikely reversal of fortune, members had come to see nothing less than God's justice at work.

But justice comes at a price, and so Deliverance Chapel had founded the Victory Songfest, a four-day festival amassing the best black talent in the Christian music world and drawing participants by the thousands. Naturally, parking and gathering space were horrendous problems, but this had been calculated to work in Deliverance's favor, creating such sympathy for the cause of expansion that donations washed in like a flood. By 1979, the factory was razed and ground broken for a new building, a megachurch facility with a thousand-seat sanctuary and an enormous education wing.

Then, just as the foundation was about to be poured, tragedy had struck. The pastor, a man of enormous energy and persuasive power, had died suddenly of a massive heart attack. Construction halted the day he was laid to rest. Leaderless, the ministry had slipped into a tailspin. By the time a new pastor was engaged, Grace Deliverance Temple had shrunk back to just twice its former size. Many of the capital building pledges were never collected. The factory lot sat empty, a giant field of uneven earth. So it had remained to the present.

A troublesome sidelight in this sad turn of events had been the strange appearance at the pastor's funeral of John Chirb, longtime congregational nemesis. No one recalled sharing a word with him that day. But memories survived of him, sitting stern-faced throughout the long and sorrowful service. What business had he among the grieving? many had asked. Was it to pay his respects or to garner some small-minded consolation that he had come? Divided opinion had lingered, so that while some had come to think of him more kindly, others came to regard him with a still deeper repugnance.

Of this whole whirlwind saga of revival and misfortune, only one tangible expression remained. Each spring, come rain or shine, hardship or ease, the Songfest went on. But chastened by shattered dreams, the people of Deliverance had fallen back on one true assurance. No longer was this great festival of song called Victory. Its new name was Amazing Grace.

We had Ed Garrett's cousin, Walter Prescott, to thank for the invitation to the Amazing Grace Songfest—Walt and his wife, Liza Mae, that is. In the 1950s, Walt Prescott had managed what few had either the courage or inclination to attempt. He had married out of his race. Liza Mae Prescott hailed from Lexington, Kentucky, the great-granddaughter of slaves in a region where life before emancipation had often been less harsh than in the Deep South. Her father and grandfather had both practiced law, and she was in the family's third generation of college-educated women.

When Liza Mae accompanied Walt to Indianapolis in the 1960s, she soon distinguished herself as an able community leader. Whether the cause was civil rights or a friendly neighborhood bake-off, Liza Mae was likely to be in the thick of it, with Walt not far behind.

Yet their path as a couple was not without struggle. Walt and Liza Mae had experienced prejudice from both sides. Segregated neighborhoods yanked them in opposite directions. Their children were ostracized by students and made to feel inferior by teachers. Nowhere did they suffer more than at the hands of the church. Prevailing wisdom identified interracial marriage as sin and the warrant against it as biblical.

This was not the case, however, at the church named Deliverance. The Prescotts were early converts to its open and invigorating spirit. Liza Mae had soon become involved in various aspects of congregational life. Among these was the Songfest committee on which, at Walt's urging, she had advocated outreach to a wider audience of the local church community.

Through Walt's cousin, Ed Garrett, Liza Mae was acquainted with our little church on the western edge of the county. Yet by the mid-1980s, the Amazing Grace Songfest was so well established that it had become by necessity an invitation-only affair. The waiting list traversed the Midwest and cut across twenty-five denominations. Even if viewed as a charity case, Ashgrove Church would have had a long wait indeed, had Ed Garrett not gone into tents and awnings. For several years running, his Little Big Top Shop had donated big tops to the Songfest, putting them up on the vacant ground of the former factory, installing lights and speakers and even electric heaters when the weather was chilly. Ed and his wife, Alice, had spoken in glowing terms of the Songfest, even expressing hope that someday Ashgrove Church might get its turn. Now, as a gesture of gratitude, Liza Mae Prescott had seen to it that our day should arrive.

There was a catch. Attending the Amazing Grace Songfest meant more than taking up precious space in a pew. It involved more than standing, singing, and swaying to the beat of someone else's drummer. To accept an invitation to the Amazing Grace Songfest was to agree to perform, to stand before the gathered and pour heart, soul, and voice into the majesty of music. It might be in a large ensemble or small, a quartet, trio, duo, or solo act, but in this great musical feast of the spirit, all participants sang for their supper.

"Why can't people just come and listen?" Gladys Hatch grumbled. "Why should I have to get up and make a fool of myself?"

It was a fair question. Gladys was as monotone as a humming bird, and her vibrato was around twice as fast. She had no business singing in front of any crowd. But at the Amazing Grace Songfest, none of this made any difference. Some of the participants were accomplished musicians. There were folk singers and jazz performers, sacred classical ensembles and rhythm and blues stylists, and, naturally, church choirs of every grade. It was not the quality of singing that mattered but the quantity of heart. As her husband, Harold, liked to say, "That's why they call it Amazing Grace!"

I embarked on my own explanation of things, sharing with Gladys a recent experience of mine in worship in an African American church. I was greeted at the door on a Sunday morning with all the warmth granted any first-time visitor. But when it was discovered I was a minister, suddenly everything had changed. The pastor had rushed to my side, put his arm around me, and whisked me to the front of the sanctuary. He had seated me on the platform in the place of honor and introduced me to the congregation in the most superlative of terms. I was a dear brother, he had announced, a true man of God, and a fine orator in the service of the gospel.

There I had sat before the admiring throng, thinking only self-contented thoughts through two hours of rousing song, prayer, and testimony. Then, just as worship reached a fever pitch, the pastor had stood and announced, "And now our esteemed brother will come and deliver to us the meat of the word which the Lord has prepared for us to receive this fine morning!" With that, he had motioned for me to rise and preach. I remember being stunned, flabbergasted, as I walked sheepishly to the pulpit and fiddled in the Bible for something to quicken my thoughts, finally settling on Galatians 5:1—"For freedom Christ has set us free." But my words themselves had seemed flat, caught in a self-conscious slavery all their own.

It was the gathered themselves who were my saving grace. They had wooed me, hung on my every timid word as if it were mother's milk. And their never-failing choruses of "Amen!" and "Praise God!" and "Thank you, Jesus!" had soon whipped me up out of myself and into a state of animation never rivaled in my preaching career since.

"Just go and keep preachin' it, brother!" they had told me in the reception line at the close of worship. "Don't let that devil stop yeh from *shoutin' it out!*"

"I think maybe that's the thing," I told Gladys, "that it is all about heart—joyous exuberance poured out as praise to God." Not outer method, I continued, but inner motive, not facility but felicity . . .

Gladys nodded her head in agreement, but her face wore a doubtful frown.

Each ensemble was to prepare a single selection of sacred music from any vocal tradition, and one thing more: churches were asked to bring their own rendition of the Songfest's signature hymn. During the closing worship, there would ring out no fewer than forty-five different versions of "Amazing Grace."

"One of those funny things, isn't it?" Ed commented. He spoke as our men's quartet had just finished its first rehearsal for the Songfest.

"What's funny, Ed?" I asked.

"That they chose a song like 'Amazing Grace' for their festival theme."

"I guess I don't know what you mean."

"Then you don't know the story?" Ed asked, somewhat surprised.

No, I didn't know it, and so Ed had filled me in on its history, sparing me none of the gory details. Its author, John Newton, had been from the age of eleven a seaman, gaining a reputation for ruthlessness and lechery. Later he had joined the slave trade, working on ships transporting captured West African slaves to markets around the globe.

"He reformed his ways later on," Ed had allowed, "but that doesn't change what he did!" I was surprised by Ed's depth of feeling on the subject. "You start to pay attention to these kinds of things when they come to touch your own family," he explained. "You learn to care more . . . "

Just days before the Songfest, the city opened the obituary page to news of the death of John Chirb, founder of Chirb Industries. In a final twist of irony, the cigarette accessory maker had lost a battle with lung cancer at age sixty-nine. Many prominent members of the business community passed by the casket to pay their final respects, but significantly fewer had attended the memorial service itself. Mr. Chirb, it turned out, had been better known than liked. His son, John Jr., had counted only a few dozen in attendance.

To his puzzlement, no fewer than eight of these were members of Grace Deliverance Chapel, including Walt and Liza Mae Prescott. The Prescotts were among those who had chosen to reflect kindly on John Chirb's presence at their beloved pastor's funeral. Now they were offering their sympathy to his family in return. And unlike John Chirb Sr., the Prescotts had addressed John Jr. with words of consolation, clearly and unambiguously spoken, leaving nothing open to interpretation.

"Your father did a precious thing, back at the time of our pastor's death," they said. "It was a gracious gesture, and we have not forgotten it."

John Chirb Jr. had not found the words to respond. Instead, he had only nodded while never abandoning that same severe countenance on which his departed father had built a reputation.

Meanwhile, the Ashgrove Baptist Church men's and women's quartets were fast running out of time. Harold, Ed, Jimmy Grimshaw, and I were feeling relatively secure with our selections, but the women were having a dreadful time keeping pitch on "Blessed Assurance." Jennifer Grimshaw, Jimmy's wife, sang a pleasant high soprano, while Polly Pruitt, our second soprano, was truly exceptional. But from there, the bottom dropped out. The lower voices belonged to Gladys Hatch and Thelma Crabtree. Each of these women in her prime had not been too fine, and that had been long ago. On the bottom rung of bearable was Gladys. She could hit the D below middle C, but once it was hers she didn't know how to hang on to it. No matter, though. She was on the bottom. The upper voices had to adjust. She would hover around the middle of the bass clef as if hugging a tree and wait for the others to find her there.

All the while, I had grown increasingly troubled over the story of John Newton, so much so that I embarked on my own study of the history of the beloved author of "Amazing Grace." The tale began much as Ed had reported. Newton had been a debauched seafaring lad, though in fairness he was following his sea captain father after his mother's death when he was only six. From there, he had landed in jail, finally serving on slave ships, living and dealing in misery. At one point, an African wife of an employer felt such enmity toward him that he became a self-described "slave of slaves."

A near-death experience at sea and Thomas a Kempis's *Imitation of Christ* had finally steered him along a different course. He renounced his old life and devoted himself to the Christian ministry, landing in Olney, near Cambridge, England, and coauthoring with William Cowper the *Olney Hymns* collection.

In my readings, I had come across a photograph of Newton's tombstone in the churchyard of Saints Peter and Paul parish, Olney. The words inscribed there were barely legible but illuminated much:

*John Newton, Clerk; once an infidel and libertine,*
*a servant of slaves in Africa, was by rich mercy*
  *of our Lord Jesus Christ*
*preserved, restored, pardoned, and appointed*
  *to preach the faith*
*he had long labored to destroy.*

Here was Saul of Tarsus in spades. Here was amazing grace in the flesh, a perfect backdrop for a festival of song at a church called Deliverance.

The Songfest arrived, and our Ashgrove ensembles brought to it their best. The women managed to go sharp and flat at the same time, certainly a singular musical achievement at this festival—probably many others as well! As for the men, we sang fairly in tune and our rhythm was impeccable, almost as if we followed the strict time keeping of a percussive instrument. Harold remarked later that it had been his knees knocking. I maintain it was our selection. At Ed Garrett's behest, we had sung "Precious Lord, Take My Hand," the popular Thomas A. Dorsey hymn. Ed knew it to be Liza Mae's favorite. More than that, it captured in many ways the original spirit of Deliverance, as Ed had come to see it.

Dorsey had written the piece shortly after the tragic death of his wife and infant child. It was thus a hymn of great faith and courage. But it was more. In composing and performing it, Dorsey, a jazz and blues musician, had also lit a fire of nonconformity in the black church against the predominant hymnody of the majority church—the white church. In time it came to symbolize a turning point in African American church identity while also gaining beloved acceptance in gospel churches everywhere. Its lilting beat and straightforward message, plaintive but pure, were irresistible. "Precious Lord" had become everyone's hymn, just as Songfest had become everyone's event. And Ed, on lead, had sung it better than he could. He pitched every phrase right to Liza Mae, who swayed side to side in her seat as a gesture of gratitude.

The two and a half days of Songfest passed quickly. Every year the event built to the same climactic cadence. Following hour after hour of nonstop singing, a large and orderly procession got underway. Out of the sanctuary and into the open field they marched—every performing group in the Songfest. There, under Ed Garrett's largest big top, each ensemble brought its own version of "Amazing Grace." Meanwhile loudspeakers carried the sound all over the lot and down the street, as people came from near and far and sat in folding chairs or spread out blankets on the ground to hear it. Here the Amazing Grace Songfest went public.

Each ensemble sang two verses only, then was replaced by the next group, which had taken the risers behind them. Through deftly executed transitions and modulations, one performance flowed into the next, forming one seamless whole.

In our Ashgrove rendition of "Amazing Grace," the men and women formed a double quartet, as Shelly Higgins slipped behind the electric keyboard and led us through. We sang verses 1 and 2, ending with

*'Twas grace that taught my heart to fear,*
*  and grace my fears relieved;*
*how precious did that grace appear*
*  the hour I first believed!*

And Gladys winked at me as we sang. Whether or not she should have been, at last she was unafraid.

Through it all, near the front of the tent, a man sat intently, soaking up the sound. For a long while, in the flurry of it all, his presence had gone undetected. Gradually, though, a few members of Deliverance had begun to notice, identifying him by those same stern features as his father. Finally, looking around the tent, Liza Mae herself had peered into his eyes with a flash of recognition. It was John Chirb Jr., son of the deceased. He was sitting under a big top parked over the vacant lot on which his father had made and lost a fortune. He had not come to sing. He had scarcely opened his mouth. But his very presence told all. John Chirb Jr. was himself the sound of grace that day, if anything was.

Later, after the voices of Songfest had at last fallen silent, Liza Mae approached him, a warm expression across her handsome face. As he met Liza Mae's gaze, John Chirb's sternness softened, the tight muscles of inheritance rearranging themselves into a broad smile.

Those of us standing near had seen it, and some had understood.

"This is big," I heard myself exclaim, "very big!"

Harold heard me. "Well you know," he said, "'grace' is an awful big word!"

And later, Liza Mae Prescott, who was accustomed to the last word on such matters, had agreed.

"Grace is the biggest word of all!" she said.

*When we've been there ten thousand years,*
  *bright shining as the sun,*
*We've no less days to sing God's praise*
  *than when we'd first begun.*

## ♪ Hymn Notes ♪

Christianity is first and foremost a religion of grace. Nowhere in the annals of hymn writing has this truth spoken more definitively than in the case of John Newton. Not only did he desert the British navy and join a slave merchant ship. At the tender age of twenty-three Newton became the commander of his own slave vessel.

Deeply affected both by a near-death experience at sea and Thomas a Kempis's *The Imitation of Christ,* Newton converted to the Christian faith, eventually abandoning the slave trade and preparing for the ministry. Through the influence of George Whitefield and the Wesleys, he became a thoroughgoing evangelical within the established church. At thirty-nine, Newton took his first parish, becoming curate to the vicar at the Olney parish, near Cambridge.

"Amazing Grace" first appeared in the *Olney Hymns,* a collection of revival hymns used widely by evangelical parishes within the Church of England. With his friend William Cowper, Newton published the hymnal in 1779, contributing 280 hymns to Cowper's 68. Other hymns in the collection by Newton include "Glorious Things of Thee Are Spoken," "May the Grace of God Our Savior," and "How Sweet the Name of Jesus Sounds."

John Newton is regarded as having been a strict Calvinist. However deterministic Newton's theology, the prime mover in this hymn is grace. Grace saves, finds, restores, brings along, leads home. And if grace prompts fear, it does so in the service of fear's relief. This personification of grace is altered only in verse 4 ("The Lord has promised good to me"), most often substituted for a closing verse attributed to John P. Rees (1828–1900) that begins "When we've been there ten thousand years . . . "

Noteworthy is the fact that the year of Newton's death coincided with the passage in Parliament of an antislavery bill. Its sponsor was William Wilberforce, in whose conversion Newton had played a role.

The tune, *Amazing Grace,* is a simple American melody, first published in *Carrell and Clayton's Virginia Harmony* (1831). It, as much as the text, has made "Amazing Grace" arguably the most widely loved hymn of all time.

CHAPTER 13

# Another Resurrection

## "Because He Lives"

C HILDREN WERE RARELY BORN INTO THE FELLOWSHIP OF Ashgrove Baptist Church. With few exceptions, church couples hadn't fussed with a diaper for decades. For most, the empty nest syndrome was but a fading memory. Neither had pastors borne the church any recent fruit. It had been half a century since an Ashgrove pastor's wife brought a baby into the world. Whether they hired them young or old didn't seem to matter. Ashgrove had come to be known as the church of childless pastors. Everyone rejoiced with exceeding gladness, then, when long-time member Polly Pruitt, following years of empty effort, turned up pregnant at the age of forty-nine.

It was the kind of curious circumstance that seems to repeat itself with unreasonable frequency, leaving the fertility specialists baffled. Only recently had Polly and her husband, Butch, given up all hope of biological offspring. Instead, they had turned to adoption. This had proven an

# *Because He Lives*

God sent His Son—they called Him Jesus,
He came to love, heal and forgive;
He lived and died to buy my pardon,
An empty grave is there to prove my Savior lives.
Because He lives I can face tomorrow,
   Because he lives all fear is gone;
Because I know He holds the future
And life is worth the living—just because He lives.

How sweet to hold a newborn baby
And feel the pride and joy he gives;
But greater still the calm assurance:
This child can face uncertain days because Christ lives.
Because He lives I can face tomorrow,
   Because he lives all fear is gone;
Because I know He holds the future
And life is worth the living—just because He lives.

And then one day I'll cross the river,
I'll fight life's final war with pain;
And then, as death gives way to victory,
I'll see the lights of glory—and I'll know He lives
Because He lives I can face tomorrow,
   Because He lives all fear is gone;
Because I know He holds the future
And life is worth the living—just because He lives.

arduous process in its own right, especially for a childless couple in the middle of life. Nevertheless an easy calm had settled over Polly. She had found the peace of acceptance, the liberating release of a great burden. In a word, Polly's fear was gone.

Naturally it caused everyone quite a jolt when Polly went public with the joyous news of expectant birth. Among the doting women of the church, only Madge Spires seemed unshaken by it. "Seen it many a time!" she said, waving her finger in the air for emphasis. "Polly needed a rest from all that worry, is all. Just let any good *older* woman catch her breath, 'n' she'll run circles around the young'uns every time!" Madge, already up in her vigorous eighties, was proof perfect of her own words.

Polly, meanwhile, was keeping her own counsel. Gradually she was becoming withdrawn, pensive. To look at her was to begin to think of Mary, mother of Jesus, pondering the meaning of such a thing quietly in her heart. Other stories from Scripture came to mind as well. Thoughts were drawn especially to time-honored tales of barren women from Sarah to Rachel, Hannah to Elizabeth. Each of these had found special cause to contemplate the mysterious ways of God. Now Polly Pruitt had joined them.

"Think it's a boy or a girl, Pol?" folks began to ask.

"Don't know," she would reply, "and don't care. I'm havin' a baby! That's all." God had opened her womb, she believed. Nothing else mattered.

Meanwhile a more immediate decision was required of Polly and Butch. After three years on the ice, heart-warming news arrived from another quarter. A caseworker at the adoption agency called with the glad tidings. "Isn't it wonderful?" she said. "You and your husband are being adopted by a little baby girl!" Polly had gasped for air. She had run straight to the supermarket where Butch cut up meat. Leaning over the meat counter, she screamed for him nearly at the top of her lungs. When he peeked out from the cutting table with a whole fryer spread eagled before him, Polly wasted no time.

"You're never gonna believe this, honey!" she said. And Butch had nearly cleaved off a finger at the news.

"What do we do now?" they asked each other. "Turn her down—or give our new baby a big sis'?"

"We'll take her!" Polly announced over the phone, not meaning for it to sound as if they'd just purchased a new Chevrolet.

"Wonderful!" replied the caseworker. "You see, patience always pays off in the end!" she explained, not knowing the half of it.

As things turned out, Polly didn't yet know the half of it either. Awaiting her at her first ultrasound was a still greater shock. She had been growing in size at an alarming rate. By her twenty-fifth week, the change in Polly was overwhelming. She was fast appearing ready to deliver in an instant. Madge had eyed her with suspicion, but she had the good sense to keep her mouth shut. Butch was a big man, she thought, but there was more at play here than just that.

At the doctor's office, Polly donned an examination gown. She reclined in a special chair as a nurse squirted lubrication jell all around her swollen belly. Then the nurse began to maneuver the probe across her middle, isolating tiny fetal parts, while Polly and Butch stared at the monitor in wonder. The procedure was taking a long time, they began to think. "There's a heartbeat!" the nurse offered, pointing to the screen. "Oh, and there!" she said again. And the same held for arms, legs, and heads. "Well, everything—seems to be there," she said, hesitating slightly.

But Butch didn't notice. He had been growing impatient for a single piece of information that had been keeping him up nights. "Well," he said, no longer able to contain himself, "so what is it—a girl, or is it a *boy!*"

"I'm afraid so!" the nurse replied.

"What—afraid what?" Polly broke in anxiously.

"Oh, no, it's wonderful!" she replied. "Just that it seems to be a girl *and* a boy—"

"Twins?" Polly exclaimed.

The nurse nodded. "Well, congratulations!" she offered. But Polly sensed her unease. She excused herself, and not long after Polly's obstetrician came in.

"I guess you're something of a miracle," he said, as he played back the pictures of tiny arms and legs, of eyes and little mouths that seemed to stare up and smile. "Here's a bit of a concern," he said, fixing on one beating heart, that of the probable boy. "There is what looks like an AV canal—a hole in the heart. Hopefully nothing gravely serious, understand, but, given your age, Polly, I'd like to run a test, an amniocentesis, on each baby, just to rule out other problems."

"What problems?" they asked.

"Nothing to worry about I don't suspect," he tried and failed to reassure them. But the test was scheduled nonetheless and took place within the week.

Several days later, Butch and Polly were called into the doctor's office without explanation.

"As you know," the obstetrician began, "we ran an amniotic chromosome test on each baby, looking for anything unusual. Now in Baby B, everything looks good. Normal little girl, we think. In the other sample, though, that of Baby A, the one with the heart defect, we found something called trisomy 21. This turns up occasionally in pregnancies among women in your age group, Polly . . . "

"What is it?" she asked.

"Trisomy 21—is commonly known as Down syndrome . . . we believe it is only Baby A, who we think is the boy . . . I'm very sorry," he said.

The doctor answered more questions, then left the room. "Take your time," he said. And when he was gone, Polly wept, while Butch sat uncharacteristically stone-faced.

It is crises and disappointments, of course, that betray who people really are. Polly was a pillar. True enough, she was tiny, standing only five feet, one inch in height, with arms "about as thick as a sausage link!" as Butch liked to say. But she was as strong as iron on the inside. Were someone to ask her where she got her strength, an unequivocal answer would likely follow. "Faith," she would say, "and my music!"

Polly sang soprano—second soprano. She sang in the car, at the supermarket, and at home in the shower. But she also sang in the Ashgrove sanctuary choir and the newly formed summer worship quartet. Each week, from June to September, the quartet led congregational hymns in four-part harmony, providing a special music selection, as well.

"They're not half bad!" people had begun to comment. "Why don't yeh tape your songs for the elderly and shut-ins?" someone suggested. And so they had. Each quartet singer chose three or four favorites, combining for a collection of fourteen hymns in all. The selections were an eclectic mix. They ranged from favored hymns of destiny like "When the Roll Is Called Up Yonder" and "I'll Fly Away" to those of commitment: "Take My Life" and "Make Me a Blessing." Others seemed to plant one foot each in this world and in the world to come. Polly's were all of this type, including "He Leadeth Me," "Victory in Jesus," and "Because He Lives."

This last selection in particular was far from incidental. One Sunday, shortly after her startling announcement, Polly had prefaced the singing of "Because He Lives" with a well-known quotation from its author, Bill Gaither, a revealing statement of the hymn's why and wherefore. In moving terms, Gaither describes the challenging time of the 1960s, as he and his coauthor, Gloria Gaither, prepared to welcome their own firstborn son into the world. Their ambivalence over bringing a blessed child into a troubled world was overcome by what the Gaithers named a "calm assurance," rooted in one strong conviction: "Christ lives." Therefore "this child can face uncertain days," and "we can face tomorrow."

"It's my favorite hymn!" Polly told us. "It reminds me how the resurrection can come alive in your life!" It was clear that petite Polly was amply equipped to face the uncertain days ahead in her own life. More than a baby was alive and kicking inside her. The resurrection power was there in strength. Polly was more than a singer, someone had observed; she was a song.

Butch, on the other hand, was as tone deaf as a T-bone steak, and just now he was falling apart. Physically large, his chest was a wall of muscle, his neck a cylinder of steel. He possessed a grip that caused other men to cringe at his approach. He would hold out his hand to them, smile, and squeeze. It made the pastor nervous each time Butch lined up for the greeting after the sermon. Sunday by Sunday, his grip seemed to tighten until finally I gave up and let him press my flesh like jelly. For all I knew, jelly is all that was left of it anyway. At least this wasn't a hugging church, I consoled myself.

Yet under all the muscle, Butch was nothing but jelly himself, a jumble of stray sentiment and unrestricted emotion. A kind soul at heart, he was prone to sudden outbursts of feeling, from unbridled bliss to red-hot anger to severe melancholy. At long last, he had broken down entirely under the strain and sobbed in Polly's arms like a baby. Then Butch Pruitt had gone to bed and stayed there.

"He won't get up," Polly confided in whispers over the phone to Madge. "His work calls, and his bowling buddies—even his mom!—but he just lies there with his head under the pillow. I don't know what to do!

"He says he can't bear to raise a retard! I told him I married one—what's the problem?"

"Yeh got to get 'im up!" Madge said. "You've got two precious babies on board, and a third on the wing. He's got to face this, one way or another!"

News of Polly's latest plight spread quickly through the church family. It was the principal subject of the monthly deacons meeting. Chairman Herb Chestnut felt obliged to exercise some sort of spiritual leadership, both for Polly's sake and to uphold the board's scriptural charter. But just what form this should take no one could say.

Herb had brought a cassette player to the meeting, loaded with the tape of fourteen Ashgrove summer quartet favorites. "For inspiration!" he explained. All through the ensuing discussion, the hymns resounded, filling the room with what little cheer the general mood of somberness could tolerate.

"But it isn't right!" Gibson Mayes complained. "I've never seen such cowardly behavior in my whole life. Why, he's givin' manhood a bad name!"

"'Course, we've all known Butch is just a little off. They say that in the meat department he's got his own butcher's block—nobody wants him too close, 'case he blows!"

"Well, it's not natural," Gibson followed.

"Has Butch ever seen a doctor about any of this?" I asked. "Has he ever been diagnosed with any sort of condition that might explain it?"

The blank-faced deacons shook their heads. "Butch'd never go to a shrink!" Winslow Cox answered. His words only confirmed the obvious. Out here, mental health therapy had yet to be discovered. Help might come for Butch from the counsel of words, but they would need to be in terms familiar, in talk of God's goodness and blessing, of courage and hope and faith beyond understanding . . .

Just now all words appeared impotent. "Why don't we just go over and *drag* him outta bed!" cried Jake Payne. Everyone laughed.

But the meeting itself was dragging on. Many commented on the eerie improbability of the whole business, from an unexpected pregnancy, to an unlikely adoption, to a big man named Butch hiding from the world under the covers like a child. Meanwhile the cassette player rolled on in the background, sending forth song after jubilant song. It was the final irony of the evening—how a little church that could produce so quaint a musical offering might also preside over such oddity.

At last all ideas were exhausted. "Well, I know Butch," Herb concluded, "and he won't face the music 'til he's good and ready!" We sat together in silence as the current hymn selection finished out. It was the final refrain of Polly's personal favorite: "Because He Lives."

*Because I know . . . he holds the future,*
*And life is worth the living—just because he lives.*

Polly's sweet soprano came through unmistakably, anchoring the other voices in a sea of blended sound.

"Beautiful!" everyone agreed. Then, adjourning the meeting, Herb turned off the cassette tape and the deacons bowed for a closing prayer.

It was at the final *Amen* that inspiration had at last struck me, and I smiled to myself. Herb was right: Better thoughts *did* come with music present!

First thing the next morning, Polly barged into the spare room where Butch was camping out, pulled open the curtains, and plugged in a cassette tape machine. She and I had talked for a long while the night before. I had phoned her the moment I'd gotten home from the deacons meeting. "I love your tape!" I had begun. Then I sprang on her a simple idea: "Play it!" I had said. "Play the tape for Butch. Make him listen—until he gets up!"

"Shut that thing off!" Butch howled, as the tape began to roll. It was the opening rendition of "He Leadeth Me":

*He leadeth me, O blessed thought!*
  *O words with heav'nly comfort fraught!*
*What e'er I do, where'er I be,*
  *still 'tis God's hand that leadeth me.*

"Stop that thing or I'll smash it!" But she didn't, and secretly Butch was glad. He buried his head under the pillow as if to block out the sound, yet in such a way that one ear could still make out every word. He clung to his wife's soothing voice, like a small child being coaxed to sleep by a mother's lullaby.

"Sometimes 'mid scenes of deepest gloom," she sang. And next, the man with the iron grip heard "Lord, I would clasp thy hand in mine" . . . and he listened.

Song after song unfolded. One message after another bore in Butch's breast the gospel message of consolation and challenge. But it was Polly's favorite hymn that finally broke through—the verse dearest to her heart:

*How sweet to hold a newborn baby*
  *and feel the pride and joy he gives;*
*But greater still, the calm assurance:*
*This child can face uncertain days because Christ lives.*

Butch listened. He listened until the pillow came off his head, and the covers were pulled back, and, after three days cocooned in self-pity, Butch sat up in bed. Polly plopped down next to him. Then, taking his massive hands, she placed them over her swollen belly. "Here," she said. "Feel."

"Because he *lives,* Butch, you've gotta get up! Because they need you! And because I need you, too. . . . Let us in, honey! Please!" Then she turned off the tape player and left the room.

Butch sat in silence for a long time. At last he got up, showered and dressed, and went to work. A life started anew that day; the hole in a troubled heart was healed. It was like the resurrection all over again—at least Polly thought so.

Our time is really no different from the one Bill Gaither had described in the 1960s. Indeed, any moment in history is a harrowing one to bring a child into a world fraught with so much evil as well as good. There are no pills to block adversity. But to believe God holds the future is to deem life worthy of the risk. It is to hold out the hand of your life, smile, and squeeze.

## ♪ Hymn Notes ♪

The music of Gloria Gaither (1942–) and William J. Gaither (1936–) has had a profound influence on the

American church in recent decades. From the creative center of their lives and work in the sleepy town of Alexandria, Indiana, they have awakened millions with a gospel message of poignancy and clarity. Of their considerable musical output, no hymn has reached further or resonated more deeply than "Because He Lives." Its signal contribution has been to incorporate the theme of resurrection into the most intimate aspects of daily life.

Together, the Gaithers have composed more than 600 songs, written a dozen musicals, and produced sixty recordings. As a composer and arranger, Bill Gaither excels at adorning a heartfelt text with an endearing tune, creating hymns that sparkle, that are at once singable and satisfying. Through his "Homecoming" videos, a treasury of Southern Gospel music and its major influences, Bill Gaither has preserved for posterity this integral stream of Christian music in America. Gloria Gaither is a best-selling author and coauthor of such books as *Because He Lives, What My Parents Did Right,* and *Let's Make a Memory.*

# CHAPTER 14

# All Churches Great and Awesome

## "Awesome God" / "How Great Thou Art"

FOR FIFTY YEARS, ASHGROVE BAPTIST CHURCH SAT alone on the county line, surrounded by farm field and woodland. Then the airport expanded, gobbling up land behind the church, bringing the scream of the city near. But ahead to the west, all remained peaceful and still. There was one good reason for this, and it coincided with countless rows of fir, spruce, and balsam lining the road opposite the church. Cobb's Nursery and Potting Shed stretched north from US 40 to Nebo Road and west from the county line all the way to Six Points. Mr. Wendell Cobb had founded the business with his brother, Wilbur. They had bought up farmland cheap in the 1950s, back when the going price was still something to sneeze at. But Wilbur had died in 1985, just as Wendell Cobb was turning sixty-five, and neither had any natural heirs to the business. Wendell Cobb had begun to think seriously about the future.

# How Great Thou Art!

Written by Carl Gustav Boberg
Translated by Stuart K. Hine

O Lord my God, when I in awesome wonder
Consider all the worlds Thy hands have made,
I see the stars, I hear the rolling thunder,
Thy pow'r thru-out the universe displayed!
Then sings my soul, my Savior God, to Thee:
How great Thou art, how great Thou art!
Then sings my soul, my Savior God, to Thee:
How great Thou art, how great Thou art!

When thru the woods and forest glades I wander
And hear the birds sing sweetly in the trees,
When I look down from lofty mountain grandeur
And hear the brook and feel the gentle breeze,
Then sings my soul, my Savior God, to thee:
How great Thou art, how great Thou art!

And when I think that God, His Son not sparing,
Sent Him to die, I scarce can take it in—
That on the cross, my burden gladly bearing,
He bled and died to take away my sin!
Then sings my soul, my Savior God, to thee:
How great Thou art, how great Thou art!

When Christ shall come with shout of acclamation
And take me home, what joy shall fill my heart!
Then I shall bow in humble adoration
And there proclaim, my God, how great Thou art!
Then sings my soul, my Savior God, to Thee:
How great Thou art, how great Thou art!

For several years, he had been watching his competition cash in on city hunger for country experience. Urban families wanted to wander through an old pumpkin patch, hunting down the perfect pumpkin to cleave from the vine and carry home to carve—so these nurseries had grown pumpkins by the thousands. Dads dreamed of a gratifying romp through the snow to cut down the family Christmas tree. They would climb a hill or round a bend and there it would be: the straightest, tallest, fullest, freshest tree anyone had ever seen. And Dad would saw it clean as the children watched, then one-hand it back to the car and home. So these tree nurseries had abandoned rows and scattered Scotch pines and Douglas firs around like Mother Nature. But city folks weren't used to walking very far at one time, except at the mall, so Cobb's competition had thrown in round-trip hayrides. And they'd never trudged in mud—mud being an unnatural occurrence in idyllic dreams of family outings in the country (who ever saw Martha Stewart with mud on her boots?)—so these nurseries had begun to pray for no rain in October. And if it didn't snow a little in December, families wouldn't come out to cut a Christmas tree, so the nurseries had fallen into praying for snow. But when their prayers worked too

## *Awesome God*

**Written by Rich Mullins**

**Our God is an awesome God,**
**He reigns from heaven above,**
**With wisdom, power, and love,**
**Our God is an awesome God.**

well, they had been forced to provide round-trip sleigh rides, since city folks didn't like to tromp through deep snow . . .

All of this seemed terribly tedious to Wendell Cobb even just to think about, and irreverent besides, as he was descended from farmers who always prayed for rain and never prayed for snow.

At the same time, the price of land at the county's edge had begun to skyrocket. When the price hit twenty thousand dollars an acre, Wendell had finally made up his mind. He had begun to sell off parcels of land to the highest bidder. If he were destined to be rich in old age, he thought, then he might as well have some fun with it as work himself to death. And, being a devout Methodist and a tither, it had occurred to Wendell that his generosity might help to save the struggling Nebo Methodist Church from bankruptcy. Soon fields lay fallow, and surveyors popped up on the horizon like dandelions. It was the end of an era, out on the edge of the county line west. Little did any of us comprehend the nature of the new one just dawning.

In the fall of 1989, Cobb's Nursery sold a ninety-acre plot of land to a housing developer. The parcel ended just south of Ashgrove Church. Soon new home construction was underway.

"Well," Winslow Cox reflected grimly, "never thought I'd see the day, but I guess the city finally found us . . . "

Others had taken a more positive view. "Don't you see?" said Ed Garrett. "With new houses come new people, and with new people come new members, and with new members come growth and change for our church!"

When Winslow Cox heard this, his face had turned gloomier than ever. That word *change* had a dire ring to it. Winslow had driven home, gone to the shed, and begun to cut posts for a new fence along his frontage.

Change might be coming, but that didn't mean he couldn't bar it at the gate.

Still, as foundations were being laid down the road, the deacons got busy laying out a strategy to welcome our future neighbors. The deaconesses were on hand as well to add the woman's touch.

"We'll need a church brochure," I suggested, "something to tell people who we are and what we do." We began to draw up a list: worship, Sunday school, prayer meeting, men's breakfast, quilters, softball league. It wasn't much, but it was a start.

"Don't forget the fish fry!" said Penny Jones.

"And the potluck dinners!" pitched in Heidi Hapness.

"We'll bake pies," said Effie Payne. "Don't care where they're from—they can't resist fresh rhubarb."

"Why, it'll bring 'em across the street with their tongues hangin' loose!" Alberta Rump concurred.

"We could take 'em a packet and a pie!" Gladys Hatch said. "Put it right on their doorstep! A little Southern hospitality oughta do the trick!"

"Okay," broke in Herb Chestnut. Herb was the chairman of the deacon board and in charge of the whole affair. "Here's where we stand. Ruthie says that Lester'll be glad to write the copy for the brochure." Lester French worked in the office at the cemetery in Plainville. Ruthie, a deaconess, was his wife.

"Lester's great with ads and such," she boasted. "He's dreamed up some catchy ones over the years!" Ruthie passed around a card for all of us to see. It read: *Don't wait until your sorrow—you can buy a plot tomorrow!* "That one's his!" she said. "And this one too!" She had handed out a second card: *By our pond with the geese, let your loved ones rest in peace.*

People were speechless.

After a pause Herb had continued. "Okay, Jenny here will take care of the layout, and Ed Garrett's agreed to pay for the printing." The deaconesses would handle the pies, he continued. Each would be fresh baked and placed in a zip lock plastic bag.

"The pies are the most important part," Effie said. "After they taste one of these, they won't care what we believe!" Not a deacon had offered a word of conviction to the contrary. The Ashgrove Baptist welcome wagon was born.

Before long, houses were springing up all over the new subdivision. For Sale signs soon dotted the development, and the outlines of roads came into view. The brochure neared completion. "We need a snappy title," Lester had suggested. "Something to get people's attention." Soon they'd settled on

COME ON HOME TO ASHGROVE,
A QUIET PLACE OF COUNTRY PEACE WITH GOD!

At Lester's suggestion, the deacons had slipped in the soothing words to the old hymn "He Hideth My Soul":

*He hideth my life in the depths of his love,*
*And covers me there with his hand,*
*and covers me there with his hand.*

"Ain't that a bit old-fashioned soundin' for the times?" Heidi Hapness had asked.

"Yeah!" agreed Jimmy Grimshaw, "Dead-soundin', too! People are movin' out here to live in a new home, not to lie flat in a cemetery plot!"

"It's peace they're lookin' for!" Lester maintained. "Tranquillity! That's why they're moving out this far. And tranquillity is what we'll give 'em!"

Somehow this reasoning hadn't seemed quite right to people, but no one could put a finger on it. They had offered no further resistance, though, and Lester had taken this as a firm endorsement.

As building progressed, it began to appear that a brochure slogan was the least of our worries.

"Those new homes down the street look awful big . . . " Gladys Hatch pondered one Tuesday morning. She'd put it out to the ladies around the quilting frame, just to get their reaction.

"Dern tootin'!" Alberta Rump concurred. "Why, I feel sure I spotted a three-car garage out there yesterday. Some of 'em look to be twice the size of our whole church!"

Madge Spires had cut to the chase. "These new neighbors a' ours are filthy rich!"

Effie thought for a moment. "Hope rich folks like rhubarb!" she exclaimed at last.

Nevertheless plans for the welcome wagon proceeded hopefully. The first two hundred brochures sat in the office in neat stacks, like new conscripts at battle ready. The pie crews were on red alert around the clock. Dozens of plastic welcome bags were each stuffed with housewarming items and a Gideon's New Testament. At the housing development, roads and sidewalks appeared, yards were newly sodded, and Sold signs replaced For Sale ones. Finally the front entrance to the subdivision went in, comprised of two terra cotta columns, one on either side of a wide road. Over the expanse stretched a fancy sign with the words we had long awaited, a tangible name on which to focus our aspirations: *Quiet Cove*, it read.

"Told yeh!" Lester French boasted.

"Quiet my eye!" muttered Winslow Cox. "Why, the whole place has gone crazy as a coot! I can't even pull out of my own driveway anymore without havin' to wait for some big truck crawlin' down there to make things worse!" But most were too caught up in the excitement to share his cynicism.

Then, just as our welcome wagon plans neared completion, something unexpected occurred. Probably it was inescapable. Wherever a housing addition springs up, a new church is never far behind. Directly across the street from Ashgrove Church, where the last row of firs used to meet the first row of junipers, an enormous billboard was posted. The sign was colorful, pictorial. It featured a white dove, flying free above two open hands as if they had just released it. The dove soared into clear blue sky, high above rolling hills, all canopied by an enormous rainbow. In the distance, at the very heart of the sign, was what appeared to be the outline of a church with a large steeple. Just above the rainbow in bright letters were the words

Coming Soon!
Awesome Church of the New Era!

The sign rose twenty feet off the ground and stood parallel to County Line Road, about ten yards from the shoulder. Adding to its imposing power was its vertical angle. It seemed to tilt forward of perpendicular, out toward the street, as if it would swoop down upon passing cars at any moment.

Or upon stationary churches! The billboard sat directly across from Ashgrove Church, nearly dead center with the front door.

"What'd they do?" Harold Hatch asked cynically. "Measure?"

The people of Ashgrove would stare at it from the church entrance. At the end of Sunday worship, they would flock there and gawk at it as if it were a UFO. But something else about the sign was altogether bewildering. The first to observe the strange phenomenon was Jeannie Simpson. She and her husband, Phil, had been trimming back a hedge against the south side of the building.

"That's funny," Jeannie said to Phil, "I thought there was a church in the middle of that sign!"

"Well there *is*—it's right . . . " Phil stopped in midsentence as he, too, stared across the street from the southwest corner of the building. The church was gone. There was nothing in the middle of the picture but sky. "Hmmm," Phil said. "That's odd! I was studyin' that church just yesterday after the service, thinkin' it looked almost familiar somehow . . . " And Phil and Jeannie had left scratching their heads.

Soon others noted the same strange phenomenon.

"Must be magic," Heidi had testified.

"Black magic, if yeh ask me!" thundered Alberta Rump.

"Now you see it, now you don't!" Billy Burton repeated, in what had become almost a chant. He intoned it to Homer Sutton, the other home-run king and Billy's archnemesis in the church softball league. Homer attended Nebo Methodist—Wendell Cobb's congregation—situated on Hendricks County Road 100 E., bordering Cobb's Nursery on the west. Awesome Church had bought up a double parcel of Cobb's land a full eighth of a mile across. A sign nearly identical to the one on the east frontage lay to the west as well.

"Why, we've seen the same thing over here on our side!" Homer said in surprise. "There's a pretty brick church in the middle of the picture—and then it's gone!"

"No," Billy corrected, "not a brick church, Homer. It's a pretty white church with a big steeple."

"Ain't either!" disputed Homer. "Not over on our side it ain't!"

"Well, how many churches you think they're plannin' to build out here?"

"How would I know? But with that much land they could put in a whole baseball stadium!" At that, both men had paused to muse.

The two congregations were abuzz with such conversation. The church, whether white clapboard or red brick, would appear in a gleam and then be gone. "I always see it on Sundays," was a comment often heard. "It shows up most after worship!" On this point, both Baptists and Methodists were agreed.

The Methodists also shared the Baptists' apprehension over the matter of church membership prospects at the new housing development. Like Ashgrove Church, they had slapped together a new church brochure, and their homemade cookie tins sat at the ready. Wendell Cobb was intent on seeing that the Nebo congregation collected members as well as money from his recent financial decisions. But the Methodists, too, worried that their wares might not find favor among the class of people likely to take up residence in Quiet Cove. Fear of change and feelings of inadequacy to cope with it are no respecters of party affiliation. They are universal, nondenominational realities.

The other nondenominational reality on the horizon was Awesome Church. As work behind the twin billboards got underway, people had begun to ponder just what sort of a church would name itself Awesome.

"For that matter," Madge Spires put it, "what in the world does 'awesome' even mean?" Having arrived early for the Wednesday evening service, she had been staring out at the sign from her parked car. "Don't believe I've ever used that word *awesome* before—not in my whole livelong life!" she confessed.

"It means . . . full of awe," I answered, "full of awe and wonder. It means grand or great with maybe just a touch of fear . . . "

"Oh. Well now, them words make sense. Why couldn't they just name their church 'Great' or 'Grand'?"

"I guess they thought 'Awesome' had an added punch to it," I suggested.

"Well, can't see anything wrong with 'Great' or 'Grand' myself," Madge said. "Not that I'd likely name a church either one," she added.

"Me either," I agreed.

But now I grew curious. Just what was behind the title Awesome Church? How had anyone arrived at such a lofty and presumptuous name? I began to watch from across the street for any official goings on, for an opportunity to step across the county line, welcome our new church neighbors to the county—and snoop.

After only five months of building, the first moving van arrived at Quiet Cove. Almost the moment it had pulled away and a welcome mat sat outside the new front door, Lester French had arrived with a hospitality packet and Effie Payne with her fresh-baked rhubarb pie. No one had answered the door, so they had simply left it on the mat—right next to the Methodists' cookie tin.

"Confound it," railed Lester. "Do they have to beat us at everything?"

"Don't you worry now, Lester," Effie consoled him. "We'll see these folks on Sunday fer sure! They'll be over for second helpin's or I ain't a three-time county fair pie-baking champion!"

"Yeah," Lester agreed, "they'll come around for your pies, Effie. That, and for some peace and tranquillity!" And the ritual was repeated at several other addresses.

Soon three Sundays had passed without the first visitor. "Should we visit 'em again?" Effie asked. She and a few others hovered together in the vestibule after Sunday worship.

"Maybe we should change flavors," put in Alberta Rump. "Maybe mincemeat or lemon meringue would suit these kinda folks better."

"Unless they bit on Nebo Methodist's cookies!" Gladys contemplated.

"No," Herb said, "I've talked to some of their members. No one's visited them either."

It was all very curious. No one could decide what to do, so they just waited.

Meanwhile work on the new church across the road was tearing ahead. Earth-moving equipment lay everywhere. Ground was being moved around on a biblical scale. Foundations were poured in intricate fashion over many acres of land. Framing timbers stretched heavenward. Work proceeded through the long, hot summer. Then one morning, as the largest structure took final shape, opportunity knocked. A BMW pulled over on the side of the road. A man wearing a chic sports coat over a black turtleneck got out and walked toward the entrance to the new sanctuary. I sprang from our little building and hurriedly crossed the street in time to call after him before he disappeared inside. He turned and smiled as I introduced myself as the pastor of the Baptist church across the way.

"Glad to meet you," he said. "I'm Jack Vance, the pastor-coach at Awesome Church of the New Era."

"Do you go by 'Pastor' or 'Coach'?" I asked.

"Call me Jack," he said.

Jack offered to show me around. Many buildings of the complex were still barely framed up, but the main structure was near completion. There were no pews in the enormous sanctuary. Instead, a thousand padded metal chairs interlocked in rows like a long string of paper clips. The pew racks were empty. What hymnals would they be using, I had asked.

"No. No hymnbooks," he said. "Two screens." He pointed to either side of the long platform. "We'll flash the words up there. And these." Jack reached into one of many identical boxes along a wall, pulled out a booklet and placed it in my hands. *Celebration at Awesome Church* was its title. I opened it to a mission statement and read:

> Awesome Church of the New Era is a community of faith, Spirit-led by our awesome God. Our mission is to celebrate Jesus as Lord of life and grow in love and grace.

On the facing page was a single praise chorus, the kind I had learned at church camp and youth retreats. Without thinking, I repeated its title aloud. "Awesome God," it read.

"We sing it every week at Awesome," Jack explained. "It's our anthem."

"May I keep the booklet?" I asked.

"Please," he responded. "Help yourself."

"One more question," I said, preparing to go. "Your big sign out front: how does the church in the picture appear and disappear? Everyone in my congregation has been asking."

"There *is* no church in it!" he answered, surprised.

"No church?" I said. "But we've all seen it!"

Pastor Vance shrugged. "It's a special-effects sign. You've driven by and seen it, haven't you?"

"No," I answered honestly. "I always turn into our drive. We all do!"

"Try driving on past sometime," he suggested with a smile. "You'll see."

Next morning I started off for the church in my cream Pontiac LeMans with a sense of excitement. I headed west on Nebo Road as I had each day for years, turned south at the Coach and Horses Diner, climbed the hill past open field and farmland, on up a mile and a half to the entrance of Ashgrove Church. But this time, approaching the gravel drive I did what I had never done: I continued on. My eyes and hands lobbied my mind to turn the wheel left, so ingrained was the movement. But on I drove, past our entrance and up to the sign, already looming large on my right. As I passed it, staring straight into its center, I experienced what ever since I have thought of as "the effect." Directly beneath the sign, a cream Pontiac came into view. Suddenly the hands in the picture came together and cradled it, driver and all, as a dove descended and fluttered just overhead. So titillating was the experience that I turned around and drove back again the other way, repeating this several times before finally pulling into the church drive to park. I got little done for the balance of the morning. One word alone ruled my attention, a word that had been pressing in upon me for weeks: *awesome!*

The following Sunday after worship, Madge Spires had come to my side. Her face wore a diffident expression, something it rarely accomplished.

"Gotta get somethin' off my chest," she began.

"What is it, Madge?"

"I told yeh a fib a while back," she said, "and I just realized it today."

"Well, Madge," I tried to console her, "if you didn't know you were fibbing, then technically you weren't!"

Quickly Madge's face assumed the more familiar posture of aggravation. When it came to sin, she had no use for technicalities.

"Quit it," she said. "I'd told yeh I'd never said the word *awesome* in my life. Well, this mornin' we sang my favorite song and—I'm embarrassed to say it—that very word's in it."

I ran through the morning hymns in my mind and, just as I got there, she'd blurted it out in her squeaky door hinge of a voice: "'O Lord my God, when I in awesome wonder . . .'"

"I've been singin' them words all my life!" Madge confessed. "So yeh see, I am a liar after all!"

"Madge," I found myself strangely defensive for her, "don't be so hard on yourself. Like you just told me, you've been *singing* those words all your life, not *saying* them! You're not a liar—not about that!"

"Hmmm!" Madge stopped to ponder. "Why, that's true, Preacher. Yeh know I hadn't considered it quite, but it's a point! Okay, then," she said. "Now that's settled." And she was off.

"Oh, Madge!" I called after her. "You know that sign out there across the road—try driving by it sometime. Don't pull into the church. Just stay on the road and watch the sign!"

And Madge nodded suspiciously. I had begun to request the same of everyone I could stop to ask. But now, once again, Madge Spires had me thinking. It was curious. Of all the hymns surrounding our congregational life, "How Great Thou Art" was arguably the most beloved. People called for it constantly on Wednesday evenings. They thanked me whenever we sang it in Sunday worship. I had never preached a funeral at which it wasn't played. It was practically Ashgrove Church's anthem! It was clearly time for me to look more closely at an awesome hymn of our own.

"How Great Thou Art" originated in Sweden. Swedish pastor Carl Boberg composed it in 1886 as a personal expression of his awe in the face of a violent thunderstorm. Equally inspiring had been the beauty and calm that followed the storm. Overwhelmed, Boberg fell to his knees in holy awe and composed all nine verses. Soon congregations began to sing his text to an old Swedish melody. In time it was translated into other languages and traveled around the world.

"How Great Thou Art" had never been one of my favorite hymns. Yet I had marveled at its emotive power in the lives of people I had come to love deeply. Its sweet words of birds and forest glades, woods and trees, and brooks and breeze were truly emblematic of the good and simple life I had come to share at Ashgrove Church. In at least a small way, Lester was right: people sought peace for their souls, and there were still a few places to find it. One of these was right out here on the county line.

Two churches, two hymns, two apt modifiers—and one God, both great and awesome . . . then the seed of an idea had formed in my mind.

On a Saturday afternoon, as across the road an enormous, newly paved parking lot was being striped, the trustees were busy displaying a six-foot sign on the front lawn of Ashgrove Church. It had taken some persuading, but in the end people had seen the point to my plan. "Be good neighbors," I'd started out. "Do what we do best." When this hadn't worked, I'd invited the whole deacon and deaconess boards onto the front lawn.

"Come and stand right over here," I said, "and stare really hard at the middle of the sign across the road." They had complied, bunching together like bystanders at a crime scene. "Now," I continued, "tell me what you see."

"It's that church again," they answered.

"But what church? Whose church?" By now they had all driven by the sign, had all seen their own cars cradled by the awesome hands of God and been visited by the Spirit in the form of a dove. All had witnessed the pyrotechnical wonder of an interactive billboard, but still they didn't see it. "Look closely!" I encouraged them.

It was Billy Burton who had figured it out. His conversation with Homer had come back to him, and the fact that Nebo Methodist Church was brick, while ours was white clapboard.

"Wait a minute," he exclaimed. "I see it! It's *our* church! The thing's like some kind of giant mirror!"

Everyone fell silent.

"So," Gladys spoke up at last. "All this time it's been sitting there, reflecting us back to ourselves . . . "

"That's awesome!" Heidi said.

"No, not Awesome," I corrected. "It's Ashgrove Baptist Church!"

Then everyone understood. We were not awesome. At best, we were something barely approaching great. It was good to know and accept who we were. But such modifiers mattered little in any case. Like Awesome Church, we were who we were only as a matter of grace. And, finally, we were all of us the same, because our God of awesome greatness is one.

And so we decided to throw a party for the neighborhood—old and new. It would be a vintage Ashgrove Baptist affair from beginning to end. Invitations were sent by mail to each new resident of the housing development. Our friends and competitors at Nebo Methodist were invited, of course. And I hand delivered an invitation to Jack Vance, who had graciously offered to announce it in their Sunday Celebration Time. Awesome Church had begun to meet on site only two weeks earlier.

"We had seven hundred the first Sunday," Jack reported apologetically, "but got up near seven-fifty last week. We'll give it some time," he went on. "Attendance is bound to pick up once people find the way . . . By the way," he asked, "did you ever see our sign from up close?"

"Yes," I reported. "It's awesome! So—think you can join us?"

"I'll do my best," he answered.

Having firmly secured the banner to upright posts, Ed Garrett stepped back to admire his handiwork. "It's not awesome," he joked, "but it's us!"

"Right!" I concurred. "It's *great!*" Then Ed read the sign for all to hear:

The Great Old-Fashioned Pie and Ice Cream Social
Ashgrove Baptist Church
Saturday, September 12, 5–8 p.m.

On the afternoon of the great event, tables and chairs were set up under a big top, compliments of Ed Garrett, of course. Balloons and streamers blew in the breeze, while gospel music danced in the air from Eddie Garrett's stereo speakers. Five whole tables were reserved for pie plates, generous slices in a large variety of flavors: apple, cherry, blueberry, mincemeat, pumpkin, pecan, lemon meringue, and, naturally, Effie's rhubarb special. Along the south side of the building, half a dozen hand-crank ice-cream makers were in motion. Each station had a team of three: a cranker, a holder, and someone to pour in the ice and salt.

Soon our guests began to arrive. They hailed from all over the edge of the county, from all the places where our members and their relatives lived. They were drop-ins, lured off the street by the sight of the big top and the aroma of fresh-baked pies. They were Methodists from Nebo, led by our old neighbor Wendell Cobb, armed with homemade cookies to throw into the mix. They came from the gated community called Quiet Cove, eager for a further taste of country life. And a handful even found their way across the now-busy County Line Road from that awesome church on the other side, led by their pastor-coach, Jack Vance—every one of them appearing to be under thirty-five. All together entered the slow and steady world of quiet greatness.

"Say, this ice cream looks great!" a woman said. She and her husband were new residents at Quiet Cove. Recent recipients of fresh rhubarb pie and oatmeal cookies, they had come back for more, just as Effie said they would. "So, is this Ben and Jerry's?" the woman asked.

"Nope, Jessie and Seymour's," Heidi answered. "And that there's Homer and Billy's."

"Well, what are your flavors?"

Heidi ran them down: "This one here's called choco-late," she said, "and that over there is called vanilla."

"Great," she said. "I'll take a scoop of each."

"Me, too," said her husband.

Lester French dipped out the chocolate and Heidi, the vanilla.

"It's a peaceful place you've got out here," the couple said.

"Yes," Lester French agreed, shaking his head up and down slowly. "It's a place of quiet peace with God . . . " And he said it in the soothing tone of an undertaker.

Meanwhile the small choirs of Ashgrove and Nebo were assembling on the lawn in two rows. Shelly Higgins was setting up her new electric keyboard. She'd purchased it the week before at the new Wal-Mart on Rockville Road. "Thought I'd better start keepin' up with the times a bit," she explained. Soon the sound of vintage hymnody swept once more across the countryside. None was certain whether the music would more likely draw a crowd or drive it away, but they didn't care. They were in the mood to sing.

For the next half hour, the hymns of everyday life issued from the mouths of an ordinary people: "Onward, Christian Soldiers," "Holy, Holy, Holy," "Take My Life and Let It Be," "This Is My Father's World," "Love Divine," "Just as I Am," "Because He Lives," "Amazing Grace." Then Shelly had closed her hymnal and placed on the stand a single sheet of music. I had introduced it to Harold and her, and they in turn had taught it to the singers. It was "Awesome God," a contemporary praise chorus from Christian singer Rich Mullins and the anthem of our church friends across the street. As we fumbled through it, several of Awesome's members had joined in, singing and swinging and clapping on the weak beats in the style of rock and roll.

"So that's how it goes," Harold said.

"Yeah," they answered, "only faster!"

Then it was our turn. For the closing hymn, we encouraged everyone to join us in a rendition of "How Great Thou Art." Together we sang of the worlds God made, and of the grandeur all about, and of God's Son, our burdens gladly bearing. "How great thou art!" we sang, over and over again in the refrain. "How great thou art!"—sixteen times in all.

"That's a sweet sound!" Jack Vance offered. He had stepped to my side holding a plate of fresh pecan pie. "'How Great Thou Art'! Haven't heard that one in a while!" he said. "Brings back fond memories."

"We sing it all the time," I replied. "It's—kind of our anthem," I heard myself say.

Then Jack turned to the road. "Well, I've got an evening plane to catch," he said. "I'm speaking at a church growth institute out in Sacramento tomorrow."

"Wow," I said, envious. "That's awesome! Before you go, though, Jack," I told him, "I'd like you to see one thing." Then I directed him to a position just outside the vestibule door. "Now, stand right here and look that way," I instructed, pointing out to the street. For a long moment he stared admiringly across the road at the fruit of his effort—a towering edifice, meticulous landscaping, and enough parking to accommodate several tank divisions. Yes, it was magnificent, truly awesome. And there in the foreground was the billboard. Gone were the words *Coming Soon!* Now it read *Come on Home!* and at the bottom, to *Awesome Church of the New Era.*

Then all at once, Pastor Vance had spotted it, the faint outline of a white clapboard church and a large steeple. He broke into a smile, followed by a howl of surprise. "Yeah!" he said. "There it is, right in the middle of the sign! It's a church all right! Say, that's awesome!"

"No!" I said, "it's not Awesome—it's Ashgrove Baptist Church!"

## ♪ Hymn Notes ♪

We live in changing times in the American church. By now, many have proclaimed the death of Christendom. Shifting demographics, controlling denominations, inelastic congregations, and stool-pigeon clergy are all cited as causes for the collapse.

At the same moment, there is a remarkable movement of the Spirit afoot. Americans are hungry for intimacy with God. New congregations are sprouting up by the thousands every year, supplanting the thousands that each year close their doors for the last time. These new congregations are learning lessons as they go about what appeals to people of the new generation: affirmation of the individual, lay-led ministries, special interest ministries, small intimate groups, fewer meetings, the pursuit of excellence—and contemporary music, strong on melody and rhythm.

There is some room for disagreement as to all the particulars, we are told. But to stray too far from the spirit of the day is to be hopelessly lost to the past. In this mad rush to the future, a question not always raised is What of the church, old and new, remains unchanging? Surely the essential point of commonality for all churches in every generation is the worship of a God through Jesus Christ who is always great, awesome, and loving.

The Reverend Carl Boberg was not only a well-known preacher but, for fifteen years, a senator in the Swedish Parliament. His hymn "How Great Thou Art" was subject to several translations and title changes. It followed a circuitous route to usage in America, finally being translated into English from Russian by Stuart K. Hine (b.1899), missionary to the Ukraine.

"Awesome God," by Rich Mullins (1955–1997), is representative of many contemporary choruses that are replacing the use of standard hymns in many church settings. From a popular song, this chorus combines many elements of contemporary pop music, including a driving duple rhythm with emphasis on the weak beat, a simple melody with vocal embellishment, repetition, and brevity.

Rich Mullins was a popular performer and an even more celebrated songwriter. His songs have been recorded by the likes of Amy Grant and Debby Boone. His untimely death in an automobile accident en route to a benefit concert in 1997 has served to further immortalize his contribution to contemporary Christian music.

Each of these hymns, "How Great Thou Art" and "Awesome God," in its own way continues to provide in worship an awesome experience of God.

# About the Author

I N ADDITION TO WRITING, WYATT WATKINS ALSO ENJOYS A ministry of speaking and performing. If you would like more information, you can write to him at 593 Woodruff Place West Drive, Indianapolis, Indiana 46201, or contact him via e-mail at watkinsdt@aol.com.